SS SHADOW EMPIRE
Apocrypha I
Queen's Books

Palais Cêlesta

author Tycoon SAITO
translator Yoshie HIYAMA
publisher Yasushi ITO
ISBN978-4-7876-0110-0
English Edition Dec.2019

SS SHADOW EMPIRE APOCRYPHA

Summary

While Cannon, according to the writer's pursuit report, is a range mark of the coming WW3 including the period before and after this war, which will reach a boiling point around August 1, 2019, or August 8, 2032, Apocrypha has its motif in the yet unclarified mistery clinging to the past WW2.

As everyone knows, SS means Nazi SS troops of NSDAP (National Socialist German Workers' Party). One thing for sure is that they are the ones that hailed around whole Europe in the firm belief that they are the very people that have been bespoken in Les Centuries of Prophecies of Nostradams.

Please understand that the word Reich (in English, Empire) has been used to mean a country ruling a multiracial people like The Roman Empire, so the writer has chosen to use the expression of The Third Reich, Reich being a German word for Empire in English.

The expression of Fuehrer (meaning President in Taiwanese English) will also not be used here. I will instead utilize the word Leader. While the only one applicable literal translation of Fuehrer into English is Leader, Communists do not like it as they feel it does not sound dignified enough to satisfy their vanity. Japan's conventional governmental administration at that time did not use the word leader either and reason why it did not is because Japan lacked the ability to view the German situation that time from the historial viewpoint.

I admit there are some literary works on the market that use the expression of SS Country-wide Leader instead of Fuehrer. But one thing that must be noted is that Heinrich Himmler was often reaching Ukraine which was the German occupied territory then but not the part of German yet. On the other hand, Japan at that time when she refers to the word the whole Japan did include Taiwan or Korean Peninsula. However, she did not include Manchurian Empire or North China District that were occupied by Kwangtung Army.

Himmler presumably must have thought that Ukraine is the extensive end of the part of SS controlling area. Fact that SS included the area where German administration had not yet been exercised would mean the application of Reich used as SS Reich is wrong and incorrect – this is the writer's personal opinion and viewpoint, so the readers' understanding of this point is kindly solicitated.

Regarding use of the word NS (National Socialist), I sense malice of people who intend to unnessessarily stir up ill feeling towards national socialists because those people cannot rationally view the historical fait accompli. In 2015 when NS Museum was opened, a press release by a certain mass communicator described this museum as Nazis Museum while the image of the museum released with the news did not show any sign of the word Nazis anywhere on the building. What I wish to stress is that there existed apparent ill feeling owned by the communicator or communicators against

NS so when they should have reported this news of the opening of the Museum as the opening of NS Museum as shown in the image they instead chose to title the news as Nazis Museum. Such media manipulation by editors who have irrelevant ill feeling

must be ruled out in future. This kind of manipulation method is nothing but brainwashing that was popular with NS or old-fashioned socialists. The unfortunate reality of there having been dictatorial leaders when the nations' own citizens were captured and shut into detention houses must be remembered as facts of the history.

Nowadays, in Italy the political party originated in national alliance which is a succeeding political party of National Fascist Party formed Berlusconi Administration. Also, in France, a fascist related party called National Front won Parliament seats. These then ongoing facts means it now is important to view and analize these facts in the light of the historical facet. In 2013, an American researcher named South China Sea the Chinese Caribbean. In there, it happened that fishermen of minor nations were often murdered. Do you, the readers, agree to the writer's interpretation and decipherment of the Caribbean issue which is written in Canon?

Apocrypha debates about the era earlier by two to three generations prior to the generation of the charactors who appear in Canon. As same as Canon, I suggest that you please use the names with English spelling attached which you encounter in Apocrypha the first time while you are reading it, as a crue to search and refer these names back on the internet. The best way to enjoy this book is to read it along with viewing the related streets, etc., without seeking bulky written explanations.

We've met before, we meet again, and we will ‼

We did meet before, and we have now met again, so we will meet you further again in the future. Thus, we will never give each other up and will keep seeking the next chance of meeting into the future.
　若草のもゆるみどりの黒髪の君が香をば袖に留めむ
　Wishing to keep the scent of your glossy black hair left on my sleeves, the flagrance that only young fresh glass can nurture⋯

May 2016

CONTENTS

SS SHADOW EMPIRE APOCRYPHA ···2

APOCRYPHA I. QUEEN'S BOOKS

1. PLACE EROICA ···11
2. People left out in the cold ···23
3. Pub crawl after the feast ···46
4. Sophie's treasure ···62
5. Marais' Mansion ···68
6. Lunch break at Lyon ···75
7. Grandma In Marseille ···85
8. Carnival in Nice ···93
9. Dinner at Hotel Le Negresco ···100
10. Report by Walter ···107
11. La Voisin in Lyon ···116
12. Hotel Lumiere ···126
13. Paris Branch Office of the Happiest Time ···133

14. Before and After ···142
15. Words of Notre Dame···152
16. The Feature Articles··163
17. Salon Kitty···170
18. Train for Zurich··178
19. Opening Bank Account at Trust Swiss Bank ·············189
20. the Ox on the Roof··198
21. French Battlefields ··206
22. German Occupation of Paris ································221
23. Capture Duke of Windsor (Operation Willi) ···············231
24. Cancellation of Operation Sea Lion ·······················253
25. Invation Strategy Against Soviet Russia ··················268
26. Challenging The Third Reich's Doom ······················277
27. Actuation of Operation Barbarossa ·······················299
28. Yummy Bait··314
Postscript ···333

SS SHADOW EMPIRE

APOCRYPHA
I. QUEEN'S BOOKS

OVERTURE PROLOGUE

Getting off the metro in Paris at the Opera station, Luc Gauric started strolling along the rue de la Paix street. He stopped at a flower shop alongside the street, stepped into the shop and ordered a bouquet arranged. Receiving the bouquet, he started walking again carrying the bouquet under his left arm.

This street ends at Place Vendome reaching there from the north. In the center of the plaza, Napoleon the First dressed in the costume of the consul of Ancient Rome was towering on the again Roman style column which was recast from cannons.

The entrance of the plaza is located at the back of this statue. This street leading to the entrance may have been named to mean peace is coming after Heroic (Eroica) Napoleon, or otherwise may have ironically meant empty peace after all residents were massacred.

This naming of the street induces people to philosophical meditation which suits the atmosphere that eristic French people produce. At many corners of Paris, such sort of hidden meanings doing exist.

However, uneducated people living there will not and cannot express what they think and feel so they just keep silence. Reason why Paris is loved and esteemed together with Rome by the whole world is not only because it is a wonderful shopping place but the fact that this kind of Paris unique atmosphere keeps attracting visitors from overseas.

1. PLACE EROICA

The long rainy season since past autumn seemed to just about clear up in the afternoon on Saturday, December 23, 1939 and it appeared that the rest of the day somehow seemed to maintain without rain. This day Luc Gauric was asked by Sophia Balthazar, my colleague at the office, to visit and join a casual party held by a couple of British husband and American wife. According to what Sophia told me she was cared by a lady for her change of job and this lady introduced Sophia to this couple.

Sophia has been asked to help the hostess to decorate the party place with flowers which may need some male power at some points and that will be my work and another reason is that she was interested in the research of Luc's astrology that will be displayed at the party.

The Paris streets were modified by Haussmannisation in the era of Napoleon the Third. With Paris Opera to begin with, all public constructions and fire prevension measures have been remodeled so the whole streets were streamlined and slums were moved away. All new constructions were height restricted so standing in the middle of the street, parallel perspective can be clearly gained. However, one space between the elegant looking 18th century style building with a balcony attached on the right side third floor level and the building beyond the other two buildings away was destroying the balance of this corner of the street.

The whole atmosphere prevailing there was something like leading you to see visions like British royal family related people were standing chatting at the gate of the building in the front, or, you may feel as if you saw a gentlemanlike person with a stick were browsing the showwindow of Cartier Main Store on his way of strolling the street after taking branch.

Height of the building where Cartier Main Store is located is in conformance to the building height regulations established to be applied to any new constructions after the remodeling plan of the city Paris was completed. However, buildings on both sides of Cartier had been built before the regulations were set so the height of both buildings are taller than the regulated height. Cartier Main Store began its business here in 1899 with beautifully decorated store presentation with platinum or gold necklaces or tiarras shown in the show window framed by black marble.

The building next to the old and tall buildings also contains a jewelry store run by Mellerio dits Meller, handling the same jewel business as Cartier. They opened this store in 1613 in response to the Imperial ordinance issued by Marie-de'-Medici. The second level of this building (in France this level is called the first floor) has an arched window and the one level up which is the third level (by French expression the second floor) is framed in a square and in the center of the ceiling a grotestic mask was decorated and this whole second level was called the noble first floor as just fitting terms. This floor is conveniently distanced from the noisy outside streets and has an easy access from the salon underneath.

As the eye shade of his fedora is cutting his view off, he took time to look those buildings up but he reckoned that the area in his viewsight where he had seldom been before was worth his observation.

Nephew of Eroica Napoleon the First, who actually was Napoleon the Third, had the streets in Paris consolidated by Governor Haussmann.

With this consolidation the streets were well laid out with good consistency, however, this corner is breaking this consistency which implies its historical transition. While Rome maintains beautiful appearance as variety of diversity, Paris has different beauty in its appearance which still is beauty coming from its consistency yet including some broken meter in several parts of it.

Luc again looked at the showwindow and talked to himself overlooking the display which was consciously arranged for the Christmas sale of their watches.

Luc　　　　[I don't see any Mistery Clocks, why…]

Then, a plump gentleman wearing moustache and a bowler hat responded and talked to Luc.

Bowler Hat [Mistery clocks are to be made to order these days. That is why you don't see them. I have been here to look at the showwindow of this Cartier Main Store ever since my childhood. This framed showwindow shows us and attracts us with Caltier corporate efforts to enrich our lives with charming wrist watches or clocks.]

Luc [Since your childhood?]

Bowler Hat [Yes, As I was living in this neighborhood. Watches and clocks are devised to utilize the restoring force of hairsprings to make human lives more comfortable. I believe the coming 20th century will become a century when restoring force will be utilized to enrich human lives.]

Luc [Do you really think so?]

Bowler Hat [If liberalism is fully utilized, even politicians can be controlled and dismissed. Such political government as socialists' government can no way prevent their politicians from running amok.]

Finishing his talk, this gentleman with a bowler hat saluted to Luc touching the edge of the hat with a couple of his fingers and left Luc there.

Luc looked at his wrist watch and started walking again. Entering Place Vendome, he turned to the right looking up the back of the eroica in Roman costume. Hotel Ritz was located at the northwest corner of this Place. The façade of this hotel building was designed by Jules Hardouin-Mansart (1646-1708) who was the constructor working for Louis XIV. Construction was started in 1705. While the above ground floors had six-metre-high ceilings, the French style ground floor had a window of oblong shape to show difference from the above ground floors though the height of the ceiling was the same 6 metres as the other floors. Another difference was seen with the French style second floor where the height of the ceiling was only 4 meteres with an arch of oblong shape with a 50% pressed down size of semilunar shape. If we describe this structure in the Japanese way, we could say that from the second-floor level to the ceiling level of the third floor one single column was set penetrating the two building levels and limestone procured in Paris was forming the outerwall of the building till that height only. Above the end of this limestone wall up, popular Paris Mansard roof was used to cover the top part of the building. The attic windows are of shapes of round and oblong alternately.

At the northwest corner of Place, a gable was rising, but the entrance of Hotel Ritz was located differently, right side next to the entrance of Ministry of Justice. The hotel entrance was marked with round sunshade at four places. A doorman dressed in neat uniform respectfully received Luc who was carrying a bouquet. Coming into the restaurant, a waiter approached Luc but before the waiter spoke to him, Luc found Sophia lightly waving her right hand, so the waiter just received Luc's hat and coat and left him there.

There Luc saw from the left to the right a rather tall man with moustache of mid fortieth of age, then a rather small lady of the sixtieth of age wearing a dress of floral pattern, and next, an eldery lady in black dress with three stranded pearl necklace together with a gentleman in black business suit with a small mastache who apparently looked like the husband of the black dress elderly lady, then Luc saw Sophia in a long sleeve Chanel suit which is again in color black.

Luc   [I'm so sorry for coming late…]

Sophia [Oh, yah, we've been waiting for you. Well, okay, let me introduce you to all here.]
  Saying so, Sophia started introducing Luc to her people.
Sophia [This is Luc Gauric. He works as a librarian at National Archives at the next department to mine where to I changed my career and am now working there. As I told you before, he is of a family that has been specialized in astrology since the past several tens of decades, or more correctly, handling astrology with an interval per several generations at sometimes in his family tree.]
  Saying so, Sophia began to introduce every attendant starting with the one standing nearest to her.
Sophia [To start with, this is Maxime Weygand. He is the commander-in-chief for The Orient Theater of Operation. He is the person who kindly checked and sought any possible position suited to me to organize the official documents of French troops. Next to Maxime is his wife Marie Renee Josephine de Forzans. She is the person that kindly relayed my request to her husband. Next to her is Gabrielle Chanel, the owner of my former place of work. There she was called Mademoiselle by everyone. Next to her is⋯]

Von D [I am Hans von Dincklage. Out from Hannover and presently working at German Embassy in Paris. I'm assigned to promote friendly relationship with France in order to protect and grow liberalism. At the moment I'm worried as the governmental instruction has not arrived from our country as to how to peace with Phoney War.]

Chanel [Von Dee, don't be so formal. Luc, you, too. Please relax and feel at home.]

After the introduction was finished Luc was seated down next to Sophia and started talking about results of fortune telling based on horoscope of Maxime Weygan for which he had been given necessary information.

Luc [The traditional method of horoscope which has been inherited from our ancestors tells the movement of planets that are visible by bare eyes; in other words, Mercury, Venus, Mars, Jupiter, Saturn and Sun and Moon only. However, as we are also interested in the method called House which we are currently studying, that is, to distribuite number in the order of arrival of Tropical Zodiac which is rising towards East soon as their birth, we are therefore inducing this method and are now half way of the study to compare the system taking the method up in our study.]

Maxime [Is that why you asked the time of birth which you wish to know even approximately?]

Luc [We also need to know latitude/longitude of the place you were born. What ought to be noted is a lady astrologer by the name of Elsbeth Ebertin writing articles about astrology on the German newspapers created horoscope on April 20, 1889 for a certain political leader born on April 20, 1889. If you are to consider what happened to this leader after the astrology was done, it is obvious latitude/longitude of the place where he was born must be made as the object of the study.]

Maxime [You are the very first astrologer that does not dare to ask about my parents. Permit of my retirement was ordered to be cancelled in August and so I restarted my duty in the eastern Mediterranean Theater of Operations. I really wish to know whether I could get a peaceful retirement or not?]

Luc [I understand your excellency's mother is Charotte of Belgean royal family and your father must be Alfred. Child born out of wedlock is not supposed to tell it to the public but the secret of birth can well be guessed.]

Marie [Well, that's a good news. So, the lineage of Maxime is not bad at all.]

Luc [Yes, your understanding is correct, but this is something that cannot be told to the public.]

Von D [You mean lineage of German, don't you…]

Von D was slightly nodding saying the above, but was pretending as if he could not hear Luc too clearly.

Luc [Your Excellency does love Paris, and I understand you must be a fan of the musical reviews of Mistinguette as she is related to Belgium, too. By latter part of May next year Your Excellency will return here to help activate your beloved Paris and

	the review.]
Marie	[For the sake of Mistinguette?]
Maxime	[Right after the world war, Mistinguette's shapely legs were insured for the amount of 500,000francs. It was a true fact that her shapely legs were the breath of life for the soldiers on the battle field.]
Marie	[She is out of any one's league even if a lot of money was thrown in. Why can't men understand this simple fact?]
Maxime	[That she is out of league is the very reason why she should be protected by men. In fact, Paris is the most luxurious city in the world, isn't it. Despite the fact that Paris does not have that much historical background as Rome, nevertheless Paris is far more popular than Rome. This is the face of Paris as a huge consumer city supported by mass culture.]
Luc	[Your Excellency is expected to protect Paris culture from devastation. The last great work is yours and you will perform this work properly. However, one thing you had better remember is the fact that your forture as well as your wife's will be very weak during December, 1943 through to May, 1945. I suggest you should behave yourselves prudently during this period so you can live a long happy life together.]
Maxime	[Thank you for your valuable advice.]
Chanel	[It's about time now. We will have to start helping preparation work of this informal party by Mr. and Mrs Dukes.]

Maxime	[The car arranged by Army is loading lots of flowers. Luc seems to know about the needed flower decorating work so he must now have realized that the bouquet he has taken with him is in no way visible.]
Luc	[Yes, I now understand from Sophie. She plans to have flowers arranged in vases by the hands of a few people and take the vases up to the salon. I wonder who can make the flower arrangements?]
Chanel	[Flower artists are abundantly staying in Paris coming from all over the world.]
Sophie	[I understand the couple is a British husband and an American wife. Is their house so big?]
Chanel	[Both of them used to stay at a suite of Hotel Ritz till they moved into the new house. This is the reason why and how they became my customer. Madam has a variety of Caltier brooches so she has chosen black dresses to make it a canvas of her beautiful Caltier brooches. Hearing this can you somewhat feel the gracious living style of theirs?]
Sophie	[Kitchen must be spacious, may be too spacious for us to help cooking, I wonder…]
Chanel	[Please let the car come around here.]

She told the waiter, then Dincklage stood up quickly and drew her chair back for her to stand up and instantly took her right hand and start escorting her. Looking at his action, other members also stood up. Suddenly, Maxime said to Sophie and Luc in an explaining tone.

Maxime [You two, come with us and ride on the car we prepared.]

Waiters handed the coats and hats over to them. They went outside and found the air there still had some warmness of the daylight and saw a Renault limousine waiting. A military officer was holding the door open waiting for them.

Maxime [Thanks.]

With ladies first, they got into the limousine. The door was shut and the car moved off looking up the huge statue of Great Eroika on the left side.

Maxime [Why did you dare to tell your viewpoint about my parents at that particular place?]

Luc [Because a German diplomat was there. Majority of astrologers have already been aware of the sign that means a world war is possibly coming. Also, very many people are noticing on their fate line a powerful fault lines are appearing. Many of ordinary people will face big hardships around 1945 and this will also happen to rulers and administrators. It is an important confidential matter that Your Excellency is of German lineage but this fact has some meaning useful to NS. Facing the huge gears of fate, humans are equal to the dust. "HOMINEM TE ESSE MEMENTO – Remember you are a mere human and nothing more!" is inevitable truth.]

Maxime [Those are the words issued by the imperator at the triumphus.]

Saying this, Maxime glanced the statue of Napoleon the First in the Roman costume standing on the tower and chuckled.

In ancient Rome, at a triumphus the imperator used to ride on a four-horse driven chariot and four on the horizontal line called Quadriga. On this chariot a slave was aboard behind the imperator holding a fresh laurel wreath on top of the imperator's head during the Republic era and after that era, the wreath was changed to a gold wreath.

Then the slave was to say [RESPICE POST TE (Watch behind you!) HOMINEM TE ESSE MEMENTO (keep in mind that you are just a mere human and nothing more!)]

Hearing this warning many times imperators in the Republic era tightened the code of the helmet specially after they won the war, but this habit has been gradually getting forgotten over the time during the monarchical period.

As a natural fact, laurel wreath was made in the morning and weathers in the evening of the same day to straightly symbolizing the human life. However, authority means to tend to pursue to keep its everlasting power, and it will explain why the fresh laurel wreath was changed to gold wreath. As an expected result, remonstrance by loyal retainers that was hard to accept tended to be turned down and consequently authority came to be surrounded only by flatterers. And they would come to care about their own luxurious lives and to spend their days in sumptuous feasts. As a result, crop failure as well as invation of the enemy across the border took place and national finance collaped. History tells us that always the last victor creats fatal decadence.

2. People left out in the cold

After a while the Renault limousine was drawn up to the front door of a building which stood at 24 Boulevard Suchet. Floors upstairs were equipped with windows of square shape and the first floor as named in French way has five arch-shape windows symmetrically equipped with the middle one in the center. The both sides of the window in the center were supported by two each half exposed colonnades which ran down to the space under the eaves of one level upper floor.

The five windows, one in the middle and two each on both sides of the so called second floor in the French way were of oblong shape and the outer wall of the building was made of limestone that was procured in Paris. The attic on top of the second floor had three windows each with an arch in the mansard roof. At both sides of the window in the middle two each Cupids are placed. This whole idea of exterior was producing perfect atmosphere of a newly built love nest.

When Luc's group got off the rimousine, they saw soldiers efficiently taking down fresh flowers off a small size truck of French troops and taking those into the upper floor level. Luc, depositing his coat and fedora with the butler, started helping arranging flowers in vases parting from Sophie. There, a man with glasses of round shape bobbed hair and a young burr-headed man were already doing the work. Luc, putting his jacket aside and rolling the sleeves of his shirt up, said hello to them and the one with bobbed hair growing a small mastache introduced themselves to Luc.

Tsuguji Foujita　　[I am Tsuguji Foujita. They call me Foufou This young man is Dentaro Hayashi. Please call him Den.]

Luc　　[I am Luc.]

Tsuguji　　[luc, won't you carry vases out from the next room together with Den. Then, these two vases are done so take them to the side of fireplace and fill them with water.]

Luc　　[May I ask what you are doing?]

Tsuguji　　[I'm trying to pursue beauty to the full end. You may think I'm doing the least useful job available in the world, but it is a known fact that there was a group of cultural figures called Doboshu (companions) serving Great General in Muromachi Shogunate in medieval Japan and doing decoration works. This fact is recorded in the book of interior design named (Kundaikansochoki)].

Luc　　[I see. That is why you are wearing such beautiful tortoise shell-made round glasses.]

Tsuguji　　[Yes? Oh, no, these are glasses made of celluloid produced in a place called Sabae in Japan. Glasses Den is wearing are the same celluloid made. Weather in Europe is much drier than in Japan so celluloid looks beautiful here as it keeps transparency and does not warp in dry weather. What I mean with the expression transparency is the one which can only be gained from living organism that could be described as squidgy transparency. To keep the transparency of the part of tortoiseshell specially at the point where the best transparency is needed must be celluloid as transparency of tortoiseshell is not enough at such point of part. Scientifically synthesized material which has excessively high uniformity is not suited to be used at such point. In addition, you do not have to kill tortoise is a fact that is friendly with nature.]

Luc [Your comments are quite impressive. This sense of yours regarding beauty is something very useful to all people, isn't it.]

Tsuguji [In the peaceful age, culture gives us a broader room to make such meditation. If I were an army surgeon like my father, I could have kept up my appearances such as my elder brother…But such job as an army surgeon will sure be destroyable to me and I shall never be able to cope with it.]

Luc [You mean war may break out?]

Tsuguji [I tell you Den's grandfather was a fortune teller and his teacher was called Kaemon Takashima. Takashima was a widely known Japanese fortune teller and was telling the fate of elder statesmen of Meiji era, rendering a great service to the nation. He also guessed right when the Sino-Japanese War and The Russo-Japanese War would start and finish. According to what Den says, to the majority of Japanese population, he sees a big difficulty would be foreseen around the year of 1945. In short, circumstantial evidence will tell that the case when a large number of human lives will be lost in a wide area can be world war or world revolution, right? Den therefore tried all he could and passed the examination of international baccalaureate, so the next target he is aiming at is to enter a university in France.]

Luc [Does he think French people should be safe?]

Tsuguji [I gather that his fortune telling does not tell him any sign of French flag officers to be sacrificed in battle.]

Without stopping their hands, they kept arranging flowers. Then 30 minutes later, they finished all the flower arrangements which were to be placed starting from the entrance via the steps to the salon area.

Coming back to the salon where the party was going to be held, Luc joined the crew of guests with Sophia who was taking the apron off and folding it, to salute the hosting man and wife. Those who gave the greeting message were The Prince Edward, Duke of Windsor and his American wife, Wallis, the Duchess of Windsor. Ahead Luc and Sophia Tsuguji Foujita and Mrs Kimiyo who was dressed in Kimono of a pattern of red and white plum flowers, decorating her coiffured hair with an ornamental hair pin designed with blur coral ball and a tortoise shell comb, and then Dentaro Hayashi, the international student.

Wallis [I did not know you have such a grown up son;.]

Tsuguji	[Oh, not really, he is Dentaro Hayashi. Please call him Den. He passed the entrance examination of Baccalaureate and is now getting himself prepared for entering the Graduate School of Medicine and Faculty of Medicine in France. As my father is an army surgeon, he asked me to help him find a proper boarding house during his stay in France.]

As a matter of fact, father of Tsuguji Foujita succeeded Mori Ougai and took the position of Army Surgeon General after Mori. In such circumstances Tsuguji could not decline the request from Army.

Mrs. Wallis looked at Den with a bit of wonder for that Den did not choose Germany for his place to study medical science.

Wallis	[I wonder why you wish to study in France particularly as you are already a medical student in Japan.]
Den	[I gather from an Army surgeon called Dr. Ishii, as regards bacterial research France which has Pasteur Institute is the most advanced country in this medical field and to study in France will give me a chance to gain significant skill and experience for the study of public health.]
Wallis	[So you mean Pastgeur Institute is the most advanced laboratory?]
Den	[Fact is death rate is much higher of infectious disease than of death at the battle field of wars. In Japan,

	many people die from tuberculosis. To combat with this disease, how to surpress growth of bacteria called Mycobacterium tuberculosis determines success to overcome this disease.]
Wallis	[I do wish to somehow contribute for development of studies of such valuable medical field some day. I do hope you will make yourself a doctor with superior capability.]

   Listening to the conversation with the two people, Luc and others could have a chance to observe the behavior and attitude of Mrs. Wallis. She looked brilliant with friendly smiles. At the neck opening of her black Chanel dress, a lily shaped brooch that is as big as her clenched fist was glittering reflecting the light of the chandelier.

   This couple looks very close to each other. On each of their ring fingers they were wearing a big Mogul emerald ring. This huge size shining emerald was of viscously thick green tea color and was cut in halves and shared by the couple. It was exactly what (Hiyoku Renri) means. To explain Hiyoku, it means two birds, each owns one eye and one wing, fly together supplementing each other. Renri is; one branch of a tree links with another branch of another tree and forms one combined big tree. This is a legend of olden time India. Here using this legend, the writer explains this couple could never been separated.

   One unhappy problem to this couple is the British public opinion then at that time was entirely against allowing a woman who is not a noble woman nor British the position of queen consort. In this sense, while they were so very popular and welcomed in Paris, in the husband's mother country United Kingdom this couple was totally unaccepted and estranged. Next to Mrs. Wallis, Luc and Sophia were asked to present a short self introductory speech, but as both of them were so excited that they did not remember what they spoke.

As the party was of a bufett style, they started choosing dishes with a plate in each hand and noticed that the arrangement of food served was being handled by Maurice Sachs who is the owner of Cabaret-Bar [the Ox on the Roof] and one other rather fat and big man. According to Sophie, the man who was cutting and serving the Cabaret-Bar's roasted beef was a cook serving at a mansion in Berlin by the name of Arthur Kannenberg. She added she had talked with him while she had been helping cooking. According to Sophie, this man seemed to have some interest in Luc's astorology researches.

After a while, Maurice Sachs started to play the grand piano in the salon. Then suddenly a lady that had been talking with Tsuguji joined him and began singing [Parlez-moi d'amour]. She was wearing a black Chanel dress but was none other than Lucienne Boyer. This song sung with her sweet voice became a hit single singing for calling a man back who was parting a woman, trying to regain the man's love that was just about to vanish away. This song that was released in 1930 sounded to be interpreted as if it were trying to take back the Golden Age of the global economy of the world which collapsed in 1929.

Lucienne　　[Next singer after me is Black Caruso; Frances!]

Singer appointed by Lucienne was Francesco Borgia who looked a bit like Enrico Caruso. The Borgias had been sealing an astorology advisory contract with the Gaurics for generations. The song Francesco sung was (La donna e mobile) of Verdi's opera, Riogoletto.

This tune sings that flirtatious Duke Mantova signing over whimsical woman's mind and saying that was why he would not believe whatever women would say to him. The tune ends with the line of [in such woman's heart, my love ought not to be tried]. It became a hit song with support by those men who were deceived by eye-catchingly charming women. At such time as 1850, at the edge of high society there existed a hidden society by the name of Dumimondo where hetaeras called courtisane lived abundantly. There was a time when such hetaeras as gathering at Restaurant Maxim in Paris. They were a dream of men at that age who eagerly hoped that some day they would achieve a big success in his courier and gain fortune to afford getting such hetaeras surround him in hand, and this same desire of men exists in any era of the history so such refined hetaeras attracted a great deal of men's attention all through the time. And that is the secret to deepen the shaded charm of Paris furthermore.

Borgia [Well, I guess now some people may be rather impatiently waiting for the dance time. Chezarina!!]

Borgia appointed a lady standing near Chanel calling her by her formal name. She was Rina Ketty and was a popular face on the jacket of records. The first song she sang was (Tornerai) singing the phrase of [I shall be back] in Italian released in 1936, followed by another named [I will wait (J'attendrai)] in French version. Those two tunes were of literally the same lyrics in different languages.

Originally, this lylic was created inspired by the opera [Madame Butterfly], however, at that very time it got especially popular among lovers who were separated because of the war with the male partners sent to the African Campaign such as Ethiopia. In France, this song was continuously kept supported through to WW2 by those who can do nothing but to wait in the homeland. Also, this tune is ideal as dancing music and there at the party several couples started dancing on the party floor. Dincklage was dancing with Chanel. Duke and his wife were also stepping. Following them, Robert, too, started dancing before the people knew it, with Sophia's friend, Roxane who happened to be there.

When the music ended, Roxane Walewska (Roxy) found Sophia and talked to her. Roxy wore shinny hair of chestnut color and had skin as shinny as her hair and looked as if she were a show model hired by Chanel to display the attractiveness of Chanel apparels, but she was smiling and laughing quite much and did not have that kind of coolness as often observed with the bluebloods. Fact that she was an aristocracy of German descent in East Europe may have been working for her to have a warm vibe about her. Holding a glass by her right hand, with her dress reflecting parl-grey color in the light of chandelier she was standing carrying a black Chanel bag on her shoulder. This Chanel bag that Roxy was carrying launched on the market at the age of matured culture of 1929 getting the hint from the haversack which soldiers use. It was devised to have enough room to contain an automobile key and un carnet de bal (a schedule book of balls) as well as a then prevalent Art Deco style perfume atomizer made of mother pearl or a cigarette lighter and other smoking tools if needs be. In addition, it has a belt with a chain attached to be hung on the shoulder which is handy for use at a buffet. Indeed, Chanel acquired in one go overwhelming support from young women and established the trend of that age.

You may wonder why the writer knows so much in detail about the description as above? Is it because he is a collector of antique bits and pieces? Or, is he a watcher of ladies who use these accessories?

The right answer is simply because he owns strong curiosity about any and everything. But above all of it, Roxy who was wearing such sexy looking dress was a conspicuous presence. She was a glamorous woman of the fiftieth age, and her appearance reminds everyone of her popurarity with men when she was young.

Sophie　　[Have you found a job since last time we met?]

Roxy　　[Not easy. Not many jobs are available for such as me of a collateral relation of an aristcracy of broken fortunes.]

Sophie　　[Could you meet your parents?]

Roxy　　[They were implicated in the mess of Poland in September and their mansion was burnt out. I am still not able to meet up with my parents.]

Sophie　　[Oh, I am awfully sorry to hear such bad news…]

Kitty　　[Sorry to cut in. I'm Catalina. Call me Kitty. If you can speak a plural number of languages, I think I can arrange a job at a service trade in Berlin if you don't mind Berlin.]

Roxy [I wonder if it is a job that I can handle?]

Kitty [Yes, you can do it no problem. And I guess you may need money to search your parents? If you wish to use this job as a temporary job, it is good enough for us, too, so we wouldn't mind it. Will you contact me if you are interested in my offer. Here is my business card.]

Finishing saying so, Kitty seemed to find out someone she knows.

Kitty [Hi, Walter! Wait a moment!]

Kitty went away to the direction where Christmas tree was standing. A business card was left in the hand of Roxy. On this card, Roxy read an address of No. 11 Giesebrecht Street and the name Kitty Schmidt.

Sophie [Do you wish to accept her offer?]

Roxy [Chanel hired me to this party just as a symbol of the nobles though I'm ranked at the lowest. What I can do is just chatting and getting nicely dressed and nothing else. So-o-o, this job may be too difficult for me, I wonder…All what I wish is to see the mansion I used to live in and meet at least one or two people that I know of.]

Rina [Next is Artur! Please sing Titine in your usual fake French. Are here any other that can talk tactful fake French? Chance is open to everyone!]

A big man Arthur who was laying the table for food and Tsuguji, followed by a British man with a little pale face came out and talked a short while together, then Maurice Saches, a jazz pianist, started playing piano liltingly. The tune was originally a French tune of 1917 by the title of [Look for Titine], but later in 1936 Charles Chaplin used this phrase as an ad-lib in his movie [Modern Times] which made this tune known worldwidely. It looked like that they were intending to revive this scene.

To start with, the rather small British man was handed a bowler from another man that had been standing near Luc. This person was the same man that Luc talked with a few hours ago at the show window of Caltier Store. Receiving the bowler and cufflinks the British man followed the action of Chaplin in his movie and tore the cufflinks off, provoking laughter of the audience.

Then, if carefully listening to him, Luc could hear that Tsuguji was enumerating many single Japanese words to make the tune sound like fake French. Lastly, the big man Artur Kannenberg exhibited his fake French constructed by enumeration of German words with dramatic gestures to finish up this farce. It went without saying that they received rapturous applause from the whole audience.

In the midst of this farce being played, Luc moved to the man with whom he had a conversation in front of the Cartier store and talked to him.

Luc [I didn't expect to meet you in such a place like this. I am Luc Gauric.]

Breguet [I am Louis Charles Breguet. I am a constructing engineer of aeroplanes. I heard you are engaged in National Archives. You are the gentleman that Your

Excellency Weygan was talking about some time before as an astrologer, aren't you.]

Then, they noticed that the British man who had also finished the fake French performance came near to them and made greetings.

Breguet [Robert, this is the astrologer about whom Your Excellency was talking. Luc, this is Robert Grant. He is a part-time British army surgeon. He used to attend Duke Windsor as his health diagnostician.]

Robert [This mansion is located in a short distance of about 15 minutes on foot from where Doctor Henri Bergson lives, so I visited him today to salute him. As he was a big man as chairman of British Society for Physical Research, I thought I should see him and report the current movement of physical research. As my specialty is more of psychosomatic medicine, my medical knowledge does not relay to the treatment of his sickness.]

Luc [Well, then, do you have interest in psychic phenomena as well?]

Robert [Taking it for granted that in the sense of psychics the state of being dead and that of being alive have no concrete difference, elan vital in Bergson's demonstration still implies existence of soul or spirit. Since our British Empire has started ruling India, many reports of research on reincarnation have been completed. To raise one example, prophecy of Les Centuries could be what the descending Entity may

	intend to show human an image of its choice. This comment of mine is based on the fact that the prophecy is of the kind that surpasses changes of the times.]
Luc	[I agree that there is a possibility that something like The Entity does exist and is letting human foresee the future. Figuratively speaking, a mistery clock is no mistery to the engineers that know the gimmick.]
Robert	[Well, if that is the case, to augurs prediction of social changes is the matter of technology and no mistery.]
Breguet	[Those such as me operating an industrial corporation, suppose I could acquire a purchase order of aeroplanes in the circumstances when a war may look to break out imminently, all what I would instantly think would be 'Oh, good, now I can cover the calculated expenses that are needed for the ongoing development program of autogiro with the fund I can gain from this sale' and would never think any more than that. Maybe next time we meet, I would wish you to tell me my fortune regarding such economic prospect.]
Luc	[Why do you stick to such short-sighted order acquirement?]
Breguet	[Our company is selling fighters to various countries in the world so that even if we receive orders, if we cannot cash the notes we shall go broke. In other words, that no war will take place is a necessary condition for an infallible collection of payment. That relates to the talk in front of the Caltier store about

	the controlled power that we had.]
Robert	[Concluding you are saying that under the multi-party system parliamentary democracy it is no way possible to draw up a budget bill under a subject for discussion of preemptive attack.]
Breguet	[You're quite right. The cabinet will crush down before the army explains such invation plans intending alteration of the Versailles system at Chamber of Deputies. This matter of course is exactly what democracy is meant for. The very first word appearing in the slogan of French Revolusion is none other than Liberty, which means the economic activities will not be handled at the ruler's ease. This philosophy is not available in socialism, and that is why USSR led by Starlin and its socialism are carefully watched out.]
Luc	[Do you wish no war to be started? In spite of the fact that you are a manufacturer of fighters?]
Breguet	[Already in my childhood I found out that mistery clock gimmick is based on the idea of regeneration of controlling power coming out of power output section. Constructing balance spring myself I came to understand this mechanism. My family business was to operate a clock store at the east side of Place Vendome so I had a good opportunity to gain knowledge of clocks and watches. Finding out the fact that mistery clock was no mistery, I became conscious without being taught by anyone, of the fact that such

as invention or contraption is a natural course of matter. You now know this explains how I came to have my own dream about such flying mechanism as aeroplane and keep talking on this subject with His Highness Maxime. French Army is also showing interest, but the true motive that drove me to produce aeroplane is passionate romanticism representing my strong desire to acquire this and such things with all my power. My desire in this regard is very similar to men's adoration to a revue actress who is out of their league.]

Robert [Yah, No argument that Muse excites man's spirit longing for romantic adventure!]

Breguet [Yes, the thighs of Mistinguett are always the object of man's romanticism. She is not in the same league as lucienne or Lena.]

Robert [I would prefer Lucienne or Rina.]

Breguet [You seem not appreciating the fact that evenings in Paris are flowering with revues. Foufou is telling me mode in Paris is relayed to Japan as quickly as just about in one-month time and is being talked about in Tokyo. We are in the era when culture spreads in the world via such media as newspaper and radio. At the same time, there is a risk that such time will come soon when communists' propaganda will affect the world history adversely even if it won't last long.]

Luc [What do you think will happen if such a case arises?]

Breguet [Well, as multi-party system democracy is now going to be the world's standard, you don't have to think this matter too seriously. It is widely believed that the spirit of French Revolution is exactly what will establish the modern nations, or more exactly, will develop the human future further, so it can be said that France gifted America the statue of Liberty.]

Robert [You, too, seem to possess a time machine with which you can see the future.]

Breguet [Oh, that is a simple device. My father was making such machine at the cost just similar to the cost of Duesenberg. Bourgeoisies that can read future will lead the whole world.]

Luc [At the price of one high class automobile?]

Robert [You're talking about skelton watch or mistery clock, aren't you.]

The automobile manufacturer Duesenberg is an American corporation that started selling in 1921 Model A that is equipped with chassis with engine. During the time from 1928 to 1938, when they went bankrupt incidentally, they produced 481 cars of the famous Model J. Their customers who purchased this model which had chassis with engine made it a rule to order the coachwork of the exterior and interior mounting of the vehicle at a mounting maker called Coachbuilder.

The total amount of payment was greater than the total amount of money that a Japanese university graduate could earn spending all his lifetime if the value at that time is capitalized as the current value. In addition, the owner of this vehicle must have enough financial power to keep funding the maintenance cost. Duke Windsor appeared as one of the top rank of cherishers of this vehicle on the list of owners. Accordingly, this vehicle was a representative vehicle drawn as an image leader on the art deco posters in 1930's. The wheel arch was bewitchingly streamline-shaped by skilled workers and tires equipped were with a number of fine spokes attached and when the tires start rolling slowly beautifully glittering – just by imagining how it would look common people would have been overwhelmed by its beauty and must have dreamed how wonderful it would be if they could own such a vehicle.

The biggest noteworthy point of appearance was the silver plated front bamper which was made not to be hidden but kept visible at all times even after the mounting work was added. This bamper was made of double tiers like a bow tie, fastened in the middle part, and the upper tier was slightly bent backward at the point between the cener and the side and this sunken part is also slightly bent upwards. This peculiar shape was devised to be prepared for such accident as should the vehicle strike a human, it was to scoop the person up before the person was run over under the vehicle that had a huge body weight weighing more than three tons. The upper metallic part of this double tier construction refleted rays of light coming out of many parts of the vehicle which gave the body of the vehicle an extra gourgeous shiny look.

Another eye-catching point of this vehicle was the design that made the curving shape starting at the wheel arch of the front ending at the connection point of the footstep outside of the doorsill, which reminded people looking at this vehicle of a coach of one singe life time ago. This was a design effective to stir the imagination of common people who didn't have a chance to look inside the vehicle. Regarding the interior, the driver's seat was made of leather following the customs of a coach , and also the back seat was covered by the fabric of the owner's choice which was the same as the case of coaches in the past times. The owner selected carpet or fabric woven in the carpet production area where he had a relationship, and oftentimes all from meter panel to door trimmings were fully covered by walnut or maple birdseye patterns.

Adding more to the interior decorations, opal lucent glass was used on the covers of the lights refecting the owner's refined taste aiming at comfortability during the travelling time. To add more, difference of Duesenberg from other highclass vehicles is the owner driver of forerunner's characteristic posture to imply a challenge of the forthcoming motor sports time, which ultimately led to production of vehicle equipped with double overhead camshaft and 395 horse power engine. The top speed of 152 miles an hour of this highest level model equals to 245 km/hr and this prompt power performance gave the same level of pleasure that could be gained by possessing and riding and running on the derby winning horse. Clearly, the largest problem that dissatisfied the owner would have been there was not enough number of such roads suitable for this fast speed run.

The first person that complied to the dillemma of the Duesenberg vehicle owners as regards road availability problem was Hitler who constructed motorway called outbahn. That this was done by Hitler may be construed as his election tactics targeting business tycoons of his relation. To realistically feel the top speed by a high-class vehicle that was manufactured at a corporation which was created and operated by a German immigrant would have given the person who made a success in the German financial circles extravagantly satisfied feelings.

One thing that can be said for sure is that a historian who is nobody except with plentiful poverty shall not have had a chance to describe the outbahn from this angle of viewpoint. Even nowadays in the 21st century, at the highest price zone of the vintage cars where average estimated auction price is as much as 2 million US dollars, there sit Duesenberg vehicles.

Now, Arthur Kannenburg came over finishing his performance and talked to Luc.

A.K.	[How did you like my performance? I have gathered from Sophie who you are. My name is Arthur Kannenburg. I am working as a cook at a cergain mansion in Berlin and occasionally go a little further to Paris to procure ingredients and partly for food preparation while my master is away from home. I understand you act as an astrologist.]
Luc	[Yes, I am of a family that has been researching astrology throughout my family generations. I am also studying Les Centuries.]
A.K.	[Les Centuries? Oh, Nostradamus⋯If it is what you are researching, I would appreciate some simple

	handbook that I can read before I come to Paris next time.]
Luc	[I remember I saw such book at a second-hand book store that I am well acquainted with. Oh, I now have an idea. The book in your pocket now is Michelin Orange Guide, isn't it. If it is the year 1940 version, why don't you give it to me? I will get the handbook of Nostradamus for you so we can do a barter trade.]
A.K.	[Yes, you are quite right. This is a copy of the year 1940 Michelin Guide started to be on sale this month. You can have it at no charge if you like. My next visit here will be sometime in early spring. Oh, I have an idea. If you know Maurice Sachs of the cabaret-bar 'Ox on the Roof', why don't you leave the book in his hand for me.]
Luc	[Yah, I visit there around twice a month…I will get a good quality copy of Prophecies of Nostradamus translated by Karl Loake. It is the year 1921 edition. Is this edition acceptable?]
A.K.	[Whatever edition it may be, it is based on the French original written either in 1555 or 1558, isn't it. I will not mind as long as it is a clean deadstock. By the way, would you mind telling my fortune with your astrological skills?]
Luc	[Well, this must be some kind of fate to meet each other now, so let me tell your fortune as you wish it. I need to learn your birth date, time and the name of the town where you were born.]

In fact, the restaurant guide book named Michelin Guide Orange Book was seldom available at book stores in France that were selling new books. This book was rating restaurants in France by number of stars ranking them from one star to three stars. Cause of the shortage was SS having bought out this edition to rate and select hotels and restaurants for SS requisition in preparation of enforcing purposes of the western front.

As a matter of course, Goring demanded to seize the three-star Hotel Ritz for use of German Air Force. Heinrich Himmler, the leader of SS Empire, thought out how to treat the important personnel headed by Hitler, in order to keep his voice powerful in National Socialist German Workers' Society. At that point of time, those who were seizing a higher position than Himmler were Hitler as the sole leader, Marchal Hermann Goring and Vice Leader Rudolf Hess, but this ranking order was later going to change. Himmler was gradually enforcing the organization in NSDAP called Black Jesuits.

A.K. [I have written down on a stationery paper the information you will need for your use to tell my fortune. Main thing I'm concerned about is safety of my family, but whether my present master is safe or not is also a bit of my concern.]

Luc [Do you wish me to tell your master's fortune, too?]

A.K. [No, it's not necessary as he belongs to a higher social position unlike me. What I wish to know is whether I will have to open and run a restaurant before my retirement. Cooking is my partner in all my lifetime ever since I served the army as a cook during WW1, though to play entertainment like tonight in the interval of cooking is also what I enjoy.]

Saying so, Kannenberg handed a piece of stationery paper which looked like showing some embossment on it. Luc quickly folded the paper and put it into the inside pocket of his jacket and predged a reunion.

3. Pub crawl after the feast

Leaving the party at the mansion of Duke Windsor, several of the party attendants went hopping to [Ox on the Roof (Le Boeuf sur le Toit)] which Maurice Saxe was running. In those days this cabaret-bar was doing its business at the eastern south side of Arc de Triomphe, which is located on the way from the northern west side of Bois de Boulogne back to the center of Paris.

Sophie and Luc thought it would be an idea to have some coffee there and moved there by a bus that Maurice seemed to have arranged to hire. There, they were again joined by Roxy and Robert, and Tsuguji and Den, too. As Luc had some interest in the performance of Japanese fortune tellers, he decided to ask Den if he knew anything about this subject.

Luc [Den, Are fortune tellers in Japan mentioning any possibity of a big disaster coming to happen in near future?]

Den [I heard quite a lot of people were foreseeing bad fate which is said to become real around the year 1945. What my grandfather told me was there would be no bad fate foreseen with French high-class officials so I should choose to rely on one of them. This is the reason why I came to ask Tsuguji to take care of me through introduction by Dr. Ishii, the army surgeon.]

Luc [Thogh this information is between you and me,

fortune tellers in Paris are telling the fortune of high social standing who visit Paris for sightseeing. Those tellers are saying at one voice that fate of people other than French nationality shows a sign of a big trying time coming and changing their fates around the year of 1945.]

Robert [Well, that leads me to wonder about a possibility of a world war or world-size revolution arising in Europe and Eastern Asia, what do you think?]

Luc [If you read Les Centuries deeply, you will come to understand there will be at least three big wars coming.]

Robert [How can you specify it for three wars?]

Luc [If you carefully analyze Volume 2 the 40th portion of Les Centuries, you will see the first line does not take too much time. But at the third line, the war on the sea becomes a quite large one. In other words, the three big countries' navies start fighting fierce battles. This implies a war of Japan against U.K.and U.S. However, in Volume 5, the 62nd portion, warships are getting melted and Trident will become dominating. But, in reality, no such strong weapon as to melt a fleet has not yet come to exist.]

5-62
Sur les rochers sang on verra pleuuoir,
Sol Orient Saturne Occidental:
Pres d'Orgon guerre s Rome grand mal voir,

Nefs parfondrees, & prins Tridental

Robert	[Well, then, what about possibility of such technology to be able to produce a weapon strong enough to melt a fleet may be developed during WW2?]
Luc	[In Volume 1, the fiftieth portion, Triple Alliance of Sea Powers shall be formed and one of the three shall be America which makes Thursday, Thanksgiving Day. This means the second war and the third were different to each other in terms of conception. For instance, re WW2, of Triple Alliance, only Japan is the country of sea powers. For WW3, Three countries of sea powers are altogether on one side and stand on a superior position with the powerful power of Trident. This means a weapon that can melt warships which were made of metals, with huge amount of calorific value. Such powerful weapon can never be made in the current century. In other words, to create such weapon, much longer interval than the past two world wars till the time when the third one can be made ready will have to be needed.]

1-50

De l'aquatique triplicate naistra,
D'un qui fera le jeudy pour sa feste:
Son bruit, loz, regne, sa puissance croistra,
Par terre ei mer aux Oriens tempeste.

1-50

Triple Naval Alliance will be united
One of them celebrate Thursday
Their bright, praise, reign will increase
At lands and seas of Orient will be Tempest (=war or battle).
(Tempest? will be used for battle at Oriental lands and seas.)

Robert [By the way, I heard Foufou returned to Japan and painted military art. Where did you go for that painting?]

Tsuguji [I went to Manchuria and near to River Khalkha, the border of Mongolia.]

Robert [According to the announcement by Soviet, they say at the battle there Soviet was superior to Japan?]

Tsuguji [What I gathered is different. According to Japanese Imperial Army (JIA), they secured as the land of Manchuria approximately the same size of the land as what Soviet announced on the south side of the land next to the Soviet's occupation. In addition, Soviet lied as regards number of fallen Japanese soldiers. Fact is number of the dead on the side of Soviet is greater than that of Japan.]

Robert [Is the number of fallen Japanese soldiers excluding Koreans or Taiwanese drafted as soldiers of colonial army like what happened with us, U.K.?]

Tsuguji [No, no way. In Japan we treat Korean soldiers and Taiwanese soldiers equally as Japanese. At the point of time when Japan annexed Korea, at some areas of Korea nearly half of the residents there were slaves which class system had been abolished in the middle of the 9th century in Japan. Therefore, it became necessary that those Korean people who did not have sir names were to be given Japanese sir names because they could escape from the past slave status if they gained sir names and became officials or policemen. 'Nuhi-slaves' are originally the survivors mainly consisting of former Kudara, Ninna and Shinra races who moved to Korea from Japan in the 4th century. Therefore, by this war, they were finally freed from slavery and became Japanese citizens.]

Robert   [Then, will it happen that Japan's enemy wait till all soldiers of Japan drafted from those in the colony were killed and the enemy's bullets were used up, Japan would have started making a dash to attack the enemy? Even Soviet is using Cossack troopers as a shield at the front line. The British army seems to think that the size of human damage which Soviet officially announced includes only Russians and not Asians.]

Tsuguji   [Japan abolished the system of Japanese envoy to Tang Dynasty China. Presumably there would have been adverse effects to continue to use this system. At that same time, slavery under the name of 'nuhi-slave' was abolished due to development of feudalism. That is the reason why you see no slaves in the novel 'The Tale of The Heike Clan' which describes life of Taira family at the ending part of Heian period. Such

	laborers as bundle shoulderers were employed by warrior bands at the bands' expense with guaranteed payment for the labor and liverty of getting married. They were no longer the object for sale or purchase and could decide to leave the job freely. The first country in the world that abolished the slavery must have been Japan, I presume.]
Robert	[In Europe, slaves did exist ever since ancient Greece till the era of Rome, but the Romans did not have slaves wear clothes that would show the wearers were slaves. Reason why was because Romans might be exposed to a hazard if number of slaves was known to be more than that of Romans.]
Tsuguji	[In case of Japan, most probably slaves were ordered to wear the same color clothes as the slaves in the era of Tang dynstry. In Tang, a different name by which they called slaves was Shoue (blue clothings) as the slaves were wearing blue color clothes. At the Omizutori (Water-Drawing Festival) in Nigatsudo Hall of Todaiji Temple, the name 「woman dressed in blue」 was registered. This must be remnants of Nara era's political system based on the Ritsuryo code. In Japan, common people used to wear many of Aizome (indigo dyed) clothes which were believed insect repellent, and this may mean blue color clothes could have been dearer in cost. It does not make sense to have slaves wear expensive clothes so this may have been the reason why slavery in Japan collapsed earlier

	than in other countries.]
Robert	[Yes, you may be right. It could have well been the case as the turning point of history sometimes comes with incredible reasons. The world war was started from the point when the prince of Austria happened to be assassinated.]
Luc	[World war does not always happen by chance.]
Robert	[You mean the next war will be different?]
Luc	[The presently ongoing partitions of Poland is clearly construed as well planned partitioning by Hitler and Soviet's socialist Stalin, isn't it. There will sure be another world war in the next century.]
Den	[I guess there a large size natural hazard may take place prior to the outbreak of the coming war in the next century so the war may have to be started all in the chaos.]
Robert	[Young person's comments are outrageous. You must know something for sure, am I right?]
Den	[In line with Les Centuries of Nostradamus, 「after literary men beat the drum in the unheard of loudness, the whole world was attacked by a calamity of 「flood and waterlogging」 and this calamity will endlessly continue till 「all are perished」 and on the areas where water damage has not been caused 「huge amount of fire and scorchingly baked stones fall from the sky」 and 「Ultimately, Mars completely finishes the century」 which can be interpreted the earth will be ended by the ultimate war.]

Luc [What you say is WW3 will be started after the natural disaster has taken place, is it what you mean?]

Den [I participate the natural disaster will be so great that countries which act as the world policemen will find the situation too serious for them to handle. Consequently, war will break out to seek the way and means to establish Ordre Nouveau. To make the whole situation worse, huge amount of fire, which is not simple fire but burning rocks, namely flaming minerals, are falling from the sky. Such weapons are what human beings have never experienced so it means this disasterious war will be coming if coming after the next century or later. In addition, Les Centuries Volume 10, the seventy-forth portion can be construed as follows.]

When the extraordinary big 7, namely 7billion are overflowned,
This overflowing will be shown during the age of genocide war,
During the time right before the millennium of great happiness arrives,
The dead will be delivered out from the tomb due to shortage of food or to extract natural resources from the bodies.

10-74
Au reuolu du grand nombre septiesme,
Apparoistra au temps ieux d'Hecatombe:
Non esloigne' du grand aage milliesme,
Que les entrez sortiront de leur tombe.

This era shows the point of time when the world population will be several times more than that in 1940. When the world population reaches 8 billion, WW3 will break out. If things go differently, the world population may not reach 8 billion, or the population may decrease due to several adverse situations as a result of natural disaster and wars.

Then, to add more, the word Hecatombe starting with the capitalized H does have a special meaning. In olden time Greece, 100 bulls were offered to Gods as sacrifice when the Olimpics ended. Considering this historical fact, the time when this WW3 breaks out is the month when the world population will be reaching the level of 8 billion as estimation and the month is named as Leo in Olimpics year could be presumed as if Les Centuries may imply this much of information as well. I read the statement of the Les Centuries this way.]

Luc [Talking about your expression of 'beat the drum in the unheard of loudness', will such announcement be like the propaganda made by NSDAP or communist party related people?]

Den [As it is stated by literary men, I guess it may be in connection with reserved copyright. For instance, like the movie of Berlin Olympics named 『Olympia』 ⋯ expert missionaries that will exceed the capability of Leni Riefenstaal or Goebbels will be coming out in future, and I think only visual images can be transmitted beyond the barrier of languages. Many

	movies that take the world's end up as the subject sponsored by world-scale industries will be publicized and shown all over the world.]
Luc	[Movies are the invension that France boasts to the world, which Nostradamus would have already known. He would have even foreseen that movies showing the end of the world and the era when ultimate weapon would be used.]
Robert	[Amazing! You are practically foreseeing some concrete thing, not just talking logics!]
Luc	[Den, can I ask you what forms the foundation of your saying about the flood and waterlogging?]
Den	[Les Centuries Volume 5, the thirtysecond version has a relation with Japan or the whole Eastern Asia area so I am keeping my eyes on this part of Les Centuries.]

5-32

Economy is smooth sailing of the sun and the moon,
Ruin will be approaching to them,
Downfall is changing their fortune,
Just as same as the Seventh Rock

5-32

Ou' tout bon est, tout bien Soleil & Lune
Est abundant, sa ruine s'apporche.
Du ciel s'auance vaner ta fortune,
En mesme estat que la septiesme roche.

Here, understanding the sun and the moon as a district that enjoy prosperity following the ways and means that Japan has chosen to achieve its economical success, the area of East Asia over to Southeast Asia may match, however, around the year of 1550 which was the age of Nostradamus, the biggest economic sphere then was Ming Dynasty and the the Chinese character of Ming consists of the sun and the moon.

Further, what the seventh rock means is a huge mill which appears in Chapter 18, Section 21 of The Revelation of St. John the Devine, where Archangel threw into the sea a huge rock of a shape similar to a hand huge mill, to ruin the great city Babylon. In other words, the huge mill is meant for such capital equipments as factories, power plants, port facilities, and so on and for the termination of the decadent metropolis. What is implied in this statement is a possibility of a big area which is the center of the world's economy being destroyed by floods or inundations in large scale caused by the falls of meteorites or heavenly bodies. This possibility involves Japan, too, and that's why I have a special interest in it.]

Robert [Mind you! Nostradamus is a French man who was dead around the year 1560!]

Luc [If future can be foreseen, he might have seen the time when books written in Japanese could be purchased in Paris. Nostradamus must have well known the time when young French boys buy Japanese books.]

Robert [What for?]

Luc [Nostradamus would have created some part in his

	book which could be understood only by Japanese or people who understand Japanese, to lock up Les Centuries.]
Robert	[So you mean even English translation is locked up, do you?]
Luc	[If this book were able to be understood easily by French people to whom the language French is naturally their native language, and if it contains such parts that such people as statemen wish not to be known by the public, it has a risk of being burnt so the book will lose the chance to be transmitted to posterity. Yes, this is the reason why Nostradums purposely made his book difficult to be understood!]
Den	[People who can acknowledge the sun and the moon as one hieroglyph are for sure Japanese, Manturians and Chinese only.]
Robert	[How do you define the race Chinese?]
Den	[Han people in Republic of China. Military clique government related people consisting of warloads who do not always follow the order of the government. Neither Tibet nor Uighur is included as people there are not Chinese character users. Qing Dynasty had its origin in Manchu people as master-race and this is the reason why on the gateplate hung on the Qing Dynasty gate showed both Chinese characters and Manchurian words.]
Luc	[Taken it for granted that Den's explanations are correct, time when books or magagines written in

	Japanese are sold shall come fairly far ahead.]
Den	[Such weapon that can fall mineral fire from the sky targeting areas where are left undamaged by water has not yet been invented to date. But who knows next century shall have such weapon or not?]
Luc	[You're right. Observing the rapid development of aeroplane manufacturing technology, there surely is a possibility.]
Robert	[I wonder if NSDAP related people have been able to decipher Les Centuries?]
Luc	[Seems they have such group of professionals. I have gathered Hess and Himmler are closely discussing this matter together with occult scholars.]
Robert	[Do you happen to know who those scholars are?]
Luc	[I once heard a rumour that Himmler was holding a gathering with SS leaders at a castle commonly called Black Cameron and holding meetings similar to sabbath.]
Robert	[Are they communicating with the psychic world?]
Luc	[I'm not that sure, but it can be said SS are doing something calling phychics all the way from India or Tibet.]

While those men were talking to each other, the showtime of dancing started and Roxy who is a regular player of short comic plays there was showing flea-up dance to the music which was a little old dance of the year of nineteen-twentieth. It is one kind of strip shows, taking veils and clothes one by one in the gesture of getting rid of fleas. She was receiving thunderous applause to her dance showing her sexy body and atmosphere. Just when the audience thought she was taking off her underwear, the spot light changed the angle and another show of singing and dancing by Josephine Baker started. Josephine was an African Jewish quarter. She was wearing white bras on her brown skin, necklace with a quadruplicate strand of large white perls and fresh bananas around her waist like a Sumo wrestler's ornamental apron and was vigorously vibrating her voluptuous body.

Luc turned his eyes to Sophie who was sitting next to him, and found Roxy there, too, who was still short of breath.

Luc [Good ambiance, good dance.]
Roxy [Yah, I'm trying hard. Need to dance by watching and imitating such dance played by others as allowance from my family in my hometown has stoppedcoming.]
Robert [I, too, really wish to be of help…]

And then, a man of age of the thirtieth in business suit spoke to her. He was together with Kitty who talked to Roxy while they were visiting Duke's mansion the other day.

Walter [Roxy, I am Walter Schellenberg. Please call me Walter. You have a beautiful body, and should you be a multiple language speaker, this Kitty could be of help to you. If need be she says she can talk with you about advancing some fund for payment of the rent of

	an apartment in Paris.]
Roxy	[Could I give you a ring in the new year?]
Walter	[She is scheduled to stay in Paris till after the new year day.]
Kitty	[Won't you come and visit me at my room in Hotel Ritz? I'm curious about what other languages you can talk as it is important for hospitality business. I will talk about the details of the work when you visit me at the Ritz.]
Sophie	[Wow, now you may be able to return the debt to Maurice.]
Roxy	[Maurice being a gay, naturally he has no interest in women. If he were straight, well, that would have been convenient to me. But as his parents are jewelers, I could refund part of debt as they kindly bought my diamonds.]
Walter	[Gay usually has a better eye to understand the charm of women. People tend not to notice this strong point of gays. They have been prejudiced in the Catholic society for a long period of time.]
Roxy	[You mean you have no prejudice against gays.]
Walter	[Maurice is talented enough to be able to run such a wonderful cabaret-bar as this place. His cabaret-bar forms and tells the charm of Paris. Decadant is certainly not a religious word but sounds somewhat attractive. The charm of Roxy is there in her a little

	tired eyes and melancholic behaviors. Those who do not feel this kind of charm in her ought not be called men.]
Roxy	[Oh, I'm flattered. Are you an Italian?]
Walter	[I'm just a German who loves Rome.]
Roxy	[May I visit you tomorrow?]
Kitty	[You're welcome.]

It sounds that Roxy seemed to have decided to listen what Kitty will tell her. Then, the bell of the grand father clock in the hall rang to tell the time of midnight. Luc and Sophie greeted to others and left the place.

4. Sophie's treasure

Luc thought he would go by a taxi and see Sophie off around the corner of Saint-Germain and go on home located in the area called Le Marais. But Sophie started asking Luc to stop at her place saying she had something to show him. Midnight in Paris in winter was covered by heavy clouds with no star showing. Her compartment was located on the third floor of the apartment which stood on the side street after several buildings off the main street.

According to what Luc remembered Sophie's parents passed away due to Spanish flu, therefore, Sophie was brought up by her grandmather. Despite her such background, he saw the apartment had a grand-looking double-doors. Her living quarter was located on the place which normally called in France the noble second floor.

Sophie, unlocking the door, pushing it forward and entered. Lightening the room receiving Luc's hat and coat, she started talking.

Sophie [I'm preparing coffee so would you make a fire in the fireplace?]

Luc [As the fireplace seems still hot enough, if I can dig out some banked fire I guess I can make fire quickly.]

Saying so, he sat by the table under the Art Nouveau chandelier at the side of the fire place.

In the center of that small table, there placed is a silver basin. He took up a box of matches which he located on the same table next to the basin and mixed the ash of the fire place with a fire hook. He found small amount of fire still there. He piled up firewood which had thin branches attached. Blowing on the firewood several times, it started flaring up. Right then, sound of steps approached and she seemed to have seated on the other side of the table without drawing the chair back.

Luc [Den who was with Foufou today may have been feeling or seeing something reading Nostradamus' Les Centuries. I'm pretty sure about this because he at least knew the world war would be numbered three… wars will not cease easily like you see the banked fire in this fire place. As the size of the war getting bigger, that much the area where France will be involved will become broader. This would mean that automatically the area to where Les Centuries are referred will be broadened…To understand the sun and the moon as hieroglyph is a brandnew point of view which has never been thought of before…By the way, what is the thing that you wish me to take a look at which you call your ancestral treasure?]

Luc turned back but Sophie was not there yet. Instead he noticed there appeared on the silver basin placed in the center of the table Latin words which were meant as the precept given to Imperator crowned by laurel wreath at the triumphus.

RESPICE POST TE (Watch your back!)
HOMINEM TE ESSE MEMENTO (Keep it in your mind that you

are nothing more than a human!)

He muttered to himself those rather archaic and Roman medallion look Latin words all written in capitals and was about to lift his eyes up from the words on the basin, he noticed a future scenery vaguely coming up on the surface of the water. He saw himself of several years older with grizzled hair and saw a little boy running out of the door and jumping at him. That boy turned around and called for someone, and a woman who looked like Sophie of slightly fatter and older came out. Luc understood what that scenery was meaning and also understood what the ancestral treasure as she mentioned was. He was also convinced that Sophie was the mistress on this water mirror. Then, with all these knowledges he gained, he noticed that the pattern of the lace on which the basin was placed was of pentacle.

Water mirror in the magics of the olden times was a technic to use water as a substitute of mirror. Then, in there, using some unknown methods, people in the olden times summoned and used the sealed spirits in order to mirror truth or future that they had not been able to tell. In Sophie's case, she sealed the spirits by placing a sheet of lace underneath the basin for fixing boundaries, but very coincidentally, Luc who could read ancient Latin happened to mutter the words which resulted in drawing magical power out. Note, however, that if a person who is not well grounded in such inspiration, the spirits will not easily respond even if such person mutters the Latin words for hundreds of times.

Then, Sophie appeared carrying a tray, on which Limoges coffee pot and creamer are put, with her right hand and a Bacarat biscuit jar, which looked heavy, with her left hand. She quickly poured coffee into a cup placed in front of Luc and pushed it nearer to his hands and put hers on the table of the seat next to him.

Luc	[Sophie, as yet..nothing has happened⋯, but I wish to do everything possible not to embarrass you.]
Sophie	[Luc, what did you see?]
Luc	[I now know you are the user of the magic called water mirror.]
Sophie	[Oh, yes? What you have just said is exactly the same as my granma told me. She said that in this ancestral silver basin the spirits called Jinn or Jinny are sealed in and these spirits let some people who have the capacity see the future.]
Luc	[From when has this been inherited in your family tree?]
Sophie	[What I heard is it was after my ancestors parted from the head family as a branch family of Count Provence. I gathered that when the ancestors were importing medicine and commodity from the oriental countries, they seem to have been quite wealthy, so this silverware could be the ones produced in the thirteenth centry. And after that time Protestant-Hunt was executed by Richelieu's army, and what I heard is that my ancestors changed their sir name to escape from the danger. Then what happened was the town Les Baux-de-Provence was devastated so they escaped

	to Marseille and started printing the book of herbs there. I understand that was the start of the presently ongoing printing business. Granma is doing a contract work of a Paris publishing company at her printing company in Marseille. Judging from the sequence of these events, this silver basin can well be a product produced prior to the Richelieu's army's attack.]
Luc	[In the middle ages, herb business was closely related to the world of magics.]
Sophie	[The best seller for those in the know is Taro Cards.]
Luc	[Was Granma producing the Marseille version, too?]
Sophie	[Part of printing woodcut is said to have existed till around the time of the French Revolution.]
Luc	[My ancesters were lovers of the Marseille version as well.]
Sophie	[What I understand is when the spirits were sealed in this silver water basin would be when my ancesters gave a lodging to a travelling astrologist in 1530s. I heard many times from my family that the person who seemed to have arrived from Italy sealed the spirits of the Vista Sanctuary in Rome. I also heard that for this reason the Latin of the fifth centry used by churches nowadays can no way revive those spirits.]
Luc	[When we have a child, we had better let our child study Latin.]
Sophie	[Do you say this as those who are sealed here are Romans?]

Luc　　　　[Some of the Roman Gods….perhaps.]

Sophie　　[I understand you, too, could see what I could see.]

　Saying this, she gazed at Luc, who crasped her hand back, nodding to her words. Sophie's earlobes got a bit reddish. It seems that the basin was foreseeing all that was going to happen, better than the couple sitting here alive.

5. Marais' Mansion

When the year 1940 started Luc and Sophie registered their marriage at the government office and started living together using the second and third (noble second floor) floors of the mansion which was possessed by Luc's family. Le Marais was a comparably old district where there were mansions of aristcrats located. It was the place where mansions that were a bit too dark to match the modern times were being scattered here and there. Among those aged houses, Luc's mansion belongs to the older style, where on the second floor there were a salon and a dining room, a kitchen, and a study, and on the third floor several extra bedrooms were making a row.

However, Sophie's search of the bedrooms excluding the master bedroom and the bathroom annexed to the master bedroom were not yet been finished yet.

The state then at the mansion was far from completion of sorting work of useful goods from the piles of goods stored in those rooms.

On February 6, the day of Shrove Tuesday, together with Sophie's grandmother, they were going to meet Luc's parents who lived in a country house in Nice. During the past week till then, Luc was adjusting the replaced awning of the second-hand convertible Bugatti.

This vehicle was given to Luc as a wedding present by Francis Borgia.

The Borgias is Luc's hereditary customer for astrology. Francis just replaced this Bugatti by a silver color Mercedes. He in fact looked like wishing to get Duesenberg which Duke of Windsor was habitually using but he settled with Mercedes as Duesenberg was a very expensive vehicle of which chasis alone cost as much as US$8,500 and the body mounting costs more than double of that cost. At such cost, even a noble man cannot but be hesitant.

 The Bugatti which Luc was tending looks like a car that was originally made by a furniture maker, so panels made to order were with birdseye maple mirror finish and on the part which looked like black braids, Brasilian ebony was abundantly heaped up.

 In addition, while white ostrich leather was attached both on the driver's and the assistant driver's seats, the rear seat was gorgeously covered by zebra fur which was producing an atmosphere of Savannah that spreads from Abyssinian Highlands over to Kenya, reminding of the series of furniture designed by Carlo Bugatti. One point which should be remembered was that these natural materials such as ostrich leather needed to be cared to maintain its softness and the zebra fur should be protected from insect infestation.

 As they were to start off from Paris in its rainy season, the most important and time-taking work that had to be done was to replace the awning. Leaving the evidence of this vehicle having been used by the voluptuary Borgia family, there came out from underneath the front seat empty bottles of Absinth, sale of which was forbidden in France at that time of the history, together with a half-used atomizer of Chanel No. 5, rouge lipstick and a lighter coated with mother of pearl which was shining in rainbow color.

 These left out goods were evidences who the driver was taking into the assistant driver's seat, but to the newly married couple these things were nothing but a nuisance. Luc was displaying these bits and pieces on the dust swept scarlet colored floormat.

While Luc was doing this display work, Sophie came over to him carrying with her right hand a basket containing sandwitches.

Sophie	[Why don't you take a break?]
Luc	[Oh, thanks. I was just feeling a bit hungry.]
Sophie	[I see you have nicely finished replacing the awning. By the way, are you going to return these women's goods to him?]
Luc	[He asked me to return a pocket book if I found that but I didn't. You know he wouldn't care about his girls in the past. By the way, do you want anything here?]
Sophie	[Abthins is still available in Provence coming from Spain. I will take this atomizer as half of Chanel No.5 purfume is still left! … I don't want the rouge nor the lighter.]
Luc	[I see. Keep it.]
Sophie	[I tell you I can smell at least three women.]
Luc	[Can you see anything?]
Sophie	[color of rouge left on the neck of the abthins is slightly different from the color of this rouge. The lighter has scent of Mitsuko of Guerlain. The Rouge smells sandalwood coming from Eastern South Asia.]
Luc	[Oh, you have a good nose like a dog.]
Sophie	[Did you notice a single blond hair is sticking to the abthans bottle?]
Luc	[You are great!! Dogs can't identify colors. Let me

	explain this trick. The blond hair on the abthins is of the Austrian nobility Luise Dietrich, and the flavor of sandalwood is of Pan Jinlian. Another woman who was using Mitsuko must be Akiko Kitsuregawa. These are the triumvirate who were taken around by Black Caruso. As a matter of course, the real target that Francesco was aiming at must be that blond hair Louise..but as she is sticking around Akiko's acquaintance called Ginji Onimaru, an owner of a trading company, he doesn't have much chance, I guess.]
Sophie	[How do you know she was so sticky to that man?]
	[Ginji is a big man with tatoo of dancing petals of cherry blossoms on his back. What I have heard from Louise is that petals of those blossoms are changing the color into pink little by little as he takes brandy, which she finds very sexy. To me, Ginji's real status seems to be the army intelligence⋯as he does not look like a real childhood friend of Akiko at all.]

Also, I guess Jinlian may be the lover of the boss of Hong Kong mafia and is enthusiastic to visit casino of Monte Carlo. In fact, she seems to be obsessed by something evil. She is indulging in men, money and alchohol and a constant winner of gambling⋯it may be her fate predetermined in her previous life. They are all cute but not trustworthy.]

Sophie	[By the way, I wish to change the color of the curtains in the master bedroom and the salon to a little brighter color. Shall we buy some nice color curtains

	at the textile town Lyon while we go to Provance.]
Luc	[Yes, that's a good idea.]
Sophie	[OK, done. Then won't you measure the size of the windows, please.]
Luc	[Yes, as soon as I finish this work, I will do it.]
Sophie	[As I finished arranging all in the cupboard, the stepladder is there besides the cupboard.]
Luc	[While I'm at this, I will finish measuring the size of the kitchen window.]
Sophie	[If our budget allows, I wish to get a curtain of such patterns as oranges or lemons for the kitchen window.]
Luc	[On our return home what about staying overnight in Lyon after we buy curtains there. Some new cinemas may be on there, too.]
Sophie	[It is a real surprise to me that every thing in the house here was made before the eighteenth century.]
Luc	[After Napoleon's capture of Italy, my ancestors were accredited for fortune telling, but while they had not yet received any significant return for the work Napoleon went to ruin. So, they had to earn their livings by leasing out the above ground floors as the mansion was given to them when they demitted to serve Catherine de Medici as her astrologist.]

Listening to what Luc told her, her eyes started shining suddenly.

Sophie	[Is here any more unopened rooms that may contain mysterious things?]

Luc	[As my father has been under treatment by a change of air at a villa in Nice since ten years ago, I haven't had a chance to ask so I don't have any detailed information about this house. Why don't you ask my mother about it in Nice?]
Sophie	[Understood. Let's take coffee while it's hot.]

Having finished light breakfast, they returned to the second floor and started the work by measuring the size of the window in the kitchen.

Sophie	[Huh??]
Luc	[What?]
Sophie	[It looks the stepladder has moved to the windowside!]
Luc	[That is called in Japan Zashiki-Warabe Spirit. Preschooler's spirits do it. It is nothing to surprise me as I have been experiencing this kind of happenings ever since my childhood.]
Sophie	[As I am holding the ladder at the bottom of it, won't you please measure the size of the window frame.?]
Luc	[Oui, madame.]

Thus, Luc put the sizes of the stone window frames of the kitchen the salon and the master bedroom on the third floor onto a sheet of stationery which he happenly took out, then slipped it back into the jacket pocket again and thought now they could purchase curtains at a fabric shop in Lyon which made him a little relieved. He was enjoying that the old interiors which he had not cared about much before was then gradually getting changed into nice light colors.

6. Lunch break at Lyon

In the Catholic ritual, the day before the Wednesday in February which is called Ash Wednesday, is the day when is the last day for Catholics to take meat dishes. This day is the peak day of the carnival when fancy dress wearing parades are programmed and is called Mardi Gras (Fat Tuesday). Mardi Gras in Nice is an event that has been continued to date since the nineteenth century and is popular as it is a fairly large size event. In 1940, Tuesday, February 6 was that day. In the morning of February 3, Luc and Sophie putting several trunks on the red Bugatti planned to go off to Sophie's grandmother's place in Marseille and to stay the first night there.

Apparently, as Luc's adjustment of Bugatti seemed to have been done well, their Bugatti Type 49 was in good condition. The part around the wheel arch was painted in black and the body in red. Tires were replaced by new Michelin tires. Number of cars of this model produced during the year of 1930 to 1934 was approximately 470. This vehicle was equipped with straight 8-cylinders, 3 bulbs and a 3.3 liter engine and was deviced to get in right off the shunt shoulder of the pavement so it does not require a sidestep which in this regard means the style of this vehicle is close to cars of the present day and it was a vehicle which evolved that much from a horse carriage.

The distance from Paris to Marseille is about 750 kilometers. They started at 05:30 in the morning and after a 6.5 hour-drive they arrived at Lyon after running about 430 kilometers. The center of

France has a large, flat plain called Ile-de-France. Roads constructed are comparably straight and old streets that ancient Rome built here and there are still left in the present day. Each village was developed surrounding a church built on the top of the hill. Running there, vehicles are shaken vertically rather than horizontally. The riding condition of vehicles then was very rough due to the poor paving construction specially at the part of stone pavement, worsened by the poor suspension system of vehicles in those days. In the center of the meter panel a big and white color speed meter was equipped which showed 160/km as maximum speed but in actuality to run the vehicle at the speed of 100 km was quite a demanding exercise.

Sophie flipped the pages over of the Michelin Red Guide Book given by Kannenberg searching a suitable restaurant for lunch. Lyon was known as the leading city of fabric formation but was also known for the fact that there was no star-marked restaurant. Because of the need of restaurants or bars for use by workers working at the weaving factories especially for lunch, such restaurants that were specialized to offer full-course menu might not be easy to survive there. As a big town of manufacturing industry, it was a place where a big volume of silk yarns was imported from Japan. There Yokohama Specie Bank had its branch and foreign exchange transaction was abundantly being dealt with. Parking Bugatti in the place of the town, Sophie looked around and suggested to Luc to enter a café next to a shop which was raising French flag.

As the weather was still pretty cold, they chose a table at the bottom of the restaurant and ordered the 'today's set menu' (plat du jour) but both of them did not talk much due to fatigue of a long time driving. At the end of the lunch espresso was served by when they got a bit relaxed.

Sophie   [I'm shopping at the store next door Dijon mustard in ceramic pot and some foodstuff, so, will you wait in the car please.]
Luc   [Do you have any choice of which hotel for us to stay on the way back?]
Sophie   [While shopping, I think I will ring Lumiere to book a reservation.]
Luc   [Alright, then while you are doing all of those, shall I finish getting a dozen of wine?]
Sophie   [A half dozen each of red and white please, Luc.]
Luc   [After I finish loading the wine on the car, I will be at the secondhand shop next door. Call me there when you are finished.]
Sophie   [Oh, I see, the next door is an antique shop. I wasn't aware of that.]
Luc   [The signboard shows 'Brocante' so most must be unattended secondhand goods. Though majority of the goods is the eighteenth-century products, I may be able to dig out some newer products if I'm lucky.]
Sophie   [Luc, I hope you can find a secondhand Art Deco stand at a cheap price.]
Luc   [I see. You wish to make the salon the nineteen-thirties style.]
Sophie   [Old pieces have nice and heavy looks, but if they are

	too heavy, it literally makes the cleaning work very hard. Another reason is the present lightening in the study is dark enough to hurt your eyes. Eye glasses are not cheap, you know···]
Luc	[You're right. Those lightenings designed in the age of Art Deco give much brighter light than those of the eighteenth century. By the way, is this the reason why you have chosen the hotel by its name Lumiere?]
Sophie	[The inventors of movie are Lumiere brothers whose home town is this place. I'm a bit concerned as France does not use movie for the means of propaganda as Nazis do.]
Luc	[To parade power blatantly is senseless. The image of Olympia was so very nice but the film showing the convention in Nurumberg was entirely meant for the personal cult of Hitler of NS.]
Sophie	[You will not call them Nazis, why?]
Luc	[As Borgia said Italy managed by Fascist Party would be facing an economic meltdown without help from NS. Those Italians will not use any name by which NSDAP related members will not call themselves. They are neuvous as to be overheard as they will never know who from where may be listening. Therefore, it's better not to use the word Nazis.]

But it is also the fact that many divinations are implying another world war. The public may have not noticed it, but researchers of prophecy or fortune tellers have already been aware of it. And as Den was saying, in the first half of the twenty-first century another world war can take place. At that time, countries that have no faith in God or to the contrary countries that believe God fanatically will attack nations of multi-party parliamentary democracy. This disaster will happen when human desire has gone out of control. What's worse is such power will never stop attacking, making a circle of transmigration.]

Sophie [Transmigration is not a Cathoric word. My granma may understand it but other people will mistake it for diabolism.]
Luc [Shall we go now?]

Saying so, he finished payment for the lunch and the couple branched out for each shopping.

Luc splurged on wood-boxed six bottles each of red and white wine that came out from the wineries around Dijon and put the box of wine at the foot of the rear sheet of Bugatti with help by the sales person.

Sales Person [Sir, do you intend to go for lion hunting?]
Luc [I'm making a killing at the casino in Cote d'Azur…I wish to say that, but you know we should not waste our good luck in exchange of such a small success.]
Sales Person [But I guess this interior is your choice to suit your taste, am I right?]
Luc [This interior was made to order of the former owner of this vehicle. He ordered this interior feeling nostalgic about his days in Ethiopia.]

Sales person [But, you bought it as a used car, didn't you, sir?]
Luc [He gave this car to me as a honeymoon gift. But it is still a very good car. The grained mirror surface finish is as good as the one of a gourgeous yacht.]
Sales person [Please drop in again on your way back, sir.]
Luc [Yes, I will.]

Finishing loading wine, he opened the door of Brocante Cocon. At the far end of the shop, an old woman was knitting. Every time when her eyeglasses started dropping off from her nose, she stopped knitting to lift the glasses up by her right hand. He said hello to her but she looked indifferent so Luc could not be sure whether she heard his voice or missed it or let it go in one ear and out at the other.

The first word of the name of the shop, Brocante, means the goods bought by this shop as second-hand goods and just put in the shop with no mending added to them. Those frequent purchasers who are lovers of antiques are often dedicated hobbyists who spend the winter time looking at the fire in the furnace, cleaning and repairing those antiques carefully watching not to lose the luster and the charm that has been gained through the passage of time. Luc, too, was attracted by those brocantes and pulled out more than ten wine tasters stained as black as coal bound by a rope.

Of those tasters, he recognized two as silver made of the eighteenth centry reading the curved seal on them, but the rest were all made of pewter called as silver of the poor. All of these were of the Bourgogne style for use to examine the refection of the color of wine on the wine glass.

Now, adding here some explanation about Hallmark, the quality guarantee standard of the purity digree of silver, those of French made has a rooster carved seal with the manufactured year carved next to the rooster on the reverse side so as not to disturb the facility of this tool. This place to have the seal curved on a wine taster, is oftentimes at the place underneath the point where the holder's finger is placed, but depending on the case, you will find this curving the outside of either side of the two sides. In case of spoons the curving is added near the handle at the scooping side of the spoon. This is because in France cutleries are placed upside down at time of table setting. This is in order to have the seal on the back side made visible to the user of the spoon.

Now, regarding the silver content, as the category of jewelry, sterling silver with the number of 925 is now mainly circulated, but as cutleries need much glutinousness so as not to be bent easily, silver contents suitable for cutleries such as folks and knives have to be average 800. Coins circulated after Middle Ages used to have this silver content in the trade area of Venetian merchant fleet. The history tells us that Denarius in ancient Rome around the age of Augustus the silver content of this coin was 98% which was the highest possible silver content that could be manufactured at that time. From the age of Nero silver content percentage kept coming down and at the age of Philosoper and Emperor Marcus Aurelius the percentage came down to 79% and after then silver content kept going down further. History tells us that the grade of silver content in Europe did not have a chance to see any improvement till Venetian trade standard was established and put in practice.

It's just an aside but the content of gold of Gold Seal used in

Former Han Dynasty of China was 95.9%. This means that this level of the gold content was the maximum that the technology could afford to achieve in the ancient age. Quality of gold as to whether the gold used on products is authentic or not can be determined only by the kinds of small metallic particles, amounts of which are different to mines producing the metals, and by refinement methods used. Therefore, dealers who tell authenticity without having such data must be watched out. As a matter of course, when appraisal is made those which are appraised to contain no impurities should form a basis of suspect of fake antiques in modern industrised area.

Suddenly, the old woman tending the shop stopped knitting and let out her voice.

Old woman [Those came from a chateau in Bourgognne.]
Luc [Why were these sold in gross?]
Old woman [At the time of the French Revolution, there happened nearby Lyon a counterrevolution. It was a time of troubles. People tried to escape and many went missing. You can have these for 5 francs if you like.]
Luc [What about this deck of tarot cards? Are here major arcana only? What about the rest of the cards?]
Old woman [Those cards were left behind by a revolusionary army related man. Quite worn-out and on one card initials which may be just meaningless scribbles or meant for a name are written in ink.]
Luc [I see initials on The Fool.]
Old woman [What about 3 francs for this deck?]

Luc	[I will take these two for a total of 5 francs. What do you think?]

And there, Sophie entered the shop, having finished her shopping. The old woman gave a glance at her and asked.

Old woman	[Are you a newly married couple?]
Old woman	[I will add a couple of the silver salt spoons here, so what about 7 francs for all those?]
Luc	[We might as well take your offer.]
Sophie	[These salt spoons are of the pattern each of Vinus and Angel! Cute, aren't these.]
Old woman	[Misses, Child of Vinus is Cupid. You will soon have your Cupid. You can serve mustard in small portions, and the wine tasters can be polished up to be used as perfect cruets and vessels for seasoning. This shop is to offer you a brocante cocon. Spin out your dreams from the cocon and weave up your life together.]
Sophie	[I see. You have told me how to use antiques.]
Old woman	[Our regular customer who is a Japanese working at Yokohama Specie Bank was saying in Japanese tea ceremony culture, earthenware of many hundred years old is being used, thinking fondly of people in the old times. This feeling is shared by people here in France as there are intellectuals who think fondly of ancient Rome.]

Finishing payment to the old woman for what they bought, they went out of the shop and returned to the car.

Sophie   [I can understand the value of the wine tasters and salt spoons, but why did you buy the tarot cards which consist only of Major Arcana?]

Luc   [I found the letters LG on the card of The Fool. I thought the cards might have been left behind by my ancesters. That's why I picked them up. In addition, fortune telling was originally done using only Major Arcana cards.]

Saying so, he had the engine of Bugatti started.

Sophie   [Why did the two letters had to be written on the card of The Fool?]

Luc   [The Fool is the only one that can make a jest of the king. This is a very special condition. There are cases when The Fool is treated as 0 or 22. If the condition changes, the strongest can become the weakest. This is similar to the case of the extinction of dinosaurs due to the change of the condition of the environments.]

The Bugatti with the couple on board made a start straight to south to Marseille again.

7. Grandma in Marseille

It is relatively close to the Marseille harvour located on the west facing slope which was consisted of four storied houses with an attic. Houses of this style seize about 80% of the houses there. Some three or two storied houses both with an attice are mixed in this block, which were houses older than the majority of four storied houses. These lower storied houses were constructed further in the older time and luckily survived till then not encountering fire. Facing this a bit old looking street, Madeleine the grandmother of Sopohia owned a house and was living there. Her house was four storied with wall of light beige color and the windows were framed by limestone of a similar color to the light beige wall color. All windows of the first floor were iron-barred. On the second floor, a balcony seized the middle part of it, which was supported by statues of angels. The stone-made handrail was retaining the former appearance of the age of plenty. The keystone which was placed in the middle part of the semicircular shape arch was covered by a grotesque mask which looked as if it were watching and guarding malicisous fellows from entering the house.

Opening the walnut double doors painted up by varnish, Sophia said hello in a loud voice but received no answer. Sophia gestured to Luc to park the car at the side of the entrance. At that time of the era motor vehicle ownership ratio was not so high, therefore, such streets as in the current age when streets were made one-way use and were crushed up by many parked cars pushing bambers of each other did not exist so at this street the side of it is practically empty so that Luc had no trouble to park their car. According to what Sophia told Luc, the first floor of the house which Madlleine, the Grand Mother owned was being used as a printing factory and a storage of printing materials and products, with second and third floors used as her living quarters and the forth floor and the attic were leased out.

All shutters of the windows facing the street were tightly closed refusing access of people outside. Two windows were attached on each side of the arched entrance and her house with this external appearance was perfectly matching and melting into the townscape which was consisting of similar big houses. France was a country where city construction planning was started in comparably early times. For this reason, height of houses was standarized in most of the towns. The neatly even height of buildings in Paris was that those buildings were built in the era of Haussmann when building height was standardized. As the area nearby the Marseille Harbor needed to provide the port workers with lodging facilities, attics or the forth floors of the houses there were leased out to those workers. And the place facing the street was utilized as much as possible to cover the demand for such commercial or manufacturing use like shops, restaurants and factories as was usual with cities of different coutries, too.

As Madeleine was already told by Luc by telephone the visit of the couple, she went to the harbor the first thing that morning and bought some fresh fish from a fisherman whom she was acquainted with. What she started cooking at the noon time of that day by simmering the fish for a fairly long time was bouillabaisse. Luc, after carrying their luggage up to the bedroom, entered the dinning room, and was urged by Madeleine to sit at the dining table. The Baccarat six-light Chandelier was the style produced in the years of 1890s which meant that Madeleine and her family used to belong to the petit bourgeoisie class or so. Cristfle catelaries which were put on the table upside down were reflecting the flickering flames of two candles. A plate of bouillabaisse soup was brought and put on the table in front of Luc. The flavor of rosemary which symbolizes everlasting love, and fennel which helps to increase apetite were filling the dining table. When each was seated, Madeleine looked at the couple and offered prayers to God.

Madeleine [Patron saint of Marseille, St. Mary Magdalene, please protect happiness of this young couple. We thank you for this modist celebratory dinner. Amen.]
Sophie [Does St. Mary Magdalene mean Madeleine, doesn't it.]
Madeleine [You're right. When I got married, people said I was a becoming bride for Marseille.]
Sophia [Luc, shall I share marbled rockfish?]
Luc [Thank you. Will you please share conger, too?]
Madeleine [By the way, Catherine rang me just past noon and told me to pay a careful attention to the words written on the margin of this year calendar.]
Sophie [She means the epigram written under the calendar that we are printing, right?]
Madeleine [May and June are not good months for France.]

Listening what Madeleine said, Sophie peeled the calendar and read out the part each of the months May and June so Luc could hear what she read.

Sophie   [In May, Schlieffen will be changed to the area nearby Ardennes, and a man who is related to Barbarossa will wield his power. In April, time when flowers blossom is short, south wind is missed…this is almost incomprehensible.]

Luc   [The month of May can be deciphered by referring it to Les Centuries of Nostradamus.]

5-45

Le grand Empire sera tost desole'

Et translate' pres d'arduenne silue:

Les deux bastards par l'aisne' decolle',

Et regnera Aenodarb, nez de milue.

Les Centuries, 5-45

The great empire will soon be devastated

Taking the place of Silue near Arduenne

The two bastards shall be discharged

A hook-nosed man who relates Barbarossa will wield his power.

If Silue is meant for a deformation of Schlieffen-Plan…and What Barbarossa with the capitalized B at the beginning does mean? Taking the great empire as France, the two bastards will be the two prime ministers in the recent years. The senior who discharges prime ministers might well be no one but Marchal Petain. But I wonder what Barbarossa is meant for. Could it be a proper noun?]

Sophie	[What does Barbarossa relate to?]
Luc	[Suppose the reason why the Latin word Aenobarbus was dare not be translated as red beard in French, might be Nostradamus' word locking tactics as Den was saying. And if this interpretation is correct, should it be originally related to NS, then this word might become comprehensible if it is put in German.]
Sophie	[I see. Then does the hook-nose come to be meaningful if put in German?]
Luc	[With hawk and nose together, the present German national emblem shows a design of a hawk glasping a harken kreuz, so that what is meant could be the man who leads Germany at the head. Also, if the forth line is translated using inversion method, this could be read as the leader of hawks supreme commands Barbarossa.]
Sophie	[What is the reason why Barbarossa is nonsensical?]
Luc	[In the fullness of time, it would come home to any one; this is what is necessary as protection of prophecy being burnt by statemen. Taking the touble of using Latin means the words are locked.]
Sophie	[Don't you have any doubts about accepting the cryptanalysis done by such a person as Den whose native language is Japanese?]
Luc	[Les Centuries has been indecipherable by any native French person for the past 400 years, so we have to seek a different way . By the way, what on earth is written on the June portion of the calendar?]

Luc [Peace is coming near and war as well, both men and women lament over blood of innocent people being spilled⋯what does this sentence mean? Did Nostradamus purposely avoid completing the sentence?]

Luc [He couldn't write more, regarding this part..]

Les Centuries 9-52

Peace approaches from one end, but war from the other

Men and women lament over innocent blood spread over the earth that has never been longed this much in past This will concern all people in France

9-52

La paix s'approche d'vn coste', &la guerre,

Oncques ne fut la poursuitte si grande:

Plaindre homme, femme sang innocent par terre,

Et ce sera de France a toute bande.

What this implies is nothing but a world war, and I presume possibility of France alone could get peace and of irritation of France for that France could do nothing but looking on with folded arms death of people of the neighborhood countries. In any case, Maxime Weygand is to be expected to keep culture of Paris.]

Madeleine [According to Catherine, when Major Arcana is fallen into the hand of the person who ought to have these cards this prophecy will be materialized.]

Luc [Major Arcana? I think⋯what I got is..]

Madeleine [It happened that French revolusionary army was sent to Lyon for putting down the counter-revolution

	power. The cards were what the fortune teller attached to the army left over there. By the way, you are planning to go to Nice. Won't you tell me about your parents?]
Luc	[My father Luc・Claude as we call him Claude got sick a few years ago and since then he has been recuperating in Nice with my mother Bice caring him there, as my clan has been living on house rent income for the past 400 years. I reckon my mother is happy as my father is always with her.]
Madeleine	[I guess you are working your job as a hobby.]
Luc	[My family in these 400 years has been the astrolosist of the Borgias. I understand our mansion in Paris was bestowed on us by Catherine de' Medici in her era. I am therefore working for both French Government and Italian nobles.]
Madeleine	[Are you working for them as astrolosist in France, too?]
Luc	[At the archives where I came acquainted with Sophie, I'm organizing documents relating astronomical observatory and also doing research work of the past war history. This war history research is my hobby work.]
Sophie	[As he showed interest in the birth date of adjutant generals or staff officers of the enemy except Napoleon, I thought him strange.]
Madelleine	[I have already had Catherine Montvoisin your fortune told. I understand that the age you live will have a

	series of difficulties but your compatibility looks good.]
Sophie	[Catherine is our family's exclusive fortune teller, isn't she, though I have not met her yet.]
Madeleine	[No, you haven't met her yet. We always use telephone or letters when we produce calendars. Lyon is fairly far from here.]
Sophie	[What is she doing in Lyon?]
Madeleine	[She sells second-hand goods at a brocante shop. I remember the name of the shop as Cocon.]
Sophie	[Now I see we have met her already.]

During such conversation, the night was getting late. They decided to go to bed for the early morning departure on the following morning.

8. Carnival in Nice

On the following day in the early afternoon, riding on Buggatti the three members arrived at Luc's ancestral villa. It was a three storied mansion standing alongside a slope leading to a hill in Cimiez District near to the harvor. They opened the gate and drove the automobile into the guarage, The state of the guarage looked more like a stable with the image of the past when there was a horse. As this visit was the very first of Sophie and Madeleine to Luc's parents, they chose to enter the residence from the main entrance. As the entrance was decorated with mosaic tile floor and offwhite marble wall with bronze lantern hanging from the ceiling which made them forefeel the life of petit bourgeoisie there, Madeleine felt somewhat relieved. If the couple had to start an extremely poor living, their newly married life would have become a misery.

The double door of three dimentional sculpture of walnut wood decorated by floral pattern was opened towards inside the house, and Bice wearing heavier makeup than usual came out together with Claude. Finishing exchange of stereotypical greetings, Bice proposed to go out to get some mimosa flowers at the event of Battle of Flowers (Bataille de fleurs). Following her idea, they walked down to the street where the festival car of the battle of flowers was parading. After about a twenty-minute walk down on the slope, there located a palazzetto which Luc's family has been possessing at Le Marais since before French Revolusion using as a rental house for their tenants.

The festival float was to parade in front of this plazetto, so the party took the local food called Socca, which was a crepe without fillings and dusted with salt and pepper, and coffee, and they waited for the arrival of the parade sitting on the prepared seats.

Then Luc noticed that Francesco Borgia, the regular customer for generations was escouting Louise Dietrich, and also guiding Akiko Kitsuregawa and Pan Jinlian.

Borgia	[I asked Bice to book the seats here.]
Luc	[You're taking a large party.]
Borgia	[I promised to take them to casino after this.]
Luc	[In Les Centuries what I read and understood recently is the Latin word Ahenobarbus matches the German word Barbarossa. Have you ever heard about it?]
Borgia	[No, I haven't heard of that.]
Luc	[And, regarding the strategy that German army used at the western front of WW1 called Schlieffen Plan, is there such news that the initiator point was shifted to somewhere near Ardennes?]
Borgia	[This news, I will send it via telegram to Italy. At Italian Embassy in France such topics can never be detected. Perhaps this news must have been sealed there. By the way, which part is it where you read and understood this way?]
Luc	[Les Centures Volume 5 Version 45. Reading this part I can understand at least half of it⋯but the word Barbarossa is still remaining as unbreakable cipher.]

Borgia	[Does French Government know about it?]
Luc	[I don't at present have any high governmental official as my regular customer. But Sophie may be able to relay this news to Mrs. Marie, the wife of Your Excellency Weygand.]
Borgia	[Weygand seldom stays in France so I don't think to pursue him will work, do you agree?]
Luc	[Nobody else but Your Excellency Weygand would be able to persuade General Petain to deal with my interpretation of this part of Les Centuries.]
Borgia	[Pursuading him then what do you expect to make happen?]
Luc	[Avoid senseless loss of human lives and protect the light of culture of Paris.]
Borgia	[You mean even if no cooperation can not be obtained from NS, Your Excellency Weygand has good utility value.]
Luc	[Yah, as he has the blood of German aristocrat.]

While such conversation was going on, a parade float carrying a large quantity of mimosa flowers came into their eyesight. Then the battle of flowers was to be started. Quantity of flowers prepared was good eough to cover all the sightseers. What matters was from which muse men there could receive the flower, consequently they rushed to the muse who was showing the most charming smiles. When all is said and done, flowers to which the charm of the young muse was brought to had much more value than flowers given by a leasury old woman knitting lace at the corner of the town. After all men went to the float, Jinlian and Akiko left there telling the other ladies they were to go to the washroom. Across the two empty seats that had been seized by the men, Louise seated next to Sophie.

Louise   [I recall Roxy is your friend. I heard she was working comfortably at the saloon of Kitty.]

Sophie smelling the scent Kitty was wearing, suddenly started feeling uneasy.

Sophie   [Now I see that was your atomizer.]

Sophie started searching it in her bag, Louise waived to her not to and said.

Louise   [That atomizer was given to me by a man of the name of Ginji Onimaru who left me and is gone, so I don't need it any more. Keep it please. Oh, by the way, here I have a small bottle of Chanel No. 5 which Black Caruso gave me. You can also have it as originally packaged. Men arbitrally misunderstand that Chanel No.5 is best suited to working women. By the way, you expect to see Akiko in Paris, don't you. I feel whatever intention the man Onimaru has, it won't be trading business. So, if you can detect whatever different from the trading business, please contact me here and tell me what you have found out.]

Sophie	[Oh, thanks. Now I see there in Paris a sub-branch of the publishing company of Happiest Time is located.]
Louise	[You're right. I'm commuting between Paris and Berlin. Should you not be able to catch up with me, please leave a message if you see Anka Stahlhelm there in my absence.]
Sophie	[Certainly.]

At the end of this conversation, the two others came back from the washroom. At this same time Louise left the seat so Akiko and Jinlian took the seat which was emptied by Louise.

Sophie	[Incidentally, Luc was wondering if Mr. Onimaru is really your childhood friend.]
Akiko	[To be honest, I was asked by my uncle who works in the Japanese Embassy in Paris to look after him. I myself don't exactly know anything but guess his stay here is not really for trading business but for something else.]
Jinlian	[No, I also can't believe that trading only is his purpose to be here.]
Akiko	[Why do you think so?]
Jinlian	[He behaves like a catholic but sometimes his behaviors show quite different facets. I travelled on the same vessel with him from Hong Kong so I had time to observe him. He was saying he was sort of similar to a hidden Christian but even so, what he said

	does not match my impression of him.]
Akiko	[He must be a hidden devil warshiper.]
Jinlian	[What!! What do you mean by what you just said?]
Akiko	[Cathoricism was handed down to Japan in 1549 but in the Edo era the missionary work was prohibited. Therefore, Christians had no other way but to keep their faith secretly. Those Christians are called hidden Christians. In case of Mr. Onimaru, he must be a worshipper of the devil which was mixed in the sailers of the vessel that carried Xavier to Japan. Onimaru is an afficiate of Que Mammon which is a sect of Mammon that was worshipped by the mercants related to the smuggling trade called 'Nukeni' in Japanese. Trademark of the international trading company that he belongs to is copying the company's president's family crest but it is designed upside down. The president's family name which is 'Jumonji' is meant for Cross in English.]
Jinlian	[Is this cross you mention the Cross of Saint Peter? Onimaru was a formidable winner of gambling or very strong at other sorts of this kind of things while on the ship. Strong men are always loved by women.]
Akiko	[The cross of Saint Peter is a symbol of strong faith, isn't it? The upside down Latin cross means blasphemy. I'm afraid you do not understand the difference of falsely similar symbols.]
Jinlian	[As he is dangerous, that much he is charming.]
Akiko	[You must have slept with him, too. You are

	unbelievably out of everyone's hand…]
Jinlian	[He spared his luck to me.]
Akiko	[What are you aiming at by spreading all bad fates to destroy men?]
Jinlian	[The guy with whom I was partnering in Hong Kong went bankrupt, but I could recover all French bonds of my portion, and all this was thanks to the information Onimaru gave me.]
Sophie	[By the way, did Mr. Onimaru return to Japan?]
Akiko	[He comes back to Paris for about a week's stay every month.]
Sophie	[He is a subject worth watching, isn't he.]

Then, at that time Louise who had been out to make phone calls came back, and at the same time the two men returned carrying bouquets of yellow color Mimosa flowers. All of them spent a little more time there enjoying coffee and the Borgia group parted to enjoy the evening casino.

9. Dinner at Hotel Le Negresco

Having parted from the Borgia party, they strolled through the streets which were busy for the carnival. Promenade Des Anglais which is commonly called Prome was very crowded with people visiting these streets after the carnival, and the shops and stores were showing nicely decorated show windows for this special event. As it was about the time to check in, Luc and Sophie looked around and easily found the hotel building even in far distance. Le Negresco was a building of which the ground level was constructed using chalky color order and on top of this ground level construction, second to forth levels (in the French expression first to third levels) which were also of chalk color were added, and on the roof a pink color dome was attached. This eye-catching appearance of the hotel building was easy to be distinguished as Le Negresco from a distance.

The steeple on top of the dome and the mint green bordering by Dormer window were producing sense of liberation and so, this building was favored by many sightseeing people. This building was constructed in 1923 by Gustave Eiffel requested by the Romanian Henri Negresco. It is the last flower that blossomed at the end of la Belle Epoque.

Off the promenade they stepped into the hotel and found Claude and others had already arrived there by taxi. Bice and Madeleine were conversing freely and friendly.

Claude   [Sophie, could you find this building easily?]

Sophie	[Such eye-attracting beautiful building is really the pearl of Nice.]
Claude	[The two domes of Hotel Carlton in Cannes were popularly known as Breasts of La Belle Otero. Nice cannot lose to Cannes. We have Le Negresco, here.]
Sophie	[What is this hotel supposed to symbolize?]
Claude	[Needless to say, it is Mata Hari. She was the sun of every one having her breasts attract all men!]
Bice	[Oh, you say the first thing in your mind! Sophie, don't take the words seriously of this Italian French man.]
Sophie	[But his talks are interesting.]
Bice	[That's exactly how I was cheated. O sole mio! What a fishy song of an Italian man!]
Madeleine	[I'm envious that at your age you still have a gentleman who wish to cheat you.]
Claude	[I agree, Bice may be right. But differently from Belle Otero whom Duke of Westminster loved, Mata Hari which name means the eyes of the sun was truly bewitching. Even the hero of France, General Petain tried to pay an incognito visit wishing to see her just for a glance, but failed as there were already a crowd to try see her, so his forceful approach caught public attention and his efforts were failed. People concluded that such action of General was to decrease his sordiers' fighting spirits so General was condemned as guilty. This was nothing but a false charge.]
Bice	[As men were too particular about such trifle matter, Goddess of Fate must have taken her away.]

Claude	[From the ancient era, it was curvaceous female body that was touched by divinity. This is a fact that is clearly shown on the statues of Greece and Rome.]
Sophie	[Whatever you say, I really think this pink color dome is very nice.]
Luc	[It's about time to start enjoying the dinner.]

Following a soup of basil and mussel, grilled squid and octopus Bolognese were served, when a man who sat at the next table to Luc's group was ordering a half portion of rabbit Porchetta (roasted whole). Lights around the tables were set dark, and only candles on each table were burning. Suddenly, Luc realized voice of the man sitting at the next table sounded familiar to him. Luc turned around and found Robert there with whom Luc had conversation at the mansion of Duke Windsor.

Luc	[Mr. Robert Grant, This is Luc. We were together at the Christmas party.]
Robert	[Well, well⋯I see Sophie the friend of Miss Roxane is here, too.]
Luc	[I have a news, I found out a new interpretation of Les Centuries in 5-45.]
Robert	[You mean a new decipherment. Won't you tell me if you don't mind.]
Luc	[The revised Schlieffen Plan seems to set the initiator point at Ardennes Forest. The man to take command is considered to be a man who was involved in Barbarossa in German. Does this bell ring with you?]

Robert	[What I have heard is in January this year, a German army related man who was caught in Belgium seems to have with him an invating plan which is exactly the same as Schlieffen Plan used at WW1. I heard this news from Duke Windsor when I met him the other day for checking his health…Regarding Barbarossa, I haven't heard anything about it. I have an appointment of medical check up of the staff of American Embassy in Berlin so I will ask at this time. To be frank with you, I am also taking the medical examination programe of embassies in the English speaking countries as my additional assignment.]
Sophie	[Talking about Roxy, I understand she is now working in Berlin at the place called Salon Kitty.]
Robert	[You mean that charming lady. Oh, it will be a pleasure If I can meet her again there.]
Sophie	[Roxy seemed to be conscious about you, too.]
Robert	[All depends on whether time allows or not. Should a new plan be issued, I shall most probably miss the chance to visit Berlin.]
Sophie	[Now that you are here, today I was with Black Caruso till just some time before. Is today a coincidential day?]
Robert	[He seems to loose his heart to all women, but as he is too irresponsible and light that women tend to ignor him after all. Did he take any ladies with him?]
Sophie	[Luise with blond hair, and Akiko and Jinlian in the eastern line. They were talking about visiting a casino

	somewhere here.]
Robert	[Suppose all this is the result from their previous life, the Borgias can be said as deeply sinful.]
Luc	[You mean the previous life has relation with the present life.]
Robert	[According to the report received from the Indian Colony, there seems to have quite a few instances of reincarnation. Christian churches are eagerly denying this report, however, should you read a confession of a killer who attacked and murdered you in your previous life, you will have no other choice but to believe in reincarnation, won't you?]
Sophie	[Me and Luc, are we related also in such way?]
Robert	[In your case, you must have succeeded in finding out the originally destined counterpart. If this guess is wrong, that is also your destiny. Point is most people can only debate on such guess deductively. As long as we study this report, authenticity of reincarnation cannot be denied. If we assume that soul exists, it may be possible that we see through future beyond space and time. Nostradamus was this type of person , or more exactly who belonged to the primates. Monkies cannot see through future, or otherwise, even if they could, they would have no means and ways to pass the information on to the others.]
Sophie	[Who is the person that you ought to seek?]

Then, the roasted half portion of rabbit was delivered to Robert's table. Robert, having once returned to his table, let a waiter fill a glass with red wine and enjoyed dinner by himself alone. Finishing dinner, he said goodbye to the Luc's party and went back to his room in the hotel. Seeing Robert off, Luc's group finished the party and had taxis called for them. At that moment, a man who wore a fedora comingfrom outside approached a waiter. He was Schellenberg of SS. He secretly handed a ten-franc bill to the waiter and asked.

Walter [About what Luc who was sitting at the side of the party seats was talking?]
Waiter [I cannot answer your question, sir.]
Walter [Is this good enough?]

He added another ten-franc bill on the waiter's palm.

Waiter [What I could hear was such words as new Schlieffen Plan, or Ardennes Forest. Also, the British gentleman was talking that he was doing the work assigned by a country in Anglosphere so he was visiting American Embassy in Berlin. He was also talking in German about something …]
Walter [German? Please try to recall that conversation.]
Waiter [He was asking the meaning of a word which if in German [would mean Barbarossa, but the British gentleman was not able to answer.]
Walter [Was the origin of that word a Latin word?]
Waiter [I don't think they referred to the original language. Then…a lady was speaking up and saying Black Caruso was planning to visit a casino tonight.]
Walter [Sorry I took your time. Thanks.]

Walter riding on the car which he had kept waiting for him, hurriedly returned to the hotel where he was staying. Borgia is a carabiniere at Italian Embassy, Italy forming alliance with Germany his duty was not so demanding as that of carabiniere in Germany, however, such information as 「new Schlieffen Plan」 and 「Barbarossa」 had to be reported back to his country Germany because Robert Grant was a doctor of the England side.

10. Report by Walter

After closely reviewing this matter for some time in his room of the hotel, Walter made a call to Reinhard Heydrich whom Walter was directly reporting to, and Heinrich Himmler.

He called Heydrich first but as he was told that Heydrich was on another line, he left with a secretary a message that he would call again and then called Himmler.

Walter [Your Excellency, I have an urgent report.]
Himmler [Does it relate to cruciality of the nation?]
Walter [The astrologist of the Borgias by the name Luc Gauric deciphered Les Centuries 5-45 and was spreading the information regarding the new Schlieffen Plan and Barbarossa.]
Himmler [I understand Schlieffen Plan, but what is Barbarossa?]
Walter [If Your Excellency does not know it, Rudolf Hess Dupty Leader may understand it. This commissioned doctor at the England side may be reporting it to his country. It seems he is also working for The American Embassy.]
Himmler [I will pass this information to Dupty Leader Hess. Hitler seems not concerned about the occult or prophecy. Our leader was reading a book today, too, of the Napoleonic wars.]
Walter [What I am telling you now is information that the England side does not know, but I observe that the

	Italian side is scheming to pull General Petain out who forced General Maxime Weygand to be the negotiating partner.]
Himmler	[Your decipherment ability is quite impressive. We cannot afford to send you to dangerous places. Let that astrologist do the deciphering work of Les Centuries for the time being. But watch him out not to leak his information to the England side. I guess this man does not understand how big the influence of such information could affect the world though he knows what he is to do.]
Walter	[What about seizing him?]
Himmler	[Calm down. Should we seize him, the relationship of Italy and Germany would be damaged. Just let him be as he is. The British doctor, too, must be set free as such touch measure as seizing him can develop to a diplomatic issue as his case involves The American Embassy, as long as America stands as a neutral power.]
Walter	[I understand, sir.]
Himmler	[Let the astrologist perspect the future as much as he can. Send the file of this person later. I think it is necessary to show the file to Dupty Leader Hess.]

Thus, he finished talking to Himmler on the telephone, then he quickly relayed the information to Heydrich. As soon as he finished this talk, he hung up and had shower. The bathroom is of the neo-rococo style and with a high ceiling, and the bathtub was supported by four Lion paws.

Walter	[Hello, this is Walter.]
Hess	[I just received an urgent call from Himmler, Can you guess who I am?]
Walter	[I understand you are Your Excellency Hess Dupty Leader. I am grateful for your call at this late hour.]
Hese	[Don't you think the name Luc Gauric sounds familiar to your ears?]
Walter	[Any person in the history?]
Hess	[Reason why the Borgias never gave his family tree up is because it is inheriting the name of Luca Gaurico.]
Walter	[Do you mean that person who was the fortune teller retained by Catherine de Medici?]
Hess	[You're right. I told this to Himmler, too. When Gaurico retired, he recommended to the queen as his successor Nostradamus who was the wellknown auther of Le Centuries.]
Walter	[Does it have any relationship with the present case?]
Hess	[Talking about Schlieffen Plan, there is a possibility that the content of it was leaked when the pilot was arrested who made an emergency landing on the enemy's territory. Details of this happening was what the Italian side could not know even if the British side could detect it. In addition, Louise reported to us the pilot was telling that the Latin name Ahenobarbus equaled to the word Barbarossa.]
Walter	[What does Barbarossa mean?]

Hess	[That's the thing that even the staff officers of Wehrmacht could not clarify. Some day Leader Hitler may externally unveil the meaning, but at this stage the contents of what this word means are in chaos. Do you have any other information about Luc?]
Walter	[He seems to have an interest in the research of the past war history and the record at the astronomical observatory.]
Hess	[According to Heydrich, a woman called Roxy seems to be a friend of Sophie, the wife of Luc, and Roxy was saying Luc alike an astrologist was showing an extraordinary interest in the birth date of the histrically known people. Luc seems to have been asking for a correct information about the birth date of the major staff of NSDAP.]
Walter	[That kind of information won't have importance to be called secret?]
Hess	[I have heard he would not tell the fortunre of the people whose lives would be terminated around the year of 1945.]
Walter	[Does it have any relation to the NS destiny?]
Hess	[He seems to set the year 1945 plus and minus three years as an unusual period based on the knowledge he piled up through the network of fortune tellers.]
Walter	[That he refuses to tell the fortune means that the destiny of the person who asks him to tell his fortune has already been expired, am I understanding it correctly?]

Hess	[Yes, I presume you're right. We, too, are in need of reviewing the use value of General Weygand and General Petain based on the information acquired from Hans von Dincklage. You, take the necessary measures regarding this matter.]
Walter	[I understand, but what do you mean by use value?]
Hess	[Both Germany and France can decrease the wasteful damage caused by the war. If we can let Paris down without damaging it we may be able to prevent unconditional jingoists in NS.]
Walter	[I agree as Paris is an international city which has communicativity of culture.]
Hess	[It is the most desirable stage for the Gestapo.]
Walter	[It will also be necessary to increase Your Excellency's leadership, won't it.]
Hess	[Taking this method, things will turn to be better without counting on Goebbels's favor.]
Walter	[As Leni's movie is more popular than the movie of Black Casanova, she is a promising existence.]
Hess	[As regards the tug-of-war by The Black Society of Jesus against Black Casanova, I am waiting to hear more good news.]
Walter	[How do you prospect this tagmatch to develop?]
Hess	[Broiler and Casanova are playing a close game, but if compared by number, Broiler is leading, while by information dissemination abilities Casanova is dominant..but in the sense of national reputation, both couldn't exceed that fatty Iron Man Hermann.]

Walter   [Fatty was against invation of Poland…does he stand for the appeasement policy with UK?]

Hess   [I don't think I can answer such question as the matter of the leader's sole prerogative.]

Then the line was cut off.

Walter asked the butler standing in the hallway to have absinth delivered to his room. In Nice it was far easier than in Paris to get absinth produced in Spain. While absinth is medical, because of its narcotic nature use of it in France was prohibited. But as Provance is the sightseeing area which is supported by the money of sightseers, at the hotel of chalk for travelers of foreign nationals assinth was secretly being served.

When Walter was putting a piece of cube sugar on an absinth spoon, Louise wearing a bathrobe was coming in. In silence she took a small bottle of brandy out from mini-bar and dropped one drip of brandy on the cube sugar. Gently she struck a match and lit it, she opened her mouth for the first time.

Louise   [Do you have something bothering you? You are taking such as absinth…do you wish to see illusion?]

Absinth is herbal liquer of transparent green color made from worm wood but the alchohol content is rather high and some are 40 to 68 percent and tastes sweet. It is taken as cocktail adding melted cube sugar thinned by the same amount of water, or sometimes nearly double amount of water to the drinker's liking. To concoct this specification, often glass for absinth has a hemispherically shape pocket into which unblended absinth is to be put. Also, on a sugar cube people normally put one drop of absinth and light the cube and when the sugar comes to get brownish, such cube is to be melted with d'eau mineral (mineral water) added and such liquid is dropped on the unblended absanth till it becomes to fit the tongue of the drinker.

For such practice, the part where the cube sugar is put is cut in the state of watermark which adds an attractiveness to the absinth glass and for this reason absinth spoon is made a collectors' item. When absinth is thinned by water, the green color of the liquer becomes clouded and produces a fantastic swaying. Looking at this swaying some imagine the body line of his lover or some others recall the lost lovers in their past.

Walter starting talking after dropping the flaming cube sugar into the glass but did not give even a glance to her face. After drinking the absinth cocktail quicky in one gulp, he put the glass back onto the table and for the first time found what to say to her.

Walter [Hess seems to be seeing through the future. We the NS members may not be able to survive the three years before and after 1945.]

Louise [Fatty as you call him often may be killed by heart attack, Casanova by cerebral hemorrhage screaming in his speech, and Broiler by mercury poisoning or otherwise strucken by thunder falling right on him due to the wrath of God?]

Walter [You, saying all this, will get thrilled to death with ecstgary on the bed, Aha?]

Louise [You are such a spoiled youngest child. Forget about

	all such silly thoughts. I WILL bring you up to be a bit better technician. It is what is needed for a spy.]
Walter	[Should I have Luc tell the destiny⋯or, would it be better to ask Ave Maria, the acquentance of Akiko Kitsuregawa, I wonder.]
Louise	[I think it may be an idea to use La Voisin in Lyon before you return to Paris?]
Walter	[Is that person a prophet? Or is she a fortune teller?]
Louise	[Though she is aged, she can read Les Centuries much better than Himmler can. Himmler's comprehension power is completely locked against Les Centuries as his mind is fully occupied by greed for power.]
Walter	[As you say, Broiler is talented to grow his evil thoughts giantly, and surely he is eagerly wanting to obtain the granary in Ukraine. On the other hand, he is growing SS as second Teutonic Knights..Does all this mean another world war? Should he poke his nose into Ukraine, it would become violation of the non-aggression treaty between Germany and Soviet and the total situation would become uncontrollable⋯]
Louise	[You're a bit queer⋯What happened?]
Walter	[You are a woman who can't predict future. That's why you are easily baffled by Onimaru.]
Louise	[You're a big worrier. What does it matter if another world war takes place?]
Walter	[Does Broiler takes humans on the same level as chickens? It is true orders can only be obtained at the sacrifice of thousands of lives. Hess may have seen

through the fates of Hitler and other leaders. He requested Elsbeth Ebertin to read Hitler's horoscope on the press in 1923. I wonder if this was to reconfirm reliability of Hess ˙ psychic reading?]

Louise [Hess by himself can see the future to some extent!]
Walter [That's what it is!]

Then he drained the absinth left in his glass. Louise darkened the light of the stand which was standing besides the sofa and put on coquettish airs to show to him. The night in Nice was just about to be started.

VENUS and OCTOPUS will be here.
See HOKUSAI MANGA

11. La Voisin in Lyon

On the following morning, after seeing Madolene off at the Nice station as she said she was going home by train, the red Bugatti was driven by Luc aiming for Lyon. Using Red Michelin Guide, the hotel had already been booked, Sophie was excited on the assistant driver's seat considering what sort of pattern of curtains she should purchase.

Hotel Lumieres was facing the square and was a six-storied 1930s art deco style building with an attic and with a sandstone outerwall. Shell shape glass eaves attached above the entrance was showing an elegant appearance. High up on the entrance, with the flag of France in the middle such flags as Japan or Union Jack were decorated which looked as if they were symbolizing the hotel's internationality receiving visitors from all over the world.

Getting introduction from the hotel concierge, Sophie took Luc triumphantly to a store where curtains were sold.

Sophie [Now, this store will help give the interior of our dining, salon and master bedroom nice and bright atmosphere.]
Luc [Next is wall paper, right?]
Sophie [Give me the memo of the measurement you took.]
Luc [Here it is.]

Sophie came to notice that the memo showing the measurements was written on the reverse side of a stationery paper so she turned the paper and found a name and birth date written which she remembered she had seen before. It reminded her that Luc had been requested by the person of that name to tell his fortune.

Sophie [Luc, this paper is the memo of Mr. Kannenberg writing his information, isn't it? Oh, the letterhead carries a mysterious mark.]

Luc in haste came to her and looked at the paper closely and passed his fingers across the embossment on the letterhead.,

Luc [This letterhead means that his work place is the prime minister's official residence in Berlin.]
Sophie [First time for me to see such an embossment as this. An eagle hooking a cross. This is his birth date. You were to tell his fortune, do you remember?]
Luc [I remember I promised to present him the Interpretation book of Les Centuries in the Germanversion in exchange of his Michelin Red Guide. Oh, my, I was forgetting this request completely.]
Sophie [The brain members of NSDAP are fond of Occult, aren't they? It may be a good idea that you take the seat of their advisor?]
Luc [Their fortune is not very promising. This is rumoured among fortune tellers secretly⋯Fortune of many Germans or British people is to be terminated one year each before and after 1945 while that of French people is narrowly safe. This is what is known even to

	Den who came from the other side of the globe. Human casualties of Asian people will also be great. It may be God's will. This is the realization of Prophecy of Fatima.]
Sophie	[France shall not be the main battlefield.]
Luc	[Whether France can escape from the danger of becoming the main battlefield or not depends on whether General Weygand can draw General Petain out to the forefront or not, as I already told Borgia.]
Sophie	[Let's choose patterns which are not too showy.]
Luc	[We had better avoid a risk to be made a target of plunder by catching attention of the enemy at such trifle matter as the pattern of curtains.]
Sophie	[We may be facing a difficult age to bring our children up safely.]
Luc	[If the situation becomes critical, we would have no other choice but to leave Paris and hide ourselves in Province.]
Sophie	[Would the protection from NS related people become necessary?]
Luc	[After the world war, there will still remain possibilities to cooperate with the survivors. One of those who will possibly survive will be Rudolf Hess and some other limited number of the leaders.]
Sophie	[What you say means you can accept Hess' request.]
Luc	[In case I cannot decline all requests, yes, that will be the only choice.]

Sophie	[In France normally there is no one whose power is super dominant.]
Luc	[You are right in this regard.]
Sophie	[Mr. Artur Kannenberg is coming to Paris for procurement of food materials so you can do something for him.]
Luc	[Then it means I cannot decline this request.]
Sophie	[Look, I can't believe Mr. Kannenberg will read the explanation manual of Les Centuries.]
Luc	[If he is intending to present the book to Hitler, well, I have to be very prudent as to whether I comply to his request or not.]
Sophie	[This is something like a puzzle ring which has no solution.]

Sophie talking with Luc till then, seemed to have started racking her brains goggling her eyes. Then both remembered that at Brocante Cocon where they dropped in on their way to Nice, they saw a second-hand prophecy related book being sold there amongst other brocantes. As their job is to work on filing documents, as professional filing workers, to observe books is part of their job and habit. Loading the purchased curtains on the automobile, they searched the place where they had parked it before, then they saw an SS Jagermark IV2-1/2 saloon painted in a deep green color mixed with glittering mica was parked there. Naturally, Luc's eyes were attracted by that 1938s model but this saloon carrying a man and a woman was just about to leave there. Leaving a glitter of the fender mascot, silver jagar, it had gone off to the direction of Paris.

Luc and Sophie came out of their automobile and hurriedly opened the door of Brocante Cocon.

Luc	[May we take a look again?]
Catherine	[Hey, newlyweds. Last time I was not aware you are the granddaughter of Madelaine.]
Sophie	[For the calendar work, I have gathered you and Madolene have been associated for a long time.]
Catherine	[Well, I guess more than thirty years by now.]
Sophie	[Where are the books that were here last time?]
Catherine	[I moved those here.]
Sophie	[Why did you change the place?]
Catherine	[Just then a German couple came here for me to tell their fortune and the man bought for someone else a book that looks relating the military history of the Napoleon era. Those two who came by the green car that was parking there and went away crossing with you.]
Luc	[Are they going to be a happy married couple?]
Catherine	[They are not a married couple. I told their respective fortune only about whether their lives can continue after 1950 as per their request. It means they are not a man and a wife but may be co-workers.]
Luc	[Did they tell you their names?]
Catherine	[The man's name was Walter as I remember it. In fact, for a fortune teller to ask the name of her visitor is a taboo.]
Luc	[The name sounds like my acquentance. I did not

	think that a German will ride on SS.]
Sophie	[Psst, this 『Prophecy of Nostradamus』 by Karl Loake isn't written in Garman? Luc.]
Luc	[This is the year 1921 version and should have 140 pages, but it looks a deadstock of which even one page has not been opened by a letter opener.]
Catherine	[If you need it, take it.,]
Luc	[Thank you very much. But why?]
Catherine	[They are going to be involved in some horrifying situation but will survive the war.]
Luc	[Are they of NSDAP relations?]
Catherine	[Most probably they may be SS. What is worthy of mentioning is such horrible symbol is appearing as the skin of victims are peeled off by a female member of SS. But no one that commits such horrifying deed is to be sentenced to death as long as they are not peeling the skin off of living people. SS male members may be judged as leaders at the higher class in a public space but so far that much horrifying instance has not happened as yet. I found him a clever man. He has a lucky star that let him manage to escape from a death sentence and does not look like an out-and-out crook, but he does not have enough power to confront the forces of evil. During the coming world war, By the holy sign of India being used upside down, a great power will hurl a storm of all kinds of atrocities. Luc is engaged in the God's mission not to allow such horror

	to go on rampage in France. Destiny of both of you has already been forcasted by me to comply to Madolene's request.]
Sophie	[How did your telling come out?]
Catherine	[Ask your husband. He has enough to tell you. You are not to worry.]
Sophie	[Luc, what are you trying to find out by handing this book over to Mr. Kannenberg?]
Luc	[I will ask Mr. Kannenberg how far his master has finished reading this book. If I get this information, I can discriminate whether his master is of the type to try to intentionally make the prophecy come real or otherwise.]
Sophie	[I don't get what you mean.]
Luc	[In this book on the 68th page, there the interpretation of Les Centuries 3-57 is written. Seven changes of England will be observed Being soaked in blood after 290 years It will have absolutely no means to escape from the support by Germany The Ram suspects that Polish of Bastarnia 3-57 Sept foys changer verres gent Britannique Taintz en sang en deux cent nonante an: Franche non point par aqui Germanique. Aries doute son pole Bastarnan. The first half of this part of Les Centuries is interpreted here to mean that during 290 years after 1649 when Charles I was executed the British system of government was changed for seven times and in this year of 1936 which is exactly 290

	years afer the execution of Charles I war will take place in Poland. And actually in 1936, German army led by NSDAP invaded Poland.]
Sophie	[If Hiler realizes this statement in Les Centuries is meant for himself, he will naturally read this book thoroughly, and it will be no wonder if he aims at accomplishment of this prophecy.]
Luc	[But, in case he does not read it···it become possible that he is haunted by Demon.]
Catherine	[Suppose Demon is haunting Hitler, what countermeasure do you think you can suggest to be taken?]
Luc	[There will be no other countermeasure but to direct the raging force of Demon somewhere other than France. I have heard that Hitler concludes his speech in the enthusiastic crowd with the word Amen like a bishop. He may be pretending God or Demon that has gained a temporary permission to use violence to God which I wouldn't know.]
Sophie	[He has a power that no ordinary person can combat with.]
Luc	[At the moment Lance of Longinus was demanded to the Austrian government and obtained, in the society of fortune tellers this deed comes to have the same effect as to declaring completion of conquest of Europe as this is the deed to take over the Holy Roman Empire. SS led by Himmler seems to pose as reviver of Teutonic Order···I also understand a fair number of

	astorologists or fortune tellers is being gathered. They will become more demanding than just to be the leader of Europe.]
Catherine	[Your foreseeing power that can see that far is quite impressive. You really are on the family tree of Gaurico succeeding the power of prediction inherited from Prophet Luca.]
Luc	[Catherine, you, too, are an authority called as La Voisin in Lyon, aren't you?]
Sophie	[Isn't your sirname Montvoisin?]
Luc	[Yes, of course. I did already notice that Catherine Montvoisin is the name which ruled the times in past.]
Catherine	[The real name of the person who summons and uses Jinn or Jinny is always hidden. I will show you something different, Sophie. Luc, do you have the set of Major Arcana with you now that I transferred to you the other day?]
Luc	[Do you mean this set?]

He took the set out of the inner pocket of his jacket and put it on the table and then Catherine shuffled the cards in front of Sophie. However, she could not shuffle them well enough as a few cards jumped out on the table. She then took her own cards out which were placed beside her and showed her tactful shuffling technic of her cards.

Catherine	[Luc, Won't you firstly shuffle my Major Arcana, then shuffle the one that I transferred to you, please?]

Luc shuffled Catherine's Arcana, and in the same way as what happened of shuffling by Catherine, he saw several cards popping out on to the table. Next, he tried his cards which could be smoothly shuffled not betraying his professional shuffling technic. Looking at this, she talked to Sophie smiling.

Cathereine [Sophie, now you know what this means? Mediums or astrologists employ spirits that are well suited to them. Whether a husband and a wife can get along well or not is up to compatibility of each other. Telling the destiny is just the same. Last time when I saw the way he handled these cards, I realized who was the one that should possess this Major Alcana, so I called Madelene in Marseille.]

Sophie [So Catherine can see it, don't you, Catherine.]

Catherine [Luc is also one of such people that have the ability to see it, so, Sophie, you can rest your mind at ease.]

Sophie [What you mean is the spirits that are to be his apostle are sealed in these cards, am I right?]

Luc [Yes, like you can use your water mirror.]

Thus Luc and Sophie were able to be handed over what they needed at Brocante Cocon.

12. Hotel Lumiere

At that night, Luc and Sophie did not go out of the hotel and enjoyed their dinner at the hotel. As it was not the hunting season, game was not available, so they enjoyed butter sautéed trout and herb-flavored grilled duck. After dinner they shifted to the bar.

At the other side of the counter, a waiter, while polishing a glass examining it through the downlight, asked what they wished to take.

Waiter	[May I take your order?]
Sophie	[Side car, please.]
Luc	[A glass of absinth.]
Sophie	[Why absinth, Luc?]
Luc	[Absinth always for alchemist has been a rule since from the old times. See Alchemists put the absinth spoon on the absinth glass this way, and putting one drop of absinth on a cube sugar, they immersed themselves in the roman of illusion. Looking at the swaying flames on the glass, you see?]
Sophie	[You are always crazy about such dubious things. Reason why I ordered side car is because I am curious about Jaguar we saw in front of Cocon. Then I remembered Side Car which was the former manufacturing company name of Jaguar I worked for previously.]

While they were talking, he was restlessly dropping mineral water on the cube sugar shaking the flames on it. Then the pale green color transparent liquid in the absinth glass started getting cloudy from where water dropped down. When the absinth was completely crowded, he glanced at Sophie and said giving a broad grin on his face.

Luc [Look sugar is getting melting with the poured water. This is the way to mix absinth to drink tasty illusion of absinth.]

Sophie [Oh, look, that person waiving hands at the right side table…]

Akiko Kitsuregawa [Sophie and Luc, why don't you join us here?]

Sophie [Luc, let's join them.]

They moved to Akiko's table taking their drinks in their hands. Pan Jinlian started talking curiously.

Jinlian [Today I procured quite a lot of piecegoods. Did you find anything interesting?]

Sophie [This. I and this passed each other.]

Sophie showed her glass lifting it up.

Akiko [Side car?]

Jinlian [Do you mean Jaguar?]

Akiko [You mean the car of walter Schellenberg. Taking Louise with him, he went back to Paris leaving us behind.]

Sophie [Ah, who is this gentleman?]

As the bar was rather dark, Sophie had not noticed a man of sturdy build sitting between Akiko and Jinlian at the other side of the table.

Akiko [Let me introduce him. He is Mr. Ginji Onimaru of Jumonji Trading Firm. Ginji, they are Sophie and her husband Luc Gauric.]

Onimaru [Nice to meet you. I am a trader of variety of merchandise.]

He casually handed his business card over to Sophie.

Sophie [That you are visiting Lyon means you are trading silk yarn and goods. Do I understand correctly?]

Onimaru [We have Japan send raw silk and purchase silk piecegoods from Lyon.]

Luc [May I ask you if your name Onimaru a popular name in Japan?]

Onimaru [My name is a rather rare one. Originally Onimaru was a name of a Japanese sword treasured by Hojo clan. My ancestors were engaged in maintainance of this treasured sword so they came to be called Onimaru. In the era of Kamakura, the Hojo clan was one of the important clans forming Kamakura Shogunate which was ruling Japan then. Spirits of the sword Onimaru must have possessed that much power.]

Luc [What is the meaning of the name Onimaru, may I ask?]

Onimaru [Oni which is Demon means the world of the dead and a monstrous creature. It is supposed to have a super

	power which does not exist in the real world. But if this power is not used for justice, it will destroy the user of this power as shown by the downfall of the Hojo clan.]
Luc	[You sound like to have professional knowledge on this matter besides your trading business.]
Onimaru	[You seem to be the type of person that can see through things and matters. What Mr. Borgia told me now sounds like true to me.]
Sophie	[According to what Akiko told me, Mr. Onimaru is a worshipper of Mammon.]
Onimaru	[Originally My clan was a worshipper of the power of the spirit world and when Europeans visited Japan my clan gained philosophy of Mammon.]
Luc	[Do you use such as Seal?]
Onimaru	[My clan oftentimes use the reverse side of God. That is why they could step on the cross. At the era of Edo when Shogunate exiled Christians, my clan was a power supportive of Shogunate. That was why contraband trade could be connived at that time.]
Luc	[I presume you must have some other purpose than foreign trade.]
Onimaru	[I had met Dupty Leader Hess before NSDAP took up to use swastika as their symbol.]
Luc	[What for?]
Onimaru	[In Japan there happened a revolution called the Meiji Restoration which terminated the Samurai age. The promoter of this restoration was Theorist Shoin

	Yoshida. His family crest includes the diagonal shape of swastika symbol. Hess may be interested in Shoin Yoshida's family crest in the hope of taking the power of this crest into NSDAP so he happened to contact my company as the name of my company Jyu means Cross.]
Luc	[Is that all you can explain?]
Onimaru	[You are surprisingly persistent questioner. I was contacted by a certain person and complying to his request with regards Mammon worshipping original model which was lost because of the influencial power of Christian churches in Europe I am now doing translation work of Japanese historical documents, namely secrets of Mammon, into Latin.]
Luc	[Is that also a request from NSDAP?]
Onimaru	[You sound like you have not heard any thing about this matter from Cardinal Borgia. Please ask him with regards this matter.]

So far the information Luc obtained from Onimaru let Luc understand existence of some kind of connection between Hess and Himmler and Vatican. He also felt that Onimaru had information about witch hunt that swept whole Europe several hundred years ago and Mammon that was lost due to inquisition.

Luc	[You must have some information regarding Mammon that is expected to wield power again in near future.]
Onimaru	[As you know, in Vatican a division consisting of exorcists openly exists. In truth, Vatican does admit existance of spirits other than spirits of Christianity.]

Luc	[Certainly, task of exorcists is to move the spirit of Demon out from the place it occupies, so that it is not meant for perishing it.]
Onimaru	[I cannot clarify why, but you, too, are living in the world of Apocalypse.]

Saying so, he looked at the glass of absinth placed in front of Luc.

Luc	[It is true that absinth is made from Artemisia absinthium extract, but I wonder if this in my glass is truly the same fruid extracted from Artemisia absinthium as stated in Apocalypse?]
Onimaru	[Bible contains many figurative expressions of which such expression as 「sweet to the mouth but bitter to the stomach」 is observed. In Apocalypse, there is a statement written as 「One third of water became to taste as bitter as artemisia so many people died」. As you should be aware, this means recepe of absinth. Actually, we hear quite a few wellknown people ruin themselves overtaking absinth.]
Luc	[Do you mean this age of Apocalypse is going to finish soon?]
Onimaru	[No way, Time of Gods is long. The age of Apocalypse might have already exceeded one hundred years. The time when absinth became popular means just the beginning of the age and some other thing that replaces the metaphor of absinthium may appear to finish the age of Apocalypse. If we do not exclude any sort of possibility, we will arrive at this conclusion, won't we?]

Sophe [I'm getting sleepy.]
So, that night was finished and all of them went to bed.

13. Paris Branch Office of the Happiest Time

By the time when Jaguar driven by walter arrived in Paris, a mantle of darkness had completely fallen. The publishing company of the magazine by the name of Happiest Time owned by Anchor Stahlhelm was seizing the second and the third floors of a building which was located alongside a street off the main street in the Theatle National de l'Opera de Paris. Louise was using this place as her hidden living quarter. Walter took the car to the garage at the back side of the building and when he started carrying the belongings to the room of Luise, he found Reinhard Heydrich waiting for him.

Heydrich wearing a Hugo Boss branded well tailored trench coat was a tall man who had another name of Blonde Beast was the superior of Walter. He keenly looked at Walter and catechized.

Heydrich [I thought I had a Bentley purchased at your request because you insisted that you would need a Bentley to operate imagery intelligence exerting your good language knowledge of English and French, but, look, the Bentley takes the shape of Jaguar. Do you realize that cost of Jaguar is one third of that of Bentley, Schellenberg?]

Walter [Louise told me Bentley is of too much bourgeois taste to use it for collecting news materials for Happiest Time⋯also Anchor said Bentley would be difficult to be distinguished by common people as a car of a magazine company⋯]

Louise	[Timing will be missed if he has to submit estimated expenses again and to wait till he gets approval. It was me that proposed the change.]
Heydrich	[Is it what it is? Then I can't say no. By the way, how much is Borgia aware of activities of our army? Even Your Excellency Himmler is making a fuss, summoning astrologists]
Walter	[The man called Luc Gauric whom I met at the party of Duke of Windsor at his mansion is the Borgias' astrologist through his family tree. What Borgia knows of is the information given by Gauric as result of his decoding the contents of Les Centuries.]
Heydrich	[Sounds like information Borgia got is rather limited. Aside Borgia, have you obtained any news regarding the imagery intelligence in relation with England?]
Walter	[A doctor commissioned by British government by the name of Robert Grant is aware of this information. I have gathered he has a health counselling schedule of U.S. Embassy related people in Berlin. I guess it will be an idea that we…]
Heydrich	[You mean to let him use Salon Kitty?]
Walter	[He seems to have an interest in Roksane Walevska.]
Heydrich	[You mean that one of brunette hair. I can see she is magnet for men. I have an idea, louise. Why don't you take her up in the fashion article.]
Louise	[Understood. You wish me to have the English version of our magazine listing this particular article provided at hotels and cafes located near U.S. Embassy in

Heydrich	Berlin.] [That's right. You have a good intuition as always. Then, when he is interested, have a waiter whisper into his ear 『you can meet her at Salon Kitty』.]
Louise	[Then what we have to do is to have her find the information or to lead him to tell it to her, correct?]
Heydrich	[I will leave this matter to your whole discretion. By the way, regarding the surplus of the expense by changing to Jaguar…Schellenberg.]
Louise	[Look, he needs funds to buy gifts for Chanel or other people of culture. By my education, this young solicitor could become a drinker of absinth just recently. Praise him for this.]
Heydrich	[Really? Can this light-weight guy drink absinth? Okay, I will accept it.]
Louise	[Yes, but he is quick to get dead drunk so I'm not yet satisfied with my performance. I guess you don't have to go home tonight, do you?]
Heydrich	[Right, tell me a bit more about the story you are to make up.]
Louise	[Yah, we need to discuss about the contents of the next issue of the magagine.]

　Saying so, she tipped Walter the wink so Walter bowing lightly left them hurriedly.
　VENUS and OCTOPUS will be here!!

The biggest shortcoming of Heydrich was his strong sexual desire which is the same as Goebbels but the difference from

Goebbels was that Heydrich will never be infatuated with women. Goebbels was a Black Casanova who got the hots for actresses one after another and got them with a promise for a better casting as a bate. At last he attempted to divorse his wife and tried to re-marry the actress Lida Baarova' and caused great tumult. It was rumoured he and Anka the president of this magazine company were lovers at their student time.

And that was the reason why he was an investor of this company secretly providing her with profitable works instead of paying her consolation money while using her as a cooperator of the work of German intelligence.

On the following morning, Walter went to see Louise at her office and found her biting into bagget sandwich. She looked a litte tired showing slightly darkened skin under her eyes. After taking a sip from a café au laite bowl with strawberries in it, she poured café au lait for him into a café au lait bowl with a design of blue swallows flying in the white background, café au lait out of a rather large Barbotine jug which was embossed a design of dull yellow amaranth colored cherries.

Barbotine is a low temperature baked porcelain created by molding clay painted by warm feeling pale and dull tone color. It was produced

In Lorraine District and during the age of Art Nouveau such design as embossed fruits or vegetables was in fashion.

Café au lait bowl is of a shape similar to Japanese powdered green tea bowl with a funnel-shaped opening but is a bit larger than the Japanese tea bowl so it can contain plentiful café au lait.

There does exist a smaller size bowl of this shape which looks very similar to Japanese tea bowl so this small size could well be used for Japanese tea ceremony.

Louise	[Good morning. Did you have good breakfast? Take café au lait anyway before you start talking.]
Walter	[You look to have been up till quite late last night.]
Louise	[That's Heydrich. He is a tough gay⋯tee-hee.]
Walter	[What's funy?]
Louise	[I tell you, the plot you are scheming now seems to be attracting more attention of higher people than Heydrich.]
Walter	[Goebbels and Himmler, you mean?]
Louise	[Don't foreget Hess either. Those evil priests look like seeking and looking forward to hearing a distortion of Les Centuries while on the other hand wishing to learn the correct interpretation.]
Walter	[You mean the draft written on the previous day? Honestly, I can't afford time to listen to absurd superstitions.]
Louise	[Les Centuries 6-34 Plot by sky flying flaming machine Shall embarrass the surrounded Overload Extreme confusion shall take place inside Those knocked down will become desperate 6-34 De feu voulant la machination, Viendra troubler au grand chef assieger: Dedans sera telle sedition, Qu'en desespoir seront les proflgez. You will interpret the first line as scattering handbills from an aeroplane. You are intending to

	falsify this statement in order to produce flyers, aren't you.]
Walter	[Flyers will of course be written this way, "Sky flying machine of Hell Will corner French Army getting surrounded Great confusion will occur inside the army Those left behind will face desparate death" I guess these wordings can inspire fear. I will also plan to send gypsy pythons right next to the corps area.]
Louise	[What at all is dear Mr. Solicitor thinking?]
Walter	[Les Centiries 1-20 Such names of places as Tours, Orleans and Blois are shown on the first line. I will use these geographical names to have understood as the line-up places though the truth is those places were where those foreign language speaking people set up tents as written on the third line. In other words, the areas where are called by those place names become battlefields, which relays to make the comprehension of the forth line arenas, namely battlefields, are flooding out like floodwaters of a big river causing a big shake of the earth and the sea. We spread this concept at the bars in the evening time from around April onwards.]
Louise	[You mean people must escape from places of the names shown as those places will become battlefields.]
Walter	[If swarms of refugees move towards the Southwest France, transport of reinforcements becomes difficult.]
Louise	[If no road can be used, can't they push through farm land?]

Walter	[Don't you think gentlemanly French won't force their way through the vineyards which are possessed by farmers of strong sence of entitlement?]
Louise	[Do they give up just to be faithful to their conscience?]
Walter	[No drafted soldiers will wish to go to the battlefields which have strong sign of defeat. That's why City of Paris must not be bombed in earnest.]
Louise	[How come can you say so. What you want is to sleep with Parisiennes, right?]
Walter	[Espionage does need red-light district.]
Louise	[What I can say at least is your project would please Heydrich and Goebbels, Mr. Solicitor.]
Walter	[Be sure to prepare one ton of flyers.]
Louise	[If we print the flyers together at time of printing the May edition of Happiest Times, I will guess the flyers will probably be ready by late March. By that time I shall be able to finish training your tongue. To obtain Parisiennes rustic pick-up line won't work.]
Walter	[What project are you planning for the feature article of the May issue?]
Louise	[The front cover will naturally show pinup of Roxy. For anticipation of this year mode, I'm thinking about an interview of Chanel. Needless to say putting an article about Duchess Wollis we must make an article that will catch the eyes of British or American people.]
Walter	[Point is how to catch the eyes of American women.]
Louise	[I am thinking about asking cooperation of Luc's wife,

	Sophie. What I gathered from her is their family of procreation seems to be an exemplary 19 century styled old flat in Paris. She seems trying to change the interior so they bought curtains in Lyon on the way to their travel to Nice.]
Walter	[If she will cooperate with you for the coverage, I will supply her with wallpaper of her liking.]
Louise	[If I take Roxy there and can photograph the scene, I guess I can easily get Sophie's cooperation.]
Walter	[Can you contact her right away?]
Louise	[No problem. Can you arrange to send the hands to do the paperhanging work?]
Walter	[I will of course cooperate to arrange it.]
Louise	[I guess you are intending to wiretap their apartment?]
Walter	[Ha-ha, are you aware of that?]
Louise	[Luc belongs to The Borgias and what's more is he is talking about persuading General Weygand to cooperate with him. So that it is obvious that we would face difficult situation if we should antagonize them. Chance is not what you just stand and wait for but is to be created by yourself, Mr. Solicitor.]

　Having said so she opend her black Chanel bag and after checking the things contained in the bag, she pulled out a small black pocketbook.

Louise	[Psst, won't you investigate how long The Gaulics have been possessing this real estate on this address?]
Walter	[What for?]
Louise	[If the Gaulics obtained this real estate in the era of

	Catherine de Medici, it would mean the Gaulics was receiving an exceptionally good treatment, and if during the time of Napoleon, we can see that the family acted as an astrologist to divine the revolutionary war. Don't you think to submit such kind of information may please Himmler or Hess?]
Walter	[Aren't you smart.]
Louise	[I guess to work under someone like a faightul dog may be one choice, but there is another style of getting a success by selling yourself to a prospective entity like a cat seeking and catching its game. It is no argument that this age is surely the time of the growth of NSDAP, but once the gear starts moving reversedly, those of the dog type responsibility shall be laid on them. Since you are a solicitor, you should shrewdly keep yourself ready to get defensive at all times. Women always keep themselves ready to do whatever possible to protect diminution of their beauty, especially beautiful women like me.]
Walter	[Women are scary, aren't they.]
Louise	[Don't be afraid. As long as you cooperate with me, I promise I won't say anything to your wife over the future.]
Walter	[Aha, You, witch!]

Saying so, he emptied the bowl of café au lait which was still warm. Sediment of tiny coffee bean shells remained faintly in the bowl forming the shape of a tongue.

14. Before and After

Louise progressed the rewarding plan of production cooperation for the change of room interiors in return to Sophie's cooperation for material gathering for the magagine and also as a wedding gift. Those curtains that Sophie purchased in Lyon were going to be used, but the cost of the wall paper was to be borne by Happiest Times under the pretence of wedding gift and cooperation to magagine material gathering. As a matter of fact, when taking photos for the magagine, Sophie and her female friends demonstrated the work of wallpapering and curtain hunging, but the fact was papering of the walls of the dining room, salon, study and the child's room was to be done by professional workmen hired by Happiest Magagine.

As Sophie could not find any suitable wall paper to her liking for the master bedroom, it was agreed that she would do this room later by herself at her own expense. For this photographing purpose, the main object of photographing was Roxane of course but additionally the magagine company asked Akiko Kitsuregawa and Pan Jinlian to join in order to add some over-the-race effect by showing international charactors.

Sophie [I think the fruit pattern is suitable for the dining room. And the salon will have an image of birds of South France playing on the green field. For the study, such design as the scenery of the remains in Rome.]

Roxy [You are surprisingly fond of Art Deco, aren't you. Luc

	looks like a lover of Renaissance style⋯the one he chose has a colour touch of Primavera of Florence. Well, but this is a good choice. This will give the study nice and light atmosphere.]
Sophie	[Isn't the paper for the child's room coming as yet?]
Akiko	[Mr. Onimaru of Jumonji Trading Company is expected to arrive taking it with him in no time.]
Sophie	[What is it which is jumping about between the vertical aquamarine color stripes?]
Akiko	[Carp. Carp is a fish very popular with the boys' festival in Japan. Oh, Mr. Onimaru seems to have arrived.]
Onimaru	[Sorry to be late. Took time to take this out of the warehouse. This is what it is.]
Jinlian	[Look, light blue color fish are jumping about in the white part between the virtical stripes of pale blue and white.]
Onimaru	[We had this wallpaper printed at a Karagami-ya, a paper-covered sliding door maker, in Kyoto. This part of silver color is painted with mica. Isn't this color a dream-like color which is different from metallic silver color?]

Louise tended to ignor Jinlian in the matter as if she had a right to ignor her, who makes eyes at any man, but Jinlian was taking it for granted that it was she that was the most charming of all women there.

Louise	[OK, then we are taking the photos of you people preparing for the work of papering the wall.]

Walter   [Hi, all of you, please look this way.]

Having a strobe flushed letting all people photographed into a film, this hustle was ceased.

Onimaru   [This camera looks a good one. Is it a Leica?]
Walter   [Yes, it is. You seem to have an eye on cameras.]
Onimaru   [Leica does the best work to show the texture of photographic subject, though I use a different camera when I have to pursue the shape of the subject···the way of lens creation technology is different to manufacturing countries.]
Walter   [Are you always take photos by yourself?]
Onimaru   [As I was helping a photo studio for photographic developing work when I was a student.]
Walter   [What mainly is your photographic subject?]
Onimaru   [Air, it is.]
Walter   [Yes?]
Onimaru   [I don't take a photo of Cathedral. What I take is the smoke coming up from the incense burner in the Cathedral, or otherwise the aura which is oozing out of great figures.]
Walter   [Till now, what sort of great fitures have you met?]
Onimaru   [Bishop of Rome, Cardinal, Mussolini, and it was just one time but I have met Hess dupty Leader.]

Some time ago, Schellenberg looked through the file of Ginji Onimaru and remembered Onimaru had received some instruction from USA, so he decided to try him by making questions.

Walter   [What about American or British figures?]

Onimaru	[I met Duke and Duchess of Windsor in Paris.]
Walter	[What do they look like; those who have aura?]
Onimaru	[Both in good and bad sense, they are people that can influence other people better or worse so much as to create a new age.]
Walter	[Can you tell whether their influence is a good one or bad by just meeting those people?]
Onimaru	[It is the history that decides whether the influence comes out good or bad. Only what I can discern is if such a big figure really has power to gather and agitate enough number of people so they can form a tidal stream to change the age. In the Christian world, those Roman gods are deemed as false gods. But at the heyday of Rome, the gods of Rome must have been the only distinguished gods.]
Walter	[I personally am not a typical Christian.]
Onimaru	[Well, if so, we may be able to understand each other more easily. We are the people in the world of polytheism and metempsychosis. A great figure is normally possessed by highly powerful spirits.]
Walter	[As Himmler is saying, could it truly happen that he is the reincarnation of Heinrich I?]
Onimaru	[You seem to be a rather theoretical person. I guess you had better discern the limit of science. There are such instances in abundance where future can be clearly seen by prophets.]
Walter	[Can you raise any example?]
Onimaru	[In Japan there existed a fortune telling style prophet

	called Kaemon Takashima. He is widely known as a person that named the assassin of the former prime minister Hirobumi Ito. He is also said to have nominated Heihachiro Togo as the general commander of the Battle of Tsushima (the Sea of Japan) at request by the statemen who contributed in Meiji Restoration.]
Walter	[Do you mean then, at the Japan's Imperial Headquarters, some people like astrologists are enrolled at all times?]
Onimaru	[To my regret, in Japan, statemen are individually employing their prophets at their expenses.]
Walter	[If so, how can they make an overall big decision?]
Onimaru	[Till the early part of the Meiji era the family tree of Seimei Abe was assigned as astrologists of the Royal Family. After Meiji, the family tree of Kaemon Takashima was related to the Royal Family. However, after politicians were assassinated by coup d'etat the means to ask for God's will was lost. This fact is the biggest concern of the nation at the moment. Doesn't NSDAP ask for God's will at the time when a big decision is demanded?]
Walter	[If I say NO, it doesn't tell you the truth. What I can say is Goebbels, Himmler and Hess seem to care too much about the movement of stars in the sky. Other than those, you know there are such people as General Goring, who are getting distracted by the number of stars on his epaulette.]
Onimaru	[What matters is the timing set by the will of God. At

	the sea war fought on Battle of Tsushima, what annihilated Baltic Fleet was not just the superior fire power of Japan. In the case of the Roman Emperor Commodus, he was poisoned and while he was paralyzed by the poison, he was assassinated because he was too competent. As this historical fact tells us, what is important is to take advantage of unpreparedness of the target.]
Walter	[You're quite right. Sometimes there happens such timing when a person cannot display his power even if he has a lot of it.]
Onimaru	[There will come the time when the Third Reich will face its power getting weakened. You better notice such sign before it develope to become a disaster.]
Walter	[When do you guess such time will come?]
Onimaru	[Dupty Leader Hess was also asking the same question though he already knew that time would come around 1945.]
Walter	[I will remember that year.]
Onimaru	[You had better be prepared to notice when the tide of destiny turns around.]
Walter	[What you say is very interesting.]
Onimaru	[I have another appointment. Please excuse me, now.]

While after Onimaru was gone, Roxy waved him from the dining room.

Sophie	[Tea is ready. Won't you come around here.]
Walter	[Oh, thank you.]
Louise	[Wow, It now looks very different and nice.]

Sophie	[Thanks. All this could happen because of your proposal.]
Louise	[No, no, you were just lucky to meet the timing of the project of our magazine.]
Walter	[I'm sure that Onimaru has something in him that attracts my big shots. But destiny cannot always be determined at God's will.]
Louise	[What makes you so concerned? To be mysterious is a source of charm]
Akiko	[His view of the world is not based on monotheism like Christianity.]
Walter	[But he does not look like a materialist either?]
Akiko	[We have an expression of All Creations. Even one single plant growing in the monsoon climate does contain spirits and human can live only with the help of those spirits so human has no other choice but to rely on the power of spirits. Human can no way go beyond Nature. The only way left for human to survive is just to accept and study the course of the stars along which they are moving through the heavens, the change of the seasons and the Aura that is given to human. But in his case…]
Walter	[Where of him is different from common humanbeings?]
Akiko	[He is trying to free the power which has long been sealed as this power is too dangerous to handle by any of religions. As I do not know for what purpose he is trying this, I have no idea of his intention to do this…]

Walter	[Sealed power…]
Akiko	[Isn't it a worthless story.]
Walter	[Oh, no, I bet it is a very interesting story.]
Sophie	[It can be surely said that Orient is full of misteries.]
Jinlian	[Is he seeing illusions taking opium?]
Louise	[No way, Jinlian. It's about time now, Sophie, I did enjoy today's coverage.]
Roxy	[The child's room was furnished very cutely. I guess It will perfectly suit a baby boy.]
Roxy	[I'm envious you now have a home.]
Sophie	[Not to worry. Your chance is coming around soon.]
Roxy	[I do hope it will be the case.]
Walter	[Destiny is a thing that can be cultivated.]
Akiko	[Do you know of an astrolosist called Ave Maria?]
Roxy	[Is she good?]
Akiko	[She is of the family tree of Seimei Abe. This family used to tell the fortune of Emperor of Japan. They lost their power in 1873 when the calendar was changed to the Gregorian calendar. Now she is doing a research work living in Paris to unite her fortune telling method with astrology. She lives in Saint-Germain-des-Pres.]
Roxy	[Do you have her telephone number?]
Akiko	[Here it is, but her fortune telling place is located beside Café Le Procope and there you can see the sign of [Words of Notre Dame].]
Roxy	[Thanks. I will visit her later.]
Walter	[Is she telling the fortune of the Japanese Embassy related people?]

Akiko   [Most possibly. I think I once heard many of her visitors are Japanese living in Paris.]

Walter [Can she tell the fortune of an European like me?]

Akiko   [Yes, but you will be asked your birth date and the place you were born.]

Walter [I will visit her later on.]

Having been watching the action taken by the NS executives, Walter was gradually started to have an interest in his own future destiny. By closely associating with Japanese he would be able to follow up their movement so that even if he arbitrarily used the expense fund for building social relationships with Japanese, he thought he would be able to justify those expenses with Himmler and Heydrich. At the same time he even thought there would be a possibility for him to see through the intentions of NS executives. What was actually happening was the invation plan of the Third Reich into France was originally scheduled to be executed in November, 1939, but since then it was repeatedly delayed for more than 30 times.

New proposals to improve this plot were being raised from time to time but it now was apparent to the public that this plot had already reached the level of a phony war as was published by the newspapermen. Leader Hitler was even having Hess and Himmler investigate horoscopes of the generals attending this plot.

Karl Kraft, who was born as a grandson of an operator of a hotel in Basel, Switzerland, worked as not only a python but had deciphered the prophetic poems of 『LesCenturies』. Goebbels created a pamphlet of propaganda with a title of 『Nostradamus bespoke victory of the Third Reich』 in six different languages. As a matter of course, the underworkers to help this pamphlet created were Walter and his colleagues.

The preface of this whole happening started when Kraft sent to his friend, Heinrich Fesel who was working at the secret intelligence service, a letter stating [life of hitler will be menanced for ten days starting on November 7]. On November 8, there happened a terrorist bombing attack at a beer-hall in Munich but Hitler survived miraculously. Hearing this news Fesel sent a telegram to Hess so Kraft was arrested and investigated by the Gestapo and as a result his ability of precognition came to attract the NSDAP executives' attention.

It was rather difficult for Walter who has the solicitor qualification to understand why by such means as horoscope that much can be foreseen. On the matgerialistic basis, such law of causality as the movement of stars in the sky is to lead individual human's destiny can no way be admitted. However, for example, that Kaemon Takashima of Japan or Kraft are both keenly interested in the mechanism of prophecy is a firm fact that cannot be ignored. Talking about Nostradamus, as he lived in the 16th century, in the materialistic sense such law of causality can scarcely be recognized, nevertheless, still now, 400 years after the age of Nostradamus, his prophecy is said to come true, exciting many people of the modern age.

15. Words of Notre Dame

The following day of the collection of the materials regarding Roxy for the magazine, turned out to be a nice sunny day after quite a while. Walter, just finishing blanch which he started to take at 11am at a restaurant called Le Procope located in rue de L'Ancienne-Comedie, was blowsing the Michelin Guide Red Book. This restaurant has been used as a gathering place for men of culture ever since the time of French Revolution. Reason why this restaurant was so frequently used by those intellectuals is deeply related to the existence of a theater standing on the other side of this restaurant. Reason why French Revolution could be the whistling arrow of the revolutions in the modern times was because the bourgeoisie stood up in the endeavor of abolishing the economic activity covenants which are maintained by feudalistic aristocracy and Catholic churches.

The prime slogan of French Revolution was nothing but liberty, however this libertyom was ultimately based on such liberty of economic activities off from the restriction caused by the Guild system. What was next added to the slogan was Equality, which means the equality of market entry opportunities and was at the same time meant for the right of objection against vested interests. Such being the case, this concept of Equality collided violently with the rights that aristocracy and Catholic churches maintained. The last additional slogan of Fratanity or philanthropy was meant for providing people that experienced financial failure with another chance to make a comeback.

Accordingly, liberty, equality, Philanthropy were all the products gained on the development of the bourgeoisie revolution. Excerting the imagination of the scene of the people heatedly arguing on how these subjects should be formed, Walter as a solicitor felt deep emotion. Needless to say, to settle political or economical matters judicially taking the methods in a verifiable way is the very opposite practice to Autocracy. But in the communist bloc, opposition faction is executed one-sidedly without the aid by barristers.

And there Roxy came back after having Maria tell her future. As she chose the today's chef's suggestion for her lunch, Walter put the money including cost of her lunch. While he was told his furture by Maria, Roxy was supposed to wait for his return. Receiving his fedora and trenchcoat back from the cloak, he went outside quickly neglecting to button the coat. He was caucious not to be noticed as a German so he was wearing an Ermenegildo Zegna branded coat which was tailor-made in Milan and a Borsalino fedora on which Chanel had put a plume to make it look different. Walter was habitually wearing these three while in France.

Incidentally, the feather on the fedora was what Chanel made by her hand to decorate a hat of Arthur Capel using feather of a bird which was hunt by him. Arthur Capel was a person whom Chanel had loved. It was a certain fact that she tended to be fond of men who looked like Capel. Capel passed away at his age of 28 in December, 1919. Under normal circumstances she might as well have got married with Von D who kept proposing to her but that she didn't would mean she was still cherishing somewhere in her mind her memory of the lost spring time life with Arthur.

The tragedy of Chanel lied in the fact that her given talent was not valued rightfully by the society then, due to the fact she was abandoned by her father and was grown up at an orphanage. Capel was a love child between a British aristocrat and his lover but he was forced to marry a daughter of another aristocrat as a son and heir. Chanel did keep association with her father but she couldn't get the position to be in public openly after all. Chanel's position in the society deemed to belong the same genre as courtesan called Demimonde. In such age as women had no opportunity to be valued rightfully only because of the reason of being women, she was an existence in the world where she was looked coldly by other women.

No one could blame Chanel in such situation if she was unable to have any interest in French males so if she got a reputation as a philanderer with British, Rusian or German males, the very cause of it could be attributed to the fact that French people were unable to value her in the rightful manner. That Walter belonged to SS did not matter to Chanel from the beginning. Rather, such a person like Chanel who drastically changed the traditional mode till she came to be called 「Angel of Massacre」 always had many antagonists so she might have some synesthesia to share with NSDAP that raised its head with the slogan of "Beat the Versailles system". Another reason must have been that Walter himself was not grown up in an ideal environment which appealed to her maternal instincts.

Next to a boutique facing the street, there was a standing

signboard showing 「the words of Notre Dame」. Going through the entrance located beside the signboard, he stepped up to what is called in France the first floor. At his knock on the walnut door painted by varnish, Abe Maria came out. Her hair was done up in a ban with a hair pin decorated by a coral bead. She was short and was wearing a Kimono-like dress which looked like she was wearing a piece of white lace fabric. Leaving his fedora and coat there, following her he entered a room where incense was being burnt. In this salon, there was a sofa placed of the art deco style of the 1930s. He was asked to wait a while sitting there so he got time to look around the salon.

In the furnace there remained some firewood which had nearly turned to coal, still showing red fire color. From the ceiling an art deco chandellia was hung injecting color of the light which is a mixed color of orange in milky white. This mixture of colors of light was creating some wondrous atmosphere there. The wallpaper was of a design of pedals of spring flowers scattered by gentle wind on the background color of moss green. On the wall, a few kinds of masks were hung which Walter could not distinguish if those were just decorations or for the use by shamans. Very probably these must have been collected on her travel via sea from Japan to Europe.
　Walter could recognize the difference of Japanese Noh masks and Gigaku-men masks from the masks of gods of Vietnumese or Hindu. In addition to those masks, there hung framed papyrus on which hieroglyph was written. Up on the furnace several cat figurines were placed. The cats looked enjoying warmness of the furnace and

half asleep. Those also looked like to have been collected from a prural number of different countries. Then he was called from inside the adjoining room, so he went there.

This second room had an altar right opposite of the door. This altar was of the shape similar to Japanese Shinto altar with a mirror of about 20cm diameter sitting in the center. Such altar with sacred festoon stretched around it was something rare in Paris. Abe Maria was sitting at the other side of a round table placed in the center of the room. The name Maria must surely be a pen name. In the business of this kind, what matters is whether prediction comes true or not, therefore, for using demon, true name of the python was usually to be hidden.

Walter had already met several of such pythons nearby Himmler or Hess. He had already told Maria by telephone several people's birth dates and first names alone. Abe Maria was sounding like casting a spell and then suddenly turned back to him and opened her lips.

Maria	[Mr. Walter, please take a seat. I understand your request to me this time is for me to tell you several people's destiny of the coming ten years. Do I understand you correctly?]
Walter	[You are quite right. To start with, regarding my own self, do you see I shall be terminated?]
Maria	[You may be cornered and may experience quite much hardship, but will anyway be able to protect your life.]
Walter	[Who else do you tell seems not to loose life?]
Maria	[The person by the name of Rudolf who has this birth

	date will live long.]
Walter	[What about the other people?]
Maria	[They will face an extreme difficulties in coming several years.]
Walter	[In your reading do you see a possibility that they are destined to die in near future?]
Maria	[To be frank, death is approaching them.]
Walter	[What best are we prepared for such danger?]
Maria	[Try not to go to the east. And should you go there, you ought not to look into an enclosure.]
Walter	[What do you mean by enclosure?]
Maria	[You may have been in an investigation room. What I say is you should not go to such closed place to enclose a large number of people.]
Walter	[What will be in such enclosure?]
Maria	[The world where humans become no longer humans shall be widened. Because of this horribleness NSDAP in line with Communism will be defined as enemy of the mankind.]
Walter	[What about Japan or Italy?]
Maria	[Japan will not enclose its people by the difference of pedigrees. Similarly, Italy will ignor any possible request of this kind by German Government.]
Walter	[Very interesting. By the way, do you know Mr. Ginji Onimaru?]
Maria	[He is a staff of Jyumonji Trading Company and at the same time has a role in a religious party. His ancestor had been to Vatican 400 years ago following the

	Japanese envoy to Europe in the Keicho Era. This envoy was led by Tsunenaga Hasekura.]
Walter	[Why did he go with them?]
Maria	[he is of the clan supervising the maintainance work of the Hojo regency's sword named Onimaru, which works to ward off evil spirits. As he is a professional researcher of exorcist, he knows what was lost in Vatican. He at the same time is serving the founder of the present religious sect.]
Walter	[Is he in contact with USA related personnel?]
Maria	[Your interpretation of this matter is not correct.]
Walter	[Does USA mean The United States of America?]
Maria	[As The creater of Que Mammon is Mr. Usa.]
Walter	[Yah, the whole matter is rather confusing, isn't it?]
Maria	[It is extremely dangerous to have the power of Rome collected in a mass in consideration of the fact Rome had been swept away by Vatican in Europe.]
Walter	[What at all are they aiming at?]
Maria	[In the original concept of polytheism, both God and Demon are altogether nothing but spirits. Perhaps the Monotheisum believers may have sorted those spirits to meet the convenience of their doctorine. If only we could control those spirits removing those which do evil alone to the human?]
Walter	[To achieve that idea, what will be the best way to be done?]
Maria	[May that have been the reason why there was a person in the heads of NS who summoned him?]

Walter	[Oh, I see, that's why Manji was turned back and used.]
Walter	[Then, as Himmler is questioning, what does Gyaku-Manji mean?]
Maria	[Do you know in 1937 Ara Pacis, the altar of Goddess of Peace, was dug out in Rome?]
Walter	[What was found there?]
Maria	[There found a wall picture which had been designed in BC13. The design is Gyaku-Manji placed in rows which was used as a dividing line of the relief of up and down side of the patterns of the altar. This Gyaku-Manji is meant for peace. As the Latin shown there tells us, it is meant for peace. Rome kept its power for the purpose of maintaining peace and did not use it for conquest.]
Walter	[You mean this symbol is wrongly used?]
Maria	[I know it won't help if I tell this to you, but if we choose to call the great spirit by the name of God, whether we can get its divine protection or not has a significant importance.]
Walter	[Without such protection, what do you think will happen?]
Maria	[Uncontrollable desire is nothing but the cause of destruction and downfall.]
Walter	[What at all can I do for this?]
Maria	[You have your superior who asked you to use me to tell his fortune. Needless to say, most of their luck have already run out, but there may still be something

	you can do for them. Also, you may be able to be of help after his luck has run out.]
Walter	[After? After the luck is gone?]
Maria	[For example, can you destroy Paris? This capital of liberty, equality and philanthropy? Does such a deed to wipe away the industrial power of Germany benefit the human's descendants?]
Walter	[I dislike the old Catholic autholitalianism, but do agree what you have just said are indispensable to our descendants.]
Maria	[I'm not a Christian, either. But I reckon I know what I should advise you. You should live your own life on your own. Those who have found out what they should do are strong. Oh, this may sound like a Zen conversation.]
Walter	[I now feel I can understand even a bit why you have many visitors asking you to tell their fortunes.]
Maria	[You know Coco Chanel, don't you.]
Walter	[Yes, but why?]
Maria	[I know she won't be loved by traditional French people. But when the 20th century ceases, she will surely be remembered as one of the three who represented France in this century.]
Walter	[I don't get you?]
Maria	[Her true value will come to be recognized when the traditional concept of values was broken down.]
Walter	[Will she be loved by Paris?]
Maria	[At this moment she is not loved by the people in

Paris. But in the French history of culture such person that surpasses her will not come out for at least 100 years after now. Reason why she is that great is what she has created has a power to go over the wall of the French language. The coming 21st century will become such a kind of age. And only when human history and concept of values will be able to find her true value.]

 Walter, having returned to Le Procope, picked a taxi up taking Roxy with him. They had some time to converse together while taking her to the station.

Walter	[What did you ask her to forcast?]
Roxy	[My life from now on. I wonder if I should meet some nice man, could I wash my hands of the present work?]
Walter	[Sure, yes.]
Roxy	[Aren't you quick with your answer.]
Walter	[There is absolutely no reason why you should work at Salon Kitty if you can find your own life.]
Roxy	[I wonder if Heydrich would agree?]
Walter	[I think he would if you can act as a mole somewhere of the side of the enemy.]
Roxy	[For what sort of compensation?]
Walter	[Every one must exert one's own efforts to find out how to live one's individual life in the best way.]
Roxy	[You sound surprisingly unselfish.]
Walter	[Facing death, yes. Religion may not be meaningless.]
Roxy	[You sound sort of dangerous.]

Walter [I tell you you had better not concern yourself to this situation any further.]

Roxy seemed to have felt something detrimental that must not be touched and so suddenly became quiet. Cirtainly, he must be showing such kind of mood around him. Taxi arrived at the station in the meantime.

16. The Feature Articles

Paris in late March was just the start of spring time and the weather was still cool. Robert, fnishing the health counselling of Duke of Windsor in a quick and orderly way, was handed his U.S. passport and the travel itinerary. In a rather large envelop, there contained a passport issued by American Embassy in Paris and a ticket to Berlin and also another ticket for a travel from Berlin to Zurich.

The instruction tells him, in view of the situation of outbreaking war status of U.K. versus Germany, to go to Berlin to do the health counselling work at the U.S.Embassy, and also to assist a Japansese to open up his bank account in Switzerland. During all while he performs the instructed works, he was to behave as a man of the name of Robin Gardner of U.S. nationality and to wear moustache to match the photo on the passport. Robert, hurriedly wore moustache in the restroom and went to the station by the car which had been waiting for him.

When he rode onto the compartment of the train, he did not yet see any one else. He hung on the wall the fedora that he had bought in Paris and the Barburry trench coat that was fitting well to his body. The newly tailored three-piece suit was felt rather hard and looked like he had to wait another season till it became more fitting to his body.

Right before the train passed the border of France and Germany, a man with a moustache came into the compartment he was seated and sat down at the other side of the seat of Robert after hunging his fedora of deep navy color and his Ermenegildo Zegna branded trench coat on the wall.

A German immigration officer came around after a while and checked their passports and tickets. After this, the man who had been wordless till then started to speak to Robert after taking off his monocle.

Walter	[I now see you are an American. My name is Walter.]
Robert	[I am Robin.]
Walter	[When I saw you in your coat, I thought you might be a British national. But you wear a France-made jacket. You look like a lover of travelling.]
Robert	[I travel quite much in Europe, but this suit is not very well tailored.]
Walter	[To choose the fabric, I guess Italian fabric is the most suited. The softly woven Italian fabric won't give a hard feel even if it is very newly tailored.]
Robert	[You know very well about Italian fashion as a German. What about your jacket?]
Walter	[I order-made this in Milan. This is Ermenegildo Zegna.]
Robert	[I see, no wonder it is fitting you very softly. Your fedora, I thought it was black but now I see this is of dark Navy color?]
Walter	[You're right. Deep dark navy.]
Robert	[Is this also made in Milan?]
Walter	[Yes, Borsalino.]
Robert	[In France this brand almost always means fedora.]
Walter	[If you wish to make a better use of your frequent

	trips, I would suggest you wear the famous brands produced in the places of your visit so as to be popular at the cabarets in Paris, too.]
Robert	[You sound like a smart person.]
Walter	[Not really, I have just learned it from someone just recently.]
Robert	[Is that person in the entertainment business?]
Walter	[She is already a retired person, but her philosophy is 『Woman that cannot be loved by man is of no value』, in the other way round, it can mean 『Man that cannot be loved by woman is of no value, either.』]
Robert	[That's the philosophy of life. In this sense, Duke of Windsor and his wife are so strongly attached to each other that Duke threw the crown away for her, which is very symbolic. Such person will seldom appear from now on.]
Walter	[Mrs. Simpson who was once divorced must be an attractive person even if she is not popular with British people.]
Robert	[The good point of America is that it is not bound by traditions and it can courageously challenge to many things. Europe maintains such old-fashioned constitution as the fact that even Chanel is left without being rightfully valued. Duke of Windsor failed to defeat such culture of Britain and had no other choice but to abdicate the throne.]
Walter	[Concluding Duke of Windsor and his wife can be the symbol of the revolution of Europe.]

Robert	[I hope this matter shall not be politically misused.]
Walter	[Certainly.]
Robert	[By the way, where is the hot spot of recent topics in Berlin?]
Walter	[Me, neither, so much about Berlin, but are you staying in Berlin tonight?]
Robert	[Yes, ..]
Walter	[Talking about the topics…if I remember it correctly..a feature article of the magazine called something like 『Happiest Time』 about DIY room remodeling is popularly talked about, but I understand in America DIY is nothing unusual, correct?]
Robert	[You're quite right. Tell me about the contents of this feature article.]
Walter	[What I gathered is the remodeling work of the rooms of an old apartment. According to my memory, workers were the newly married young wife and her friends. Those friends helping the wife were all quite goodlooking women.]
Robert	[The name of the magazine you are talking about is an English name. Does it mean they publish an English version, too?]
Walter	[Most probably. Especially at those cafés that are located in the neighborhood of American Embassy, I guess.]
Robert	[Well, what you told me looks interesting.]
Walter	[You may find such information as the sightseeing guide of Berlin. It may have some useful information if

you can find the magazine.]

Walter Schellenberg then spent the rest of time with Robert who possesses a fake passport of U.S. listing the name of Robin, by talking about wild game and other safe topics. When the train was just about to arrive at the Berlin station, dinner time was getting near.

Getting off the train, Robert checked in Hotel Liberty where he had reserved a room and left the baggage there, and took dinner at the hotel restaurant located next to the front desk.

He ordered rib stake and salad. While waiting, a waiter brought draft beer first, when together with the beer he brought to him English newspaper published in Berlin and the month May version of the magazine 『Happiest Time』 which is the latest version just started to be sold. Robert felt he had seen the woman on the front cover of the magazine before. That smiling woman is much alike Roxy with whom he had a dance at the mansion of Duke of Windsor in Paris.

He quickly checked and confirmed that magazine is for sale on March 28 and read the article which he found in the middle part of the magazine. He reckoned the place photographed in the magazine must be the procreation of the residence of Luc and his newly wed wife whom he met at that party. After a short while, waiter brought salad and put it on his table but he was busy keeping his eyes on the magazine. Then, when the rib stake of delicious flavor with oil flicking by heat was brought by the waiter, he for the first time looked up at the waiter.

Waiter   [So, all's ready of what you ordered.]

Robert	[Right.]
Waiter	[you seem to be interested in the article of this magazine.]
Robert	[I recognize one person who is a bit alike to a lady I know of.]
Waiter	[I have seen the one on the front cover a few times here.]
Robert	[This looks like an article of Paris?]
Waiter	[I guess her friend lives in Paris. I am sure she stays in Berlin.]
Robert	[Do you happen to know where she lives?]
Waiter	[You can ask concierge for that information.]
Robert	[Thanks.]

Finishing dinner, Robert went to the concierge desk taking the magazine.

Hotelier	[How can I help you?]
Robert	[Is this woman on the front cover living in Berlin?]
Hotelier	[You can see her at Salon Kitty. Shall I make a reservation?]
Robert	[A bit after 3 o'clock tomorrow afternoon would be convenient to me.]
Hotelier	[Mr. Gardner, Before you meet Rosina, please tell the salon [I came from Rothenburg]. Then speak up to them telling them you have an appointment at 3pm with Rogina.]
Robert	[I need the address, too.]

Hotelier [You see the address and telephone number of Salon Kitty on this memo, but if you pick up a taxi waiting in front of any embassy buildings of the world's major countries, you can just say Salon Kitty to the driver, as all drivers know the place.]
Robert [Thank you.]
Hotelier [Please enjoy Berlin, sir.]

Then, Robert returned to his room.

17. Salon Kitty

Robert went to American Embassy and engaged himself in the scheduled health counselling work. He had a message of Duke of Windsor to American Embassy in which Duke of Windsor stated he would like to ask a speedy imprementation of peace mediation by U.S. Government should war break out between U.K. and Germany. The response representing U.S.A. was that U.S.A. would certainly act as a peace mediator between the two countries. After the luncheon, Robert received a written reply to this effect from U.S.A. Putting it into his bag, Robert took his leave from the Embassy. Riding on one out of the crowd of taxis gathering around the embassy, he quickly asked the driver to take him to Salon Kitty.

Around the area of Embassy such people in uniform as SS related persons or policemen were notable in the crowd. Though this measure is to care about the safety of other countries' diplomats or visiting foreign people, if such scene is too notable, those like Robert who are accustomed to the atmosphere of luxirious city Paris were made neuvous. The taxi stopped in front of a five storied building at No.11, Giesebrecht tree-lined Street.

Coming off the taxi, he went to the entrance of Salon Kitty using elevator. On his knocking on the walnut door which was decorated by a gorgeous three dimentional flower sculpture, one side of the bi-parting door was drawn back towards inside and a woman past middle age peeped out. She was Kitty Schmidt, the proprietor of this salon. At the neck opening of her black Chanel dress, a jaguar shaped brooch glittering the saphia eyes of mysterious atmosphere with jewelries of Cartier scattered on it was clinging to the neckline of her dress.

Robert [I came from Rothenburg.]
Kitty [Please point any one you like of the photos of this file..]
Robert [I made a reservation at 3pm of Rosina?]
Kitty [Oh, please excuse me. Mr. Gardner.]

She walked leading him and showed him to the bottom room of the corridor and knocked the door and opened it.

Kitty [Please enjoy your meeting.]

After she was gone, he recognized there Roxy wearing a thin silk fabric. She was no Rosina.

Roxy [Robert. You did find me out!]
Robert [You will have to call me Robin here.]

He took out the American passport from the inside pocket of his jacket and passed it to her.

Roxy [I see, Robin.]

As soon as she finished to confirm the name on it she returned it to him.

Robert [Were you since able to meet again with your family?]
Roxy [My mother who had been heavily insured passed away last month. I am now all alone in the whole cosmos. I work at this salon as courtesan but the whole streets are in no way as pleasant as Paris. Lots of army uniforms and no fun at all.]
Robert [You are not at all becoming to this town.]

Roxy shut Robert's mouth with her hand.

VENUS and OCTOPUS will be here!!

Roxy [What I heard from a Japanese diplomat is… At the revolution when the era of Samurai came to the end, those who flourished and managed this period were the middle to low class warriors and the Geisha courtesans.]
Robert [Tell me the story you heard.]
Roxy [A Samurai by the name of Kogoro Katsura was chased in Kyoto by the Samurais of the old regime Shogunate and hid himself at the place where Ikumatsu his favourite Geisha lived. But he was pursued by Isami Kondo, who was known as a great swordsman, to the Ikumatu place. Ikumatsu courageously faced Kondo and drove him back.]
Robert [How could she do that?]
Roxy [Isami Kondo was going to check a big and long wardrobe box called Nagamochi but at her words of 『Are you gone crazy to wish to see women's underwear! If you find nobody in there but women's underwear, shame shall be on you.』,Isami Kondo gave up searching the inside of Nagamochi.]
Robert [So it means Isami Kondo was a highly proud Samurai.]

Though he said so, he had no idea of what sort of underwear Japanese women at that age were wearing. As such, he imagined a Samurai beried in women's langeries which he knew.

Roxy [What is making you grinning? Kogoro Katsura later

	got married Ikumatu formally. He was a devoted husband so he ordered a diamond ring for her in 1875.]
Robert	[Japan is located at the reverse side of the globe, isn't it.]
Roxy	[Correct. Where did he place this order then?]
Robert	[If London, in 1870 Garrard manufactured the diamond crown of Queen Victoria. If Paris, it is possible that was Cartier which had a close connection with Napoleon III…but if for 1875, I guess it may have been Garrard of London, I wonder?]
Roxy	[To coordinate with the Chanel dress, I wish to have a Caltier ring and a brooch like what Wallis wore.]
Robert	[I will think about it for you If you help my life like Kogoro.]
Roxy	[No invalid promissory note, OK?]

Then suddenly there was a knock at the door. She quickly wore a bathrobe slipping off the bed and found Louise in black SS uniform holding Luger P08 at the ready. Luise entered the room with the skull shaped metal on her uniform cap which was dully refecting the room light.

Roxy	[What's the matter?]
Louise	[We need to find out a U.S. espionage.]
Roxy	[I'm afraid your guess is wrong. He is an American by the name of Robin Gardner.]
Louise	[Kitty was saying she had missed to acknowledge his passport so I am here to do it.]
Robert	[Is this what you want?]

As he pointed the inside pocket of his jacket, Roxy pulled the passport from there and handed it over to Louise.

Louise　　[This passport was reissued at the American Embassy in Paris. Why is this reissuance?]

Robert　　[I lost it when I had a business suit made in Nice.]

Louise　　[As you say so this jacket looks like French made. American passport is targeted so be careful to keep your passport.]

Robert　　[OK.]

Louise　　[Have a nice trip.]

　Bowing slightly touching lightfully the brim of her cap, she went away taking the soldiers who were carrying assault rifles.

Roxy　　[Ever since she was appointed to the case officer, she comes in quite bluntly. It is pretty disturbing to the classy atomospere of this place, isn't it?]

Robert　　[Why don't you quit here?]

Roxy　　[I have no place to go, you know.]

Robert　　[I am going to Zurich by the train of 8am tomorrow morning. Are you coming with me?]

Roxy　　[I will wait for you at a bit before 7:30am at Café Odyssey which is located in front of the station.]

Robert　　[Okay.]

　Now that their decision was made, both quickly wore clothes and she saw him off at the door of the salon. Coming back to her room there she found Walter Schellenberg waiting for her.]

Walter　　[It looks that the day for you to leave here has come.]

Roxy　　[Aren't you quick to find it out.]

Walter　　[Half of this package is a farewell gift from me. 100,000

	pounds and 100,000 U.S. dollars and Uk bonds and I put a special pass of Gestapo. Porlish passport cannot work till Switzerland.]
Roxy	[You, too, do believe the Maria's fortune telling at 「the Words of Notre Dame」 !]
Walter	[Suppose the peak of NS comes in summer, next year, our ways of approach are to be varied in many ways. The black note-book in this package states code names of persons who may contact you in London, Paris, Zurich and New York. As there is no need of your contacting them back, no contact details of those persons are listed in the note-book.]
Roxy	[What action do you expect me to take in such situation?]
Walter	[You are not in such a position as to consider how to make the world war ceased as long as you are unable to prevent the war from happening. There will come an occasion when peace will become needed at a certain timing.]
Roxy	[You wish to have someone act the role of modification of the situation in between war and peace.]
Walter	[I guess your interpretation is not out of forcus, though nothing definite can be said at this moment.]
Roxy	[Chanel can play the role both with U.K. and Germany and I can decode her writing, too.]
Walter	[It is a good hint, Roxy.]
Roxy	[I'm sure she will not get married with that shadowless Von D. Her preference of men is still a

	shadowy person such as Capel in her past.]
Walter	[What is making you such comment? All of sudden.]
Roxy	[What I wish to say is that she will help you if such a person as you were a self-supporting student like Capel. She will most probably help you.]
Walter	[I haven't thought about such possibility.]
Roxy	[What you have told me about the heroes at the time of Japan's Meiji Restoration who married to Geishas is a very well composed story. Walter, you are a good story teller.]
Walter	[Oh, No. it is not a fiction. It is a true story. In the era of Meiji when was the time of revolution in Japan, people's sense of values was greatly changed. Failing to follow the change, oftentimes daughters of families of culture became Geisha. The first prime minister called Hirobumi Ito married to a Geisha. Wife of the foreign minister Kaoru Inoue was a divorced woman and Inoue met her at a salon and married her. Another instance is Munemitsu Mutsu whose wife was also a Geisha. Those exGeishas married to Japan's great feagures were the stars at the Japan's social watering hall by the name of Rokumei-kan. In other words, Japan's diplomacy was developed under the influence of such women. In this modern world, such time as when only if women can obtain a proper chance, they will become an existence of leaving their names in the history.]
Roxy	[Chanel may be the forefront of such women.]

Walter	[When the 21st century arrives, her name will be known as the first representation of the 20th century France. Like the era of the nobles is now finishing, time will come when what has been done will be valued in place of the origin of clan, like NS.]
Roxy	[I'm surprised you can talk like a solicitor.]
Walter	[No one can tell what value NSDAP can leave in the history. As for the size, it will surely leave a large footprint, but..]
Roxy	[You always tend to say too much. That's why you are said as a good-for-nothing lawer.]

There, Louise who was here just then knocked the door and came in.

Louise	[I have arraived tickets. Can we see each other again?]
Roxy	[Thank you. I hope destiny makes us meet again.]
Louise	[Take care.]
Walter	[I will not see you off.]
Roxy	[You don't wish to have your tear noticed.]
Walter	[No, I don't wish to notice your tear.]

Thus, after the two people went out of her room, Roxy started packing her belongings into just one trunk. She decided to take the black Chanel dress which contains past memories of hers and which also is easy to wear. Those dresses which she wore as Rosina are nothing but a reminder of the disturbing past. She decided to ask Kitty to dispose all those clothes at her will. People who see a ray of light in their future will not hesitate to throw off the past decidedly which is just like a pupa turning into a fascinating butterfly.

18. Train for Zurich

On the following morning, Robert and Roxy met in due course at Café Odyssey at the station front and rode on to a compartment of the train. There Dentaro Hayashi had already been on board waiting for them.

Robert	[This is Mr. Dentaro Hayashi from Japan. He is helping you to open an account at Trust Swiss Bank in Zurich. You can call him Den. This is Miss Roxane Walewska, Roxy.]
Roxy	[How do you do. I'm sure we will get along though for a short time.]
Den	[Likewise.]
Robert	[Why at all, do you wish to open a bank account in Switzerland?]
Den	[It looks necessary to cash American bond and put it in a bank.]
Robert	[Can you give me more details?]
Den	[My father's acquaintance has some connection with America and gathered such information that American Government is currently studying a possible asset freezing measures to be applied against Japan. If this comes true, bonds of American Government or State Governments will become unrealizable assets. This is why I deposit the funds in the Swiss banking account.]
Roxy	[Listen, I wish to cash U.K. bond in my possession and

	half amount of pounds I have, Robin.]
Robert	[Do you have such assets?]
Roxy	[I have the profit of sales of the right of the mansion which used to be there in Warsaw.]
Robert	[So both of you will change your assets to higher current assets.]
Den	[Correctly saying, I just change my assets to a safer type of assets.]
Robert	[Which means?]
Den	[Sign of divination has appeared which tells chaos will be rolling in the whole world. This sign has already been noticed by fortune tellers who have above the average power. In any case this chaos will no way be possible to be avoided.]
Robert	[In actuality, the present jerky relationship between Germany and the two countries of England and France has been treated and reported by press as a phoney war. I am inclined to feel nothing may happen after all?]
Den	[In future there will be at lease two world wars. The next one will happen in the near future, but the other one will need much more time till it takes place.]
Robert	[The second one, in other words WW3, do you know when it will break out?]
Den	[I am not in a position to define the breaking out date of WW3. All what I can say by studying Les Centures is WW3 will have a totally different scheme from that of WW2.]

Robert   [As you say so, I remember one of my acquaintances was telling such kind of comprehension of Les Centuries.]

Den   [Didn't that acquaintance of yours tell you anything about the forth line of Les Centuries 7-14?]

7-14
Faux exposer vindra topographie,
Seront les cruches des monumens ouuertes:
Pulluer secte, saincte philosophie,
Pour blanches noires, & pour antiques

Robert   [No, but I'm curious to learn those particular contents in the second line of Les Centries 7-14. Won't you mind telling me about it?]

Den   [The line states black in the place of white, new system in the place of old. Interpretation of the first line is fascism taking the place of capitalism…]

Robert   [If we read the latter line as the old resime will take the place of the new resime, does it cause any inconvenience?]

Den   [Such comprehension is possible only when the latter part of latter line is understood as relating to the former part of the first line, but suppose the latter line covers the word black only, the sentence can be translated such as the white capitalism changes to black fascism or nationarism when fascism or racialism changes from the old resime to the new resime. Then, if 7-14 implies the date when Bastille Day takes place,

	it definitely means this dramatic turnabout will happen in France.]
Roxy	[You mean fascists' resume will be formed in France?]
Den	[As the contents of fascism keeps phase-changing, it had better be called nationalists'.]
Robert	[I understand when racialism hails around Europe at the second time, resume will change from white to black. But why didn't Nostradamus make Les Centuries more comprehensive to French people instead of using cryptic figures?]
Den	[It may be because he knew WW3 was to break out. For this reason even in English he used the word July instead of Month of Seven. I think the reason why is that Nostradamus thought about the necessity for Japanese or the like to decipher this part of Les Centuries.]
Robert	[By the way, though this question of mine may sound queer to you, how do you medically understand the meaning of reincarnation?]
Den	[Japan is the world where spirits dwell in all and every thing. There, spirits can lodge even in the habitually used handtools. Robin, do you see any difference between that you know your former life and that you can foresee your future?]
Robert	[Considering the result of the well-known researches of the reincarnation that happened in India, I do understand the human past could be observed. But can future be seen as well, I wonder?]

Den	[Those people as mistics or fortune tellers can at least feel the past even if they cannot visualize it in images.]
Robin	[Robin, What is it like of your reincarnation of the past?]
Robert	[After all, I will take it as reincarnation of a person as a result of revived memories of his former life.]
Den	[If one can see some kind of image and if he knows that image is familiar to him, then such image is a image of the past. For instance, if one can see Roman warriers aboard a four-horse driven chariot, it is obvious that that was an image of the past. Likewise, if the image is of the clothes of current mode the image belongs to the near past or the present day or the near future. But if it is a completely different image?]
Roxy	[You mean a very distant future?]
Den	[The person who can see that image will be called a fortune teller and that's all.]
Robert	[That won't mean to have analized the mechanism.]
Den	[If what does not exist at the present time can be seen and if the time when the particular individual is no longer living can be seen, both future and past comes to be one same thing and no difference.]
Robert	[What you wish to say is that there is such possibility as, if past can be seen, future can also be seen, right?]
Den	[Probably, we can at least see or feel those.]
Robert	[Okay, then, if for instance someone insists that the contents of Nostradamus' Les Centuries are out of forcus, how do you hit him back?]

Den	[Well, that may happen if Nostradamus' statement was meant to explain some matter other than what is argued about, in other words, some happening in further more distant future, also it can be the case that people lived in the further distant past can no way understand what the matter is or means. For example, if a person who lived 500 years ago trys to explain the radio broadcasting system in the present day, he shan't no way be able to tender any bit of proper explanation. for what he has never seen or even never had any idea what it is like.]
Robert	[If the thing or the matter is truly made visible to Nostradamus, I think he should have written the exact name of it.]
Den	[If the statesman should have known the book wouldn't do any good to him, he would have burnt the book. Even the first emperor of Chinese Qin Dynasty in BC200 or thereabouts had the book burnt.]
Robert	[Was that book stating some harmful prophecy against the emperor?]
Den	[According to the statements in the book called Shiki that was written by Shibasen, there listed a prophecy telling that it would be Ko that would destroy Qin. Following this prophecy, the first Qin Emperor built the Great Wall of China for the purpose of preventing the invation from a tribe called Ko which was a tribe consisting of barbarians of north side. However, this invasion did not happen and at the death of the first

	Qin Emperor his youngest son called Koga who was in fact not the nominitee for the successor of Qin Emperor derived the position of the next emperor, being carried out by the eunuchs. But as Koi was incompetent enough to control the country as an emperor, consequently Qin died out. This sequence of events was recorded by the Chinese as a proof of the prediction having come true. The first Qin Emperor was a notorious tyrant for the fact that he had books that inconvenienced his position burnt and buried his objectors alive. As you will see by this instance, that Nostradamus' writing was done in the very way to be understood is very meaningful.]
Robert	[Is this also applicable to Apocalypse of John??]
Den	[Yes, there is that possibility.]
Roxy	[By the way, shall we have some tea? Let's go to the dining car.]
Den	[Do you like to try Japanese Maccha tea. I can make it for you.]
Robert	[Is what you mean the one of the traditional style?]
Den	[Yes, it is.]
Roxy	[Oh, that sounds great.]
Den	[I have here some hot water that I was given at the hotel this morning.]

 Finishing his talk, he took out from his baggage a tea basket made of cane. Then he put on the table besides him three tea bowls of 10cm and 12cm diameter out from the tea basket. Those bowls looked alike café au lait bowls but had some deformation with unevenness on the surface of the bowls. He then took out of a lacquerware a small bamboo spoon of a shape similar to an earpick and he used that spoon to scoop green tea powder from a tea powder container.

Next, he poured vaporing hot water into the tea bowls and stirred the tea and hot water into mousse form. He then took off the plug at the top end of the small gourd-shaped container of about 5cm long, pulled out several pieces of confetti candy onto the palm of his hand and showed Roxy to take the candy in this manner. Next, Den handed the larger and fully glazed tea bowl called Karatsu over to Robert who was calling himself Robin and the smaller tea bowl of black hand-molded earthenware to Roxy.

Den [These bowls are made of earthenware so they do not heat easily, but the tea inside the bowl is pretty hot so you be careful. The drinking manner is that you sip the tea for three times and make a sound of drinking with the last sip.]

Roxy [That sounds an unreasonable request. Tell me what purpose is such manner for?]

Den [Originally it was a go-sign to the tea server who was sitting on standby in the adjoining room. This matter was formed in the age when no glass partition between the rooms existed.]

Robert [Is tea ceremony culture for people who use servants?]

While talking, Den was making tea using a café au lait bowl which he found at a flee market.

Den [Samurai used to gather at tea rooms for discussion of a coup d'etat or the sort and when they entered the

	tea room through the small entrance they made it a rule to hung their swords on the sword hanger placed outside the entrance panel of the tea room.]
Robert	[It equals to 'put the gun belt off!' in America, isn't it.]
Roxy	[Is the size of the tearoom similar to this compartment?]
Den	[You're right, but there equipped a space called Tokonoma in addition, where art objects are decorated such as a picture drawn paper roll to be unrolled and hung on this space or framed paper on which caractors written by a high rank priest in the first half of the ceremony, and then at the later part of the tea ceremony such paper roll is replaced by a flower vase with a monocyclic flower put in it. Most of the walls of tea rooms are straw mixed mud walls. With such mad walls on the back, a monocyclic flower of vivid color symbolizes the delight of life. For those Samurais who were at all times facing death at the battlefield, such thoughtful decorations might have worked very impressively.]
Roxy	[A new war is just about to start here in Europe, so I guess every one must now have courage to face death.]
Den	[Your comment sounds interesting to me. Do you have any such information to lead you to have this comment?]
Roxy	[I gathered at Salon Kitty that Count Charlo who is the foreign minister of Italy said Hitler is making a

	wrong choice so Italy would not agree to the alliance with Germany. If a large size order of arms is placed to hide the failure of domestic economy, the public will take it for sure as an expansion of armanents?]
Den	[Yes, as you say, many researchers are analizing that the name Hitler could be Hister in Les Centries.]
Roxy	[Information about Ciano seems to be comig from Borgia of National Gendarmerie of France. I once met him. He is a good singer.]
Den	[The Borgias look to have an old family tree.]
Roxy	[Yes, their family tree is so old that they believe Renaissance is their ancestors' biggest contribution.]
Robert	[Is that family tree the one with a lot of scandals such as incest…]
Roxy	[I heard the family placed the young brother or cousin in the position of Cardinal in their endeavor to have their family member get the seat of Pope.]
Den	[Information about Vatican comes out from the Borgias onto Chiano. By the way, shall I tell what may happen to Robin in near future?]
Robert	[Whose prophecy is it?]
Den	[This is based on Nostradamus Les Centuries 9-83. 9-83 Sol vingt de Taurus si fort de terre tremble Le grand theatre remply ruinera L'airi ciel terre obscurcir & troubler Lors l'infidelle Dieu & saincts voguera 9-83 On May 10, the land of fortress Maginot line will shake. The French battlefields will collapse and be buried. The air will be darkened both in the sky and on the

land. Those miscreants try to make gods or saints more popular. The great nationals often mean French people and the word theatre means battlefield in the military terms, therefore, the great theatre would mean the battlefield in France. As the 20th of Taurus comes to be May 10, starting on this day, pagans try to spread propaganda to popularize gods and heroes other than Christiasm. Typical of atheism is socialism but nationalism is also quite similar to socialism in this regard. One thing I can advise you on your behalf is that to protect yourself you should not be in the district near Maginot Line.]

Robert [Are you warning me that Phoney War can well develop into a hot war?]

Den [When you choose a new place where you are going to live together, I suggest you to ward off this district.]

Robert [Well, our conversation resembles that of the Samurais of a few hundred years ago, doesn't it.]

Den [Yes, that is the case, indeed.]

The rest of time was spent exchanging such common subjects as culture or historically known sightseeing spots and around 10pm, the train finally arrived at Zurich. The three people agreed to visit Trust Swiss Bank at 9am on the following morning and checked into each hotel room.

19. Opening Bank Account at Trust Swiss Bank

Robert taking Roxy with him arrived at the entrance of Trust Swiss Bank and found Den there already, waiting for them. They therefore entered the bank just at 9am and told the bank staff that they were there for the purpose of performing the procedures of a new account opening. At their words, the staff guided them into a private room. Then a man in charge greeted to them handing his business card to each one of the three.

Bauer [How do you do, I am Salomon Bauer. I am to be in charge of your account.]

Robert [In addition to the account opening of Mr. Dentaro Hayashi, we wish you to help opening an account of this lady, Miss Roxane Walefuska.]

Bauer [About the account establishment of Mr. Hayashi, I understand we can receive an introduction letter.]

Den [This letter from Duke of Windsor is what you will need.]

Bauer [Yes, I have certainly received it now. You wish to cash bond of British pounds and U.S.dollar bond. Here, we will certainly keep those.]

Roxy [I did not know you need an introduction letter.]

Bauer [No, that is not really the case, but we will need some time for you to wait. What do you wish to deposit with us?]

Roxy [These U.S.dollar notes and British pounds.]

Bauer [I understand. Please give me some time.]

Robert	[Is there any problem because of absence of an introduction letter?]
Bauer	[Mr. Robin Gardner, we have an information from our profession that half amount of the British pound notes were fake notes. Were those U.S. dollar notes and British pound notes the ones gained through transactions done in the Germany?]
Roxy	[These notes are the gains from sale of fixed assets in Warsaw.]
Bauer	[Please tell me where you received the payment.]
Roxy	[In Berlin.]
Bauer	[Sorry to say, we do need some time. The application of Mr. Hayashi can be processed pretty quickly, though.]
Robert	[Understood. Den, as your account can be processed in no time, we are going to part at this place.]
Den	[Sudden farewell. This is exactly what is said 'treasure every meeting, for it will never recur'.]
Robert	[We know we must not involve you in our situation.]
Roxy	[That tea was delicious. Thank you.]
Den	[I'm sorrowful to part, but wish you good health.]
Roxy	[Have a good day.]
Bauer	[Mr. Hayashi, these are the whole butch of the relative documents. You are rest assured as regards safety of your assets as Switzerland is a permanently neutral country.]
Den	[Thank you. I have acknowledged the receipt.]

 Finishing talking to the bauer this way, Den left the bank.Though he was not aware of it, there were eyes that were gazing at his movement coming out of the bank and heading towards the station. Walter with a monocle wearing a Milan tailored business suit and Louise wearing a chestnut color wig were both watching Den while pretending to be browsing Paris mode magagines.

Walter	[Oh, Gush, only the Japanese fellow came out.]
Louise	[As same as the last month?]
Walter	[Though I thought the notes this time should have no problem.]
Louise	[In the last month deal, both U.S.dolars and 1.000 dollar U.S.trading bills failed to be accepted.]
Walter	[Forgery of pound notes is very difficult to be performed. I wonder if the ones used this time works or not.]
Louise	[I understand a new mold has since been used.]
Walter	[It certainly is an extremely difficult work for even the top class forgers.]
Louise	[Look, the secretary of Rothschild is entering the bank.]
Walter	[I see. The bank must have requested appraisal of the notes to their fellow trader.]
Louise	[Do you think that man's appraisal ability is trustworthy?]
Walter	[The Rothschilds' family business is originally an old coin dealer. Can you guess their former name before they gave their name as Rothschild?]
Louise	[Did you research that much, Walter?]
Walter	[Bauer, the same name as that bank's President's clan.]

Louise	[I see. This bank is also funded by Juwish capitals.]
Walter	[That may be the case, but if so, it does not matter.]
Louise	[Why? As this is Switzerland?]
Walter	[Do you ever think it is at all possible to avoid birth of Jewish blood mixed descendants?]
Louise	[You, you think it is not possible, do you?]
Walter	[Jewish people drifted into Egypt, and at the time of Babylonian capitivity jews were exiled to Methopotamia and what's worse is several Jewish tribes were completely terminated. Do you know all of these historical occurences?]
Louise	[What you wish to mean is that Jews exist everywhere?]
Walter	[Yes, they exist everywhere in the world. At Ise Shrine in Japan, a symbol called Kagome is nothing but Star of David. What's more is this God is who plays a role of preparing food for the highest ranking deity, Goddess of the Sun.]
Louise	[Which part of this story is a problem, Mr. Lawyer?]
Walter	[The ancient Japan was based on matriarchy, therefore records of male successors are not accurate. Doesn't this explain that the story of God of Ise feeding Goddess of the Sun every day would mean their relation is like husband feeding wife?]
Louise	[Any other more convincing arguments?]
Walter	[Ancient Emperors of Japan were called Sumerogi. The spelling of Sumero of this word Sumerogi is quite alike the spelling of Samaria.]

Louise	[Do you presume the emperor of Japan which was allied with Germany could be the family tree of Samaria?]
Walter	[There is an information of Japanese Navy letting Jews live in Shanghai. Doesn't this imply there are some people at the Japan side who are feeling this possibility as a true fact?]
Louise	[Oh, Walter, that is a very strained interpretation!]
Walter	[Before the age of Babylonian Captivity,jews used to call months not using a particular name per month but called like the first month, the second and so on, and this numbering method of calling months also coincides with the Japanese month naming habits. Duration of Babylonian Captivity was about 70 years from around 607 BC and the first enthronement of the emperor in Japan was close to this period of Babylonian Captivity. In the Japanese interpretation of years, this year comes to be the 2600th Anniversary of Japan.]
Louise	[Our highness Lawyer seems to have a vast knowledge.]
Walter	[According to what is written in the Chinese book 『The History of The Wei』, there is a statement that Japan was using iron arrowhead which is different from Korea. In addition, the book has a statement which reads that if people go down to the south about the same distance of the half of the mileage of the width of the Korean peninsula, the land is directly connected

	with the land of Japan. Both Japan and the south part of Korean Peninsula already entered the iron age, however, that technology to cast iron was not imported from China. Moreover, in the one former age of the iron age, namely in the bronze age, the bronze casting technology at its beginning part of the age has a possibility of that it did not come from China.]
Louise	[Then, via what route that technology propagated from the Hittaitis?]
Walter	[The route could be the Stepped Road of the ancient Scythians. In other words, there is a possibility the tribe lost after the Babylonian Captivity may have entered Japan through this route.]

Here, the writer wishes to add a brief explanation. It happened that in August, 2013, a mold of Ordos style dagger of 350BC through to 300BC was dug out in the west coast of Lake of Biwa in Japan. In view of the fact that this type of dagger was never dug out in the whole in the area from the mainland China to the Korean Peninsula, this implies the possibility of Eurasian nomads having taken it into Japan.

As regards Japan's iron casting culture has a possibility of its having spread down via the north area of Japan, Hokkaido, and that spreading route may have needed a special additional statement to emphasize that Japan used iron arrowhead. Problem of iron is that due to humid weather in Japan, it is difficult for iron ware to survive the years, and also a possibility of those having been melted and recycled as iron was a very precious natural resource. This latter explanation may sound more reasonable. Buddism spead over Japan via Paekche, but such logics to set other cultural things to have come through the same route has already been proven not applicable with the instance of unearthed iron mold of Ordos-style dagger. Regarding rice farming, as a result of gene analysis which was made possible in the 21st century, it was proven that the Japanese rice plants is the tyle of Fujian rice plants and not the major and popuar types of rice grown in the Korean Peninsula. On the other hand, the gene of rice plants which was made grown in the Japan seazed area of the etreme south of the peninsula has the same gene as Japan's and China's Fujian grown rice.

Bauer [Sorry to have kept you waiting so long. Miss Roxane Walefuska, We have accepted the total amount of UK pounds and US dollars to be deposited in your account at our bank.]
Roxy [Oh, good! Robin.]
Robert [Good thing that these notes were proven to be not fake.]
Bauer [We do hope your long patronage.]
Roxy [Mr. Bauer, Thank you sincerely.]
   Then they went out of the bank.
Louise [Look, Roxy is wearing glasses.]
Walter [Which means the printing this time was successful. Let someone check at which ticketing window she is going to buy her ticket.]
Louise [Are you going to trace her?]
Walter [Don't you agree she still has some more use value.]

Louise   [What a scary lawyer you are.]
Then, they proceeded onto the next action.

After Roxy and her companion were gone, the man who discriminated the notes Roxy brought in as to whether these are forged notes or not came into that small room in Trust Swiss Bank.

Karl   [Won't you exchange this 100 pound note of mine with one of the notes you have at your bank?]
Salomon   [No problem, but why?]
Karl   [The printing is undoubtedly genuine, but the quality of paper used doesn't feel quite right, though it may stay in the production tolerance.]
Salomon   [With this one added, you may have built up a collection of monies which you feel hesitant to use, right?]
Karl   [As my ancestral profession is the old coin dealer, this is a kind of destiny that I have to face.]
Salomon   [Even the Rothschilds will take this note as genuine?]
Karl   [If my doubt is staying at this level, even British bankers won't be able to distinguish it as fake. But this level of doubt could still be my personal objective of study.]
Salomon   [Do you mean that it is what NSDAP is intentionally programming to order the production?]
Karl   [the feel of the material paper may have caused by the quality of water when the paper was produced, though it is only my intuition.]
Salomon   [Is coin discrimination more difficult?]

Karl [Purity of Genuine ancient Rome Denarius silver coin keeps around 98% but at some other later times the degree of purity came less than 98%. Melting the silver coins which were cast at much later time, copies made in such manner won't keep the same level of glitter as the genuine Caeser silver coin and subtle difference of glitter cannot be avoided. . The most difficult ones for discrimination are the coins of lower grade with scars on the surface or of worn out surface which were melted and recast. Those ones of this time have a possibility of being such kind of coins.]

20. The Ox on the Roof

Robert and Roxy having been back to Paris, found an unoccupied room in Saint-Germain and started living there together. This couple thought it a good idea to eat out occasionally and dropped in the cabaret-bar Ox on the Roof. Stepping in there, they found their acquentances sitting at the counter taking surved dishes.

Luc	[Wow, fancy meeting you here again.]
Den	[Hi, Robin and Roxy.]
Luc	[He is Robert, Den. Aren't you so quickly intoxicated having just half of the glass.]
Robert	[So these are Mr. Librarian and Mr. Doctor, Aha.]
Roxy	[A doctor of bacteria reserch, right?]
Luc	[I knew at the first glance when we met for the first time you looked a very becoming couple.]
Robert	[That's what an Astrologist thought.]
Maurice	[Didn't see you for a while. What can I serve you?]
Roxy	[Prosciutto salad and a glass of red wine.]
Robert	[Whole roast quail poruketta and a glass of red wine.]
Maurice	[Price could be less if you take one bottle for both of you.]
Roxy	[Thank you. Please give us one full bottle.]
Maurice	[Okay.]
Luc	[By the way, Hasn't Mr. Kannenberg come yet to get the book?]
Maurice	[I expect him today.]
Luc	[Strange he hasn't been here for a whole one month

	after I left the book here.]
Maurice	[Speak of the devil..here he is.]
A.K.	[Long time no see. Hi, Luc, It's been quite some time since we met before.]
Luc	[Maurice, please pass him that book.]
Maurice	[Ar, here it is.]
Ar	[Thank you! This looks pretty clean as I see it.]
Luc	[It is a dead stock. Not a single page has yet been read.]
Ar	[All depends whether this book can please my master in Berline.]
Luc	[When do you plan to present this book to your book loving master?]
Ar	[I think I had better keep it till he decides to start some big event.]
Luc	[I can easily know to where this book has been read, so when you know it, please tell me.]
Ar	[I understood. Do I have to seek another master in your astrology?]
Luc	[There will come big difficulties in the year of 1945. I suggest you to resume your profession after this year.]
Ar	[Regime change or the like?]
Luc	[I should say, yes.]
Den	[Why are you refrained from clearly saying the world war?]
Ar	[Please teach me.]
Luc	[I need to learn if your master starts all his planned actions after he has finished reading the whole book or

	otherwise if he may start to take all actions just following at his will without reading the book.]
Den	[Will you be able to come to Paries on May 10? I wonder you may not.]
Ar	[Why May 10?]
Den	[Because I feel if something happens it must have some relation to Germany.]
Ar	[I'm just a cook. Sometimes I do take dishes to the study, but I'm never in a position to advise anything to my master.]
Den	[Please time when you present that book in the afternoon of May 10. If you can do it, it will become clear that your master is now taking actions for the purpose of realizing the prophecy.]
Ar	[I do understand. I will cooperate with you.]
Den	[World war is foreseen by 〖Les Centuries〗, as well.]
Robert	[Very interesting. Is Destiny chosen by the will? Or are we to go with the already fixed destiny? Which do you think?]
Luc	[Prophecy means to observe development of situation beyond the time and space. No one can surpass this set frame.]
Robert	[Future means a difference of the memory of the former life, doesn't it.?]
Luc	[It comes to the same result whether you go to the future or the past surpassing the time and space for the point that the image other than the real fact at this present moment can been seen.]

Den	[Suppose you have seen a certain scenery, if people appearing in your sight are wearing clothes that you have never seen to date, possibility of its showing the future will be high. If those people wear a toga or an armor, it is meant for the past. Nostradamus recorded his vision of a part of the future in a random way.]
Ar	[You are giving to me, namely, to Artur, the chance to verify that happened or did not happen.]
Luc	[I think You are the only one who could make such verification. By the way, could you lay in a stock of any good food ingredients?]
Ar	[Fresh vegetables and delicacies which arrived at the market on Monday. As I cook for quite many vegetalians, point I care about is if nutrients are enough or short.]
Robert	[It is important to have food with well balanced nutrients to make your idea a good one.]
Ar	[Incidentally, what is the art object on that table?]
Den	[That's for the flower festival.]
Ar	[I'm lost. Here in Paris it is a bit too early to talk about the flower blossom season.]
Den	[Foufou engraved wood into a statue of an infant to celebrate the birthday of Buddha. In Japan we set the birthday date on April 8 of Gregorian Calendar and have the celebration on that day. The liquid which is filling the basin has to be sweet tea originally in Japan, and people pour this sweet tea on the infant Buddha and drink the left-over tea by themselves.]

Ar	[Sweet tea in Japan···what are you using here instead?]
Den	[English tea sweetened with sugar as a substitute.]
Maurice	[If you like, why don't you celebrate the birthday of the Budda and pour a cup of tea on it and take some tea?]
Ar	[For what kind of joke did Foufou engrave the German mark?]
Maurice	[Put it the other way round, then it becomes Gyaku-Manji. This one is Manji and not German symbol.]
Ar	[Manji? Oh, yes, the German symbol is surely the other way round. So, today April 8 is the birthday, I see!]
Den	[Peace to all people.]
Ar	[Then let me join and be a Buddhist for today.]

　Thus, the night was getting late and in the next small room there was Walter Schellenberg looking at what was happening in the next room, who was not in the disguise for that night.

Walter	[Busy night tonight, too, isn't it.]
Maurice	[Yes, Thanks to frequenters. This place is a gathering spot of people of culture.]
Walter	[All depends on how you cooperate with us, but you know I have a power to arrange on a priority basis this cabaret-bar get relocated on the street where it was located previously.]
Maurice	[I would very much like to have a bit more space than here.]

Walter	[I guess you are in need of a few more small rooms.]
Maurice	[You seem not to wish to share the same room as Al.]
Walter	[As I must be cautious not to say much to him as he reports all what he hears to his superiors right away.]
Maurice	[I will of course keep it to myself that you are here.]
Walter	[Thank you.]
Louise	[Look, Roxy seems to be seeking somewhere to work again. What about your hiring her at your Cabaret-bar?]
Maurice	[Roxy is an attractive looking person, but Robert may not like such an idea.]
Louise	[I understand they anyway found a lodging in Paris.]
Maurice	[I guess Mr. Grant may return to London in the coming summer?]
Walter	[Till then, he is supposed to work for U.K. and American Embassies, am I right?]
Maurice	[Yes, so I understand.]
Walter	[Incidentally, I heard that at the office of Ribbentrop a plan of transferring jews to Madagascar is getting formed.]
Maurice	[Jews in Germany?]
Walter	[It seems to include the occupied area by Germany. Profession of minister of Foreign Afffairs is deemed to concentrate on diplomacy, so what he is doing is overstepping his authority. You have no relation to this matter of course, as you are cooperating with me.]
Maurice	[Thank you, sir.]
Walter	[The biggest problem that NSDAP is facing is there

	are uncontrollably too many grandstanders in its members.]
Maurice	[Number of stars, other than sgrandstanders, right?]
Walter	[Yes, they are making noise about stars in the sky as wellas those on their shoulder loops. Don't you think such things are mere superstitions?]
Maurice	[Yes, I wish to think so.]
Louise	[Human life is to be carved by oneself.]
Maurice	[On this table I see materiarism predominantly going on.]
Walter	[But Communism won't work either. Marx failed to calculate and take human desires into his theory. Heads of Soviet are spending all their time to destroy each other's lust for power.]
Maurice	[Yes, I have heard of that.]
Walter	[Such person who is detested by Starlin will never come back from a dance party. He just suddenly vanishes away in the air without leaving any trace.]
Louise	[purged out.]
Maurice	[With what reason?]
Walter	[Depends. What I gathered is sometimes according to the person's degree of loyalty, or only because he is a Russian. Starlin tends to trust Asian blood, but hates most of Jews. But as regards doctors, he trusts and promotes jews as long as they are doctors.]
Maurce	[What is the reason why?]
Maurice	[Why?]
Walter	[To avoid assassination by Russians. He is afraid of

being assassinatd by Russians. A possible political backlash, namely. Jews will in no way form a political power in Soviet.]

Maurice　[Oh, sounds the guests over there calling me. Excuse me, now.]

After Maurice left them, they started taking the tea which was now cooled off.

21. French Battlefields

On May 8, when is the flowering time of horse chestnut trees (marronnier), at 1800hours of that day, an urgent telegram was despatched to the attention of Cardinal Borgia at the Vatican and of the Foreign Ministry of The Netherlands to inform the start of military action in the French theatre that includes Holland and Belgium. This particular date and hour were the scheduled time when the declaraton of war was notified to Holland, so that this telegram meant that this declaration had been already leaked out. The Belgian Government had concluded a military secret agreement with U.K. and French armies, therefore, any additional declaration of war conflicts the duties of a neutral country so declaration of war was not announced to Belgium.

Also, France had declared war at time of her invension into Poland so Germany and France were already in the battling state.

On May 10 at 0:10am, a warning was alerted at the Belgian army, and starting at 0130 hours a rapid development of army force was started. At 0400 hours, fighters with the mark of swastika on the tail fin started to dive bombing at the Belgian army airports.

This fighter called Stuka is a single-engine dive bomber equippd with such features as inverted gull wing and non-retractable landing gear. The big difference of this bomber from the other coutries' bombers was that this bomber had a siren called Trampet of Jericho which firstly attached to this bomber after the Spanish Civil War. The only countermeasure against the attack of this bomber was just to escape as soon as hearing the bomber's roaring sound which was the sign of immediate bombing. Then what had to be done next is to lift the face up and counter shoot by a machine gun the bomber flying away high up into the sky. To make this style of fighting easier, the pilot fought back from the reverse side of the turret and blindly hit the gun in the air from where Stuka might possibly make another attack.

Then, into the army force on the ground that was no longer much protected by the sky fights, tanks of the caterpillar shaped beasts rushed into the battlefield. This was the beginning scene of the mortal combat at the Western Front about two hours ahead of the original plan. On the woodlands at the south edge of Belgium where U.K./French troops found difficult to pass through, the German tanks got going mowing down the trees with the power of the caterpillar. The French reconnaissance aircraft did find this caterpillar marching on May 11, but though the French headquarters were somewhat surprised but did not take it too seriously as they seemed to conclude that the goods to be transported must have been limited due to this highly disturbing route condition even with caterpillers.

On May 31, German troops attempted river crossing in Sedan, which action made France aware for the first time of its past negligence of building a protection guard in this district. Reason why France overlooked this possibility of danger was because France had been taking the B army group as the main-force unit instead of taking the German troops, the A army group, as the main-force unit. In the south of those troops existed as a fact of course the maginot line, and on the alert for the German C army group, General Maurice Gamelin kept his reserve forces as was at the maginot line. Should he have been a bit more cautious of the movement of the German troops, he could have had time to transfer part of the U.K./France troops staying in Belgium to the backside of the German A army group. If it had been done, the stampede of U.K./France troops to Dankirk must have been avoided. Armour corps needs a constant supply of fuels and bumbs, otherwise, they would be put in a more difficult situation than the case of foot soldiers.

Going back a little previous time, in the evening of May 9, Schellenberg in his military uniform was seen nearby the German C army group. There he met with Gypsy fortune tellers of a number of about 20. Those people spoke fluent French and so they were assigned to visit around cabaret-bars in each city telling people that calamities which were talked about in Les Centuries would take place in France.

After the bus on which those fortune tellers had been aboard, SS field officer level personnel was gathered in the bought-out dining room of a hotel. Schellenberg, standing on a turned-out wooden box of wine bottles, propagated a secret military instruction.

Walter [Sieg Heil]

Every one [Sieg Heil!]

Walter [Please check and acknowledge the contents of the bag just handed to each of you. You have one envelope which includes French francs as a maneuvering fund, another for pound sterling and one Red Michelin

Guide. The troops you belong to is to be the end of the line of the A army group and bypassing the side of the C army group you are to invade into France. Tomorrow on 10th at first light our friendly air force is to start scattering our propaganda handbills. By this battle plan, the French border will be stampeded. This is exactly what Nostradamus presaged 400 years ago! Our mission is to materialize his prediction and to make a big contribution to the third Reich which our leader Hitler is going to establish. Then, when we have broken through the border, we will have Paris surrender. We must requisition such as Hotel Ritz which is listed as the representative top-class hotels as typed on the list you have, to be utilized by Marcial Goring. We must secure the Imperial Suite for use by Marcial, and the Windsor Suite for the stay of the distinguished. Which troop is to be in charge of this mission depends on which troop will be the first one to succeed this requisition. Each one of you on a command post vehicle is to take two trucks and 50 soldiers. Keep it in your mind that we are now given a chance to shine as vanguards. Sieg Heil!]

Every one [Sieg Heil.]

In this way, a large stock of the restaurant guide book of the so-to-called Orange Guide or Red Guide which had been scarcely found at book stores in and around Paris was distributed to each attendant of this meeting. The distributed books were marked the dorm per use of the headquarter officers, officers and soldiers in accordance to the number of stars they were bestowed. Needless to add, the dress code for dinner time of the headquarter officers was a dress suit with a tie.

Schellenberg at a later date wrote that this dress code was demanded by the empire leader Himmler at his hosting parties even at the last stage of the war. Ritz in the Place Vendome was selected for use by the air force headquarter officers and for Paris martial force Le Meurice was appointed. This means quality of hotels in Paris and the wine stock status of each hotel had been secretly researched in advance. At the same time, geographical easiness of guarding those officers was an important condition to maintain security.

By that time already, in Schellenberg's blueprint of plan there may have been a plot to set Duke of Windsor up as the leader of Europe. Gayful ex noble Hermann Goring who can serve Duke of Windsor and his wife as a good crony is a person that has good knowledge of art objects and can talk much about this art genre. And what's more was that the old friend of the couple Coco Chanel was lodging at Ritz.

In the early evening of May 9, Hitler dressed in military uniform shut himself up in a wooden hut discreetly built on the half way up of a small mountain. At mid night, he pressed the shutter release button of Leica on the tripot.

It was his habit to record the condition of the sky of the day when he was going to do something important which would evidence that his decision was always influenced by stars. By then, the invation program to France had been postponed for as many as

58 times influenced by his study of the horoscope and weather map to time the execution of his decision. The war plan was also established in consideration of compatibility of each and every general. Traudl Junge who was Hitler's secretary testified in 2001 that Hitler had been believing the existence of power that could move the whole world and was beyond human understanding.

The French border area was quiet showing no sigh of invasion despite time progressed to 0400 hours on May 10 except that a big stock of fliers showing embellished Nostradamus prophecy began to be scattered from the sky. French people living in this area heightened their anxiety to the utmost all in one gulp when the tank corps led by General Rommel crossed the French border. At this very moment when this invation took place, Duke of Windsor was commanding as major general of U.K. army the effective strength of the reserves to protect Maginot Line but did not receive any order from General Gamelin except the order to keep watching and waiting.

Despite the surrender of Holland to Germany on May 14, Belgium continued its resistance. In the morning of May 15, diplomatic confidential documents were burnt out in the courtyard of the French Foreign Ministry building. The German tank corps passing the river at Sedan moved towards north and began surrounding U.K/French armies, but no hot war took place in the area where Maginot Line was built.

However, reaction of the public was different. In the beginning when the handbills were scattered from the sky, they did not react much to this propaganda. However, as the gypsy fortune tellers at the cabaret-bars in the town rumored that siege using the machines of hell that fly around the sky will be achieved which means the Nostradamus prophecy comes true. Then they caught the news that Amsterdam was burnt out in the late afternoon of one previous day which inevitably led them to believe the fortune that was told by the gypsy would come true.

At that point of time, no one could deny the fact that Holland and Belgium were getting surrounded and as the hand bills show the only way to save life was then believed to run away to the southwest of France. Owners of factories and shops and stores closed their work places and loading their household goods on trucks, and those bourgeoicies who do not own trucks joined the run-away using their passenger automobiles being afraid of plunderage by the enemy troops. Seeing such long rows of evacuating carriages, farmers, too, joined them loading their household goods and even live chickens on carts. Into such a narrow road that is just about good for only one car to pass, it then became totally impossible to have the army vehecles move towards the battlefield. In that situation, not only to General Gamelin but to any people it became totally impossible to send the reinforcements to the north.

On Thursday, May 16, Borja of Italian Embassy, who was nicknamed as Black Caruso was having a secret meeting with Edouard Daladier of French Ministry of Defence.

Ed [Caruso, what about for today? You must remember that if I meet you it would cause nothing but misinterpretation in many concerned parties.]

Borgia [As this is concerning the matter about which the ambassador can not act officially, I came here to see

Ed	you secretly in order to protect the city Paris.]
	[I am leaving this matter to General Gamelin⋯ but as you say so, as is in the ongoing situation France is surely disadvantaged.]
Borgia	[I presume if we can carry out Marshal Petain, the hero of WW1, the French citizens will accept him regardless of whatever results shall be due.]
Ed	[That sounds a persuading comment⋯No one wishes to pull someone's chestnuts out of the fire.]
Borgia	[I believe this measure is a good one not to hurt Your Excellency's established career.]

Somewhile after this conversation, Daladier extended his arm to the telephone.

Ed	[Hellow, Oh, are you his Excellency Marshal yourself?… May I ask you what you will you do in your capacity of his Excellency Marcial? Gamelin could well be incapable to handle this situation, don't you think so?… Oh, I understand, sir. Your recommendation is always followed in the first. At the Cabinet meeting tomorrow morning we will obtain the prime minister's agreement and call Max back. Needless to say, please keep this subject in your confidence, sir.]
Borgia	[His Excellency intends to call General Weygand back, is my understanding correct, sir?]
Ed	[As Holland drew their hands from making a decision to surrender, the reshuffle of Maurice Gamelin is a matter of time now.]
Borgia	[When will his Excellency Weygand will take up his

	post?]
Ed	[That will happen on Monday, the 20th.]
Borgia	[Let us try our best not to allow Paris to fall into the same disaster as Rotterdam by the German troops!]
Ed	[Do you think Mussolini will be able to offer his good offices to Germany?]
Borgia	[I am one of the lovers of Paris, too. I do not wish to see the light of Paris distinguished. Your Excellency does know that I have a good connection with Vatican, don't you.]
Ed	[Oh, yes, I remember your relative is a cardinal···I do rely on you in this regard.]

By exchanging such conversation, Borgia set about helping to solve two important pending problems. One is to have General Weygand out and the other his implication of the release of guard against the Italian army when the ongoing battle does not settle quickly.

In addition, to secure Daladier, who had the experience of the prime minister position, as a pipe of below the surface diplomatic negotiations could contribute to the national interest of Italy. This Borgia's capability to do political horse trading was the very secret of the Borgias that kept survising the difficult age since the renaissance period.

On the morning of the 20th, Maxime Weygand changed places with Maurice Gamelin at the control office. Finishing his assigned duty, Gamelin looked completely exhausted and did not even speak clearly.

Max [Maurice, is this map showing the current battle situation?]

Maurice [Yes, as you see it.]

Max [I don't see the defence line of France other than the Maginot Line. Where are the others gone?]

Maurice [We did have an agreement with Belgium and the main force of the U.K/France allied forces were ready to confront the approaching main force of the enemy… how come could they break through the Ardennes Forest…]

Max [Your explanation is totally inconherent!!]

Maurice [No French troops can ever closely follow the marching speed of the German troops that crossed the river in Sedan. Our tank corps were almost completely annihilated by severe dive bombing.]

Max [Why didn't you think about having our troops stationed in the middle part of France go for the rescue?]

Maurice [All the roads to Benelux were occupied by the refugees' vehicles and cargos. Even food and ammution can not be smoothly transported.]

Max [What happened to the retreat of U.K./France allied forces from Belgium?]

Maurice [The supply of fuel could not be made in time, so they cannot even move quickly enough.]

Max [Is what you mean the friendly forces in Belgium are feared to face the encircling and annihilating

	operation?]
Maurice	[Y-yes, as a matter of fact…]
Max	[When German operation of the encircling and annihilating attack is finished, the next target of Germans will naturally be Paris. In order to earn some time till this happens we must serisously consider the possibility of moving all the army power now stationed in the middle part of France for the sole purpose of protection of Paris.]
Maurice	[If I can make any helpful comment at this stage to you as successor of my present assignment, it is just one fact that we have lost air supremacy so we are desperately at a definitive disadvantage. To our deep regret, Black Nazi troops are organically handling the movement linkage of the attack up from the sky and armored cavalry on the ground so that the movement of the troops are done by the superhuman speed.]
Max	[We must definitely report all this situation to His Excellency Marshall Petain.]

　The changing marking from moment to moment on the map of the Benelex countries which were consisting of Belgium, Holland and Luxembourg, to show the battlefield getting enlarged rapidly was evidencing that the situation was driven into a desperate situation. In addition, Maginot Line stood meaninglessly.

　Time passed further quickly and on Sunday May 26, surrender of Belgium became definite. General Maxime Weygane visited Edouard Daladier of Department of Defence taking Deputy Prime Minister Philippe Petain with him. At the side of the sofa in the

Minister's broad room, a huge size map showing Benelux and the northeast district of France was spread and the spot where each troop of both sides was stationed was shown by placing a piece each on such spots of both sides on the map. As a matter of course, friendly armies were shown in the blue color, use of which color had become habitual since the time of French Revolution.

Studying the map, it looked like that at the Maginot Line there seemed to have some possibility left to continue to fight, but the problem was even tanks that could be used were not left at all. The major French force as well as U.K. army force were getting cornered to the direction of Dunkirk, and as regards Belgium, it was very questionable how long it could hold out. Such actual critical phase was clearly shown on the map

Ed [I understand that your visit today with Dupty Prime Minister Petain is for consultation about an important change of policy. Does it mean you have any ingenious idea? Unfortunately, my secretary is taking a leave today so I apologize I cannot serve you even a cup of coffee.]

Max [As we understand that Your Excellency must also understand it, if we leave the situation as is, it will be extremely difficult to keep the present battle line. We believe now is the time to make a cease-fire negotiation so we can negotiate our conditions with the German side. I would appreciate your instruction.]

Phillip [Ed, at the end of WW1, though France won the war, the human damage at our side, especially the damage of young generation was great which seriously

	influenced the economic activities of our country after the war, which I know you are clearly aware of. Now, this time again, 300,000 lives of young French men were lost already by now. Max is now detailing the reason why the continuance of the present war is difficult. Don't you think now is the time to review and reconsider the whole present situation?]
Ed	[What you mean is that the arrival of the reinforcements from the middle south France will not be in time. What do you think to keep going by transferring the location of the government?]
Max	[Ed, number of refegees from the northeast area keeps increasing day by day which is disturbing the force going north. However, we cannot order the troops to walk through the vinyards.]
Ed	[That's out of question. If we dare to let them march through the vinyards, we will certainly loose the next election.]
Max	[Where to maintain the government also depends on the transportation power of the army. Timing of a truce will be lost once we have lost our fighting power.]
Ed	[Paul, the Prime Minister, is insisting on resistance. How should we mediate this matter with him?]
Phillip	[There would be no other choice but to ask either Franco of Spain or Vatican.]
Max	[We must try by all means to have Paris the international city escape from being destroyed.]

Ed	[Will the German side accept such mediation?]
Phillip	[I did hear that the NS foreign minister Ribbentrop slept with Matahari.]
Max	[What about trying encouraging the enjoyable divertissement such as reviews of Mistinguette somehow to go through this difficulty?]
Ed	[I agree the cancan might work but I wonder if those dancers will remain in Paris?]
Max	[Should Paris be the target of bombing, we must immediately announce the open city declaration to the world. What about using American journalists as reporters?]
Ed	[To use American journalists as witness⋯It seems worth considering. Point is how to persuade Paul.]
Phillip	[If Paul's will of resistance is unmovably firm, the cease-fire negotiation shall not only collapse but Paris will be burnt to ashes.]
Ed	[In case we ask for the meditation of peace to Spain, it will become necessary that Phillip is to be the prime minister.]
Max	[Ed, why not you?]
Ed	[I think in consideration of the nation's trust and popurality, Phillip is the only one that can make servicepersons keep a cease-fire. Spain will trust us if Phillip does the work. For me, let me do negotiations as foreign minister. The early release of the French prisoners of war and their return to the homeland are important negotiation subjects. We cannot afford to

lose any more French lives. When that time comes, in order to enable Phillip to act as prime minister and Max to coordinate the cease-fire terms and conditions, we will be able to have a chance to persuade Paul to retire.]

The discussion on that day failed to bring forward any promising conclusion, however. when in the morning of Monday, June 3, the factory of Citroen was bombed, people living in Paris began running away gripped by fear. On the 5th when Dankirk surrendered, it then became obvious to any one's eyes that the major German force would rush into Paris. In an endeavor to protect the confusion possibly caused by the refugees, the French government announced an Open City Declaration on the 10th. The fear-ridden Parisians escaped from Paris and as a result the population of Paris decreased from 5 million down to .7million. In other words, 4.3 million refugees ran away to the direction of southwest of France. This situation arose nothing but great hindrance to the advance of the reinforcements. On Friday, June 14, the German force entered into Paris in full scale.

On June 16, when the new cabinet with Philippe Petain as the prime minister, Edouard Daladier took the post of the minister of foreign affairs as was planned and the preliminary negotiation for a truce through the Spanish Ambassador's mediation was started on June 17.

22. German Occupation of Paris

At the dawn of Friday, June 14, prior to the advance of the German Defence Force into Paris, Walter Schellenberg joined one of the SS hotel requisitioning troops. Following the black Mercedes taking Walter aboard, several cars with officers and four trucks with soldiers aboard ran together. This group of vehecles arrived at Place Vendome and parked in front of Ritz. Barricades were placed at the two gateways to limit the passage strictly of other than the people living there.

The German officers announced the requision of the hotel at the front desk and ordered the hotel staff to cancel all reservations. At the same time, a group of the soldiers sealed the door of the wine cellar and ordered the staff to present the wine list. They selectd the wine which meets Goering's taste and listed the brands up so his nominated brand can be quickly taken out at Goering's request. The similar listing and sealing exercise of the tea and coffee beans per producing districts was also being worked out. In fact, there are many in the NSDAP leaders who do not take any liquer nor cigarettes, so that this work has a more importance and significance in order not to fail serving Goering's needs. In addition, some other SS officers with the origin of the nobles started to examine the art objects decorated in the suite and the restaurant to determine if those pictures and objects of art might suit Goering's taste or not and also if those are suited to the season of the year.

And, needless to say, the secretarial group of Goring brought something like enigma in and started fixing the transmission equipment. Then, all the goods that showed the French tricolor flag were removed and swastika banners were hung on the both sides of the walls of the imperial suite to proudly show that was the place where Marshal Goring was staying. Also, the Windsor Suite was not touched at all and sealed as was as originally programmed. This part of the hotel had the need to be kept untouched for the exclusive use by Duke of Windsor and his wife. When the time comes of receiving Duke of Windsor as a uniformed symbol of the Third Reich of unified U.K./Germany, this place Ritz as is would be expected to turn into a comfortable palace for their use.

    Walter, while checking the reservation status of the suite, urged the hotel manager to have the then staying hotel guests leave there by 11am, but while he was checking the hotel register, he found the name Coco Chanel. He then thought about her influential power to those men of culture who were surrounding her. He had the manager tell him which room was the least exposed to the outside and having called several soldiers he ordered them to clean that room and help her to move her luggages into that room. Then afer finishing the breakfast and when the room service took the emptied tableware away, he went out following the room survice and entered Chanel's suite.

Walter	[Mademoiselle! Long time no see.]
Chanel	[Oh, that was you. I was seeing you when you came into the Place but was not aware it was you. You look great also in this military uniform.]
Walter	[As I seldom wear this⋯]
Chanel	[But it is suiting you quite well.]
Walter	[The cut is of Hugo Boss but the fabric is the soft

	Ermenegildo Zegna branded fabric.]
Chanel	[Now I see why it doesn't have the hard feel of the military uniform but I reckon it must be comfortable to wear. By the way, what can I do for you?]
Walter	[I wish you to please move from this suite which can look over Place Vendome to a room at the side of Cambon Street.]
Chanel	[Do you mean by saying such a thing that I am an obstruction to you and your people?]
Walter	[All suites are always monitored from the side of the Place. This must be annoying to you.]
Chanel	[You mean our meeting is also been watched.]
Walter	[I will have our soldiers to help you move your property.]
Chanel	[Okay, but before I move there, let me take a look at the room I am moving to.]
Walter	[Yes, I will. Please understand I have a room selected which is not easily been viewed from outside as I cannot make casual calls to your room under the strict surveillance.]
Chanel	[So you mean my privacy will be kept.]
Walter	[Incidentally, do you happen to know any news about Duke of Windsor and his wife?]
Chanel	[I heard a rumor that Wallis ordered one dozen of large size vessel trunks at Louis Vuitton.]
Walter	[Do you know where he ran away?]
Chanel	[These days my memory is getting poor, Walter.]
Walter	[Mademoisell, which do you prefer, the cancan of Moulin Rouge or the Ox on the Roof?]

Chanel   [Well said!]

Chanel's property was not so many. a folding screen finished with Coromandel lacquer, a Chippendale wardrobe, a large stand mirror framed by the Baroque style design, and an extra-large quilted sofa. All of her clothings and accessories were carried to the new room by Cecile who was serving Chanel as her room clerk for a long time, and by Manon, Chanel's seamstress. As Chanel had no family, her belongings were very few.

On Friday, the 21st, the cease-fire agreement between Germany and France was signed and sealed. On Tuesday, the 25th, this agreement came into effect. On that day Paris began to regain its serenity. In the afternoon of that day, one silver Mercedes appeared at the gate of National Archieves. The driver of that Mercedes was Borgia. Following his car, two black color Mercedes appeared. The man with round shape glasses in a military uniform who came out from the car which arrived in the first place stood straight in front of the second car and at the same time a batman who got off from the assistant driver's seat opened the rear door. The round glasses lifted his right arm and at the same time Borgia also lifted his right arm high.

Himmler   [Sieg Heil]
Hess   [So he is here, is he?]
Borgia   [Yes, our family's successive astrologist.]
Hess   [Don't tell me he has run away.]
Himmler   [I had Walter monitor his whereabouts so he is here today, too.]

They went through the gate and came inside. Borgia who was dressed in the uniform of an Italian Carabiniere led the party and they were received by the director and shown to a small room. There, Luc Gauric who had been summoned was waiting. The director went away without entering the room. The entrance of the room was guarded by two SS soldiers.

Borgia [This is in regard to the telephone conversation we had this morning. From now on you are to work as a librarian directly reporting to SS. However, NSDAP are to esteem the fact that you are still the advisor of the Borgias. Let me introduce him. This person is Luc the astrologist who succeeds the name Gaurico. Luc, let me introduce you to those two gentlemen. Your superior to whom you are directly reporting is His Excellency Hinrich Himmler the leader of SS Empire, and the gentleman next to him is NSDAP Dupty Leader, His Excellency Rudolf Hess.]

Luc [How do you do.]

Himmler [Hi, I'm counting on you.]

After bowing Borgia went out. Having seen Borgia off, Hess opened his mouth for the first time.

Hess [You ought to predict the fate of our Third Reich. In addition to this important mission, I wish you to read 『Les Centuries』 of Nostradamus.]

Himmler [We already know that your ancestor recommended Michelle Nostradamus to the Queen as his successor.]

Hess [Is Luca Gaurico the author of Mirabilis Liber which was published on May 25, 1522?]

Luc	[It seems part of that book has some relation to him, so that the person who inquired this point to the publishing company could have been Nostradamus. Suppose this was the case⋯]
Hess	[Then it could have happened that Nostradamus was chosen because of the fact he could make hit-a-nail-on-the-head questions.]
Himmler	[We understand you have the first edition of 「Les Centuries」 of Nostradamus here in this place.]
Luc	[The book you mean is here, but please note this is a special book.]
Luc	[This book is one of the books which are called Queen's Books among some people.]
Himmler	[Queen's Book?]
Luc	[This is a book that was inherited from Catherine de Medicis to queens of successive generations. She was in a position of making questions in person to Nostradamus.]
Himmler	[Which means?]
Luc	[It means that what is meant can be found in the scrubblings into the book or incomprehensive signs. Of course, those which were not written by Catherine herself must be excluded.]
Luc	[That is Mary Stewart of the queen of Scotland. She was the queen of France since 1556 till 1560 when Francois II passed away. Nostradamus lived till 1570, but the marrage of the next king of Charles IX was in 1570. This means that Queens who had a chance to

	ask questions directly to Nostradamus were only these two queens.]
Hess	[Where is this book now?]
Luc	[I believe British Royalty possesses it.]
Himmler	[Do you wish to submit a report as regards Operation Sea Lion (Invation of the U.K.)?]
Hess	[I'm afraid to convince Goeing to resort to that means just for getting that book.]
Himmler	[Luc, do you think which one of those books of Mary's and Catherine's has more value?]
Luc	[As Catherine has too much power, Nostradamus may not have clearly given the answer to her if the answer turned out to be such one as to inconvenience the regime at that time, however possibly she must have made more number of questions that can be asked only by the one who has the true power.]
Hess	[What you mean that the Catherine's book may have more deals of what was going to happen in future.]
Luc	[That is a matter of possibility. Don't you think that Mary's way of living has some problem as to the degree of carefulness in executing politics?]
Himmler	[Yes, your answer has a valid point. It now looks to me that those markings in the book sounds to have more value.]
Hess	[Such possibility that at Mary's innocent questions Nostradamus carelessly leaked what he really meant might be appearing in Mary's book.]

Himmler	[It would be great if we could obtain Mary's book like Austria obtained the lanse of Longinus.]
Hess	[As the possessor of the lanse of Longinus, we NSDAP have already secured the dominion of Europe…]
Himmler	[Uklaine which possesses prolific land is located in the communists' territory. We need an object to which a spirit that dominated the force of Mongolia to be drawn or summoned.]
Hess	[Are you confident of success to secure such object?]
Himmler	[A Soviet scholar, Mikhail Gerasimov is now applying for an official permission to unearth the tomb of Timur. If Barlas Ruby which was the talisman of the Mongolians is unearthed, we are planning to capture it.]
Hess	[Is it a ruby?]
Himmler	[It is a large red spinel. It is the same as the Black Prince's Ruby of Imperial State Crown. Till around 1890 it was not possible to do nondestructive inspection but later on an eminent German scientist classified it as ruby definining single refraction for spinel and double for ruby.]
Hess	[Then is the 33 carat on the Crown of Saint Wenceslas determined as ruby?]
Himmler	[That is the talisman to protect Europe, but as a talisman to rule the plain of central asia I believe the Barlas ruby of Tamerlane is the most desirable.]
Hess	[When it is obtained, I will leave the storage management to you.]

Himmler	[As you please. By the way, in the Leader's libraby, I found a German edition of the Nostradamus' book.]
Hess	[That was gifted to the Leader by Artur Kannenberg, his cook. Kannenberg presented that book to him at the dinner of the day when the invation plan into Holland was successfully carried out.]
Luc	[Are you sure of the information you just gave me?]
Hess	[That is a book of which the cut out pages by a paper knife can only be read, but why are you concerned about such a trifle thing?]
Luc	[The Leader is being moved by the power of some huge spiritual body.]
Himmler	[Luc, I need your explanation.]
Luc	[His highness Empire Leader is not acting to realize the contents of the prophecy but is driven by a certain huge spiritual body which makes his action look like the action by his own will. In the 『Prophecy of Nostradamus』 written by Karl Loake, of its 68th page, according to the Loake's decipherment, such statement is written that Germany will attack Holland in 1939. If Empire Leader understood that Nostradamus' prophecy had come true, he would no doubt have continued reading the rest of the book. But that he did not would mean he had already known that the prophecy would come true having already read that part of the book.]
Himmler	[That's the reason why our Leader had kept the jewish former senior officer Ernst Hess alive!]

Luc	[What does the Leader know about?]
Himmler	[When he was taking a rest in the shade of a tree at a recess, he heard a voice saying 「Adolf, that place is dangerous. Move and come here」 so he called for other members around him and changed the place.]
Hess	[Then the shade of the tree where they had just been was bombed and those who did not move there were blown away. These similar instances happened for several times. The Leader is the live witness of these happenings.]
Luc	[Till the time comes I will keep watching the future.]
Himmler	[I'm counting on you, Mr. Astrologist of the Borgias. Walter Schellenberg is to resume the task of liaison between you and me.]
Luc	[I understand.]

23. Capture Duke of Windsor (Operation Willi)

On Friday, July 5, 1940, Walter Schellenberg was in his secretariate chamber of Gestapo Headquarters in Paris. At sometime past 11am the telephone rang. It was a call from the foreign minister, Joachim von Ribbentrop.

Foreign Minister [Walter, I have just obtained the agreement of the Leader Hitler. We have been informed that Duke of Windsor who is currently staying in Lisborn, Spain has a schedule to participate in a hunting event with Spanish nobles on Saturday, July 27. Can you possibly take him out from Spain to Switzerland so as to have him out of reach of the watchful eyes of U.K.? The Foreign Ministry prepared a fund of 50million francs which I will have Hans von Dincklage deliver to you. You are to receive it in Ritz.]

Walter [Has the Leader any special instruction for me to follow?]

Foreign Minister [You are to win favor of Duchess Wallis and lead her to persuade Duke to particiate in the hunting game of the Spanish nobles passing the border from Lisborn to Spain. I trust you can make this happen. If needs be you can consult with Coco Chanel as she may have a good idea to materialize this plan.]

Walter [Whatever you say.]

Foreign Minister [I understand you are Mademoiselle's favorite far more than Hans.]

Walter　　　　[I will ask Mademoiselle to select at Cartier the most suitable gift to Duchess, as she knows much better than I regarding the knowledge of the clothes that Wallis possesses in her wardrobe.]

Foreign Minister　　[Duke of Windsor has a possibility to be enthroned as the Emperor of The Third Reich.]

Walter　　　　[You mean Hanoverian Dynasty, don't you?]

Foreign Minister　　[As Hans is a noble of Hanover, he wishes that to happen. However, I think if annexation of the British Empire would be possible, we wouldn't mind Windsor Dynasty. Don't you agree? As regards the emperor coronation, we are now asking that greedy Cardinal Borgia to work on realization of participation by the Pope of the Vatican. If this plan is materialized the German side would be able to seize the seat above Mussolini. I will wait for a good report from you in August. One more point for you to care about is Franco of Spain. He is shrewd so watch him fully. Possibly he may be thinking to secure Willie and demand gratitude for that from U.K.]

　　Finishing his talk, he hung up unilaterally. Then Walter consulted with Hydrich how he should react to the foreign minister's instruction.

Walter　　　　[Just now I received a call from the old man and was told to seize Willie.]

Hydrich　　　　[Yes, I know that. It was me that told him your telephone number as he called me in the first place. Take two men that can talk English and Spanish. Also,

	I had Japanese Embassy introduce me to a person working at a trading company so talk to him and find out any information about the mansion in Lisbon.]
Walter	[You are awfully thorough in your preparations, aren't you.]
Hydrich	[Regarding this case, the Leader, and also the Dupty Leader Hess, too, are very aggressive for what reason I can't figure out. Do you have any idea why they are so eager?]
Walter	[I have absolutely no idea why.]
Hydrich	[Won't you move to Madrid secretly without catching the attention of American pressmen.]

In the afternoon of that day, Walter met Hans at the entrance of Ritz and received a trunk and the key. He then went on to meet with Chanel and looked for several brooches or rings that would be becoming to Duchess Wallis.

On Friday, 12th, two men came to meet Walter. They were the ones chosen by Hydrich in Berlin for the assistants and interpreters to work with Walter. The skinny and rather tall man told his name was Arbert and the other sturdy looking man called himself Carl. Walter told them to go by separate ways and respectively buy several tickets instead of a through ticket and meet at a bar in Madrid taking a few days before the meeting. On the following morning, Walter had Louise ride next to him like his lover and drove the green color SS Jaguer down to the south. France in July had dry wind browing and mornings are especially pleasant. In this way they escaped from the eyes of journarists or of the spies of the enemy countries.

After staying overnight in Lyon, he changed with another man of similar height to Walter and he in the driver's seat and Louise in the assistant driver's seat started back to Paris. About one hour later, Walter was at Lyon Station. He travelled down to south to Marseille and at Marseille Station, he spent about one hour reading a book at a café. Confirming no one was watching him, he rode on a train for Barcelona. He was wearing a Milan tailored linen shirt and dark brown cotton pants and kept himself nondescripting.

Arriving at the station in Barcelona, he took a taxi and went to a park from where the façade of Sagrada Familia could be looked up at and sat on a bench there. Taking out of his leather trunk a pair of mother of pearl opera glasses and started watching the statues on the steeple. The stone sculptures in the setting sunshine were showing a little rosy color and those sculptured human figures looked as if they were blood circulating bodies. He still kept looking up the steeple, perhaps nearly twenty minutes, when all of sudden an Asian look man spoke to him in French.

Obnimnaru [Haven't you been keep looking at the statues very earnestly, have you?]
Walter [As my study of Christianism is just surficial, I cannot recognize which scenes those statues are meant for.]
Onimaru [Are you of the Black Jesuits?]
Walter [I like royal blue.]
Onimaru [Shall we go and have some paella?]
Walter [Just as I thought.]

Then, for the first time these two men looked at each other. After this short conversation, they went to Hotel USA where Onimaru had made reservations for both of them. Having checked in the hotel they went to the hotel restaurant where they were served two portions of paella dishes. They toasted pouring cooled tea into glasses.

Walter	[Why did you take almost thirty minutes till you spoke to me?]
Onimaru	[I had to confirm you had not been followed.]
Walter	[What is the reason why a person in trading business like you cooperate with us?]
Onimaur	[My ancestor was a member of the envoy that Tsunenaga Hasekura sent to Rome in 1615.]
Walter	[So they were religious Catholics.]
Onimaur	[Regretfully, the other way round. They possessed religious faith for Mammon.]
Walter	[Mammon? Were they demonolaters?]
Onimaur	[In Christianism the opposite religion is the side of the devil, isn't it?]
Walter	[You're right.]
Onimaur	[In that sense, Japanese gods equals to devils, don't they?]
Walter	[What is the reason why Japan joined to the envoy of Catholics?]
Onimaru	[They concluded an agreement with the Vatican minister in charge of exorcism of Vatican.]
Walter	[What for?]
Onimaru	[The Japanese are to receive the spirit that Vatican wishes to ward off.]
Walter	[Does Vatican intend to make the devil god?]
Onimaru	[That's not correct. No human has the power to

	destroy a mighty spirit. That is why we Japanese take over the spirit that Vatican cannot afford to keep. In addition, in the Monsoon region all the great spirits are either Gods or Devils.]
Walter	[Is that still going on now?]
Onimaru	[Yes. For your informatin, the family seal of Hasekura who led the delegation out of Japan is Gyaku-manji, the same as the symbol of NSDAP.]
Walter	[That means to Vatican our Gyaku-manji seal was not a news.]
Onimaru	[In addition, the minister in charge of exosism at Vatican at that time was Cardinal Salvatore Borgia.]
Walter	[We, SS, are also called as Black Society of Jesus, but the third chanceller of the Society of Jesus was Francesco Borgia which has the same name of that Black Caruso. This may be a result coming from some predestination.]
Onimaru	[Histroy repeats itself, though a slight development can be noticed.]
Walter	[No, history does not keep to be the same, as evidenced by that Americans achieved a greater growth than U.K.]
Onimaru	[That's another misunderstanding. This hotel is capitalized and possessed by the Japanese Usa family. This is why this hotel is called USA.]
Walter	[I see.]
Onimaru	[In near future, for the purpose of showing the language English, the flag of Stars and Stripes may be

	used. Likewise, for Spanish, Mexican flag and for Portuguese by flag of Brazil.]
Walter	[To show German language?]
Onimaru	[The transition of the age could be much more fierce than what we imagine. Japanese at the time of the Samurai era, did not imagine that the Japanese language would be spoken in Taiwan or Korea. In a hundred years of time, the age may come when books written in Japanese are sold in Paris. As long as the power of culture exists the world could be getting multilingualized.]
Walter	[You mean language will not be converged to the language of the forceful country.]
Onimaru	[Force does not equal to millitary force. The way of living, folkways and culture are also forces. Only, these are difficult to be quantized.]
Walter	[I tend to believe only what is quantized.]
Onimaru	[When you love a woman, you won't quantize her, will you?]
Walter	[It is absolutely not the right way to love the opposite sex based on balancing the profits and losses.]
Onimaur	[It can be said that it was the German military force that proved the power of culture which made Paris loved and escaped from destruction at this time. Don't you agree?]
Walter	[Certainly. The currently considered strategic operation may develop to that extent where monarches of the whole Europe might be carried out

	to join it.]
Onimaru	[Roman Emperor? Holly Roman Emperor? Third Reich Emperor? The naming of Third Reigh sounds no fun.]
Walter	[As Mussolini is aiming at forming Mediterranean Empire, I don't think he will smoothly accept the naming of Rome.]
Onimaru	[There will be a possibility of formation of federal system when Rome in the new system is established. The Emperor is to be crowned by Vatican and the spirits that are no longer needed will be taken by Japan where 8 million gods are already habitant.]
Walter	[What at all is Japan aiming at by collecting so many spirits?]
Onimaru	[Japan does not hold shrines only.]
Walter	[What at all do you mean by what you have just said?]
Onimaur	[The roads connected with shrines that have Torii, the divine gateway to shrines are not the only roads to divine places in Japan. There are a lot more divine places in Japan which do not belong to the hierarchy of the Ise Shrine only.]

With this convertation, that evening came to the end.

On the following day, Walter rode on a train and arrived at Madrid. He went to German Embassy and saluted to Ambassador Schuettler. Then a clerk took him by car to the hiding place. This house was facing towards about three blocks inside of a lane by a square and looks just like an average house, namely, not too shabby nor too gourgeous. The wife of the owner of the house was in her fiftieth and rather fat and a typical wife of a merchant's home. The room allocated to Walter was the attic of that house which was about 300 years old showing dried up beams and the hard core of the wood was exposed with the soft wooden part sunken.

In that attic, a comparably simple single-use bed which only had a sheet of walnut headboard attached, and a chestnut-made night table with three-layer drawers. As regards telephone, the line was already been connected. In this attic, there were several more rooms so it was possible to have the other two people use them.

On the next day, Walter was called to come to the Embassy, and he met there the German ambassador Hyune stationed in Lisborn, so he handed to him the Cartier accessory that he purchased in Paris for a present to Dutchess Wallis Windsor. This present was to urge her to attend the hunting gathering scheduled on 27th as a surprise guest to strengthen the ties of friendship of Spain with Portugal. According to what Hyune told him, as Wallis here could not freely go out or meet her friends like when she was in Paris, she now was a frequent visitor to parties held at embassies of respective countries, and her Portuguese guard was always following her secretly at her outings.

On that day at 6pm, Walter visiting a bar called Val Sonbura sat at a table where his upper half of the body could be seen from the square and put his panama hat on the table as a mark. Having ordered a glass of fresh orange juice, he kept looking at the Madrid part of the Michelin Orange Guide for about 30 minutes, when Albert wearing a hunting cap appeared and after a few minutes Carl, too, came and sat on the table next to Walter.

Walter   [This is the map of the hunting place, but the

	Portuguise guard is not to enter the Spanish territory.]
Albert	[Where shall we keep our car to wait?]
Walter	[I understand there is a big tree of cork alongside this road that goes through the valley.]
Carl	[Can we get a supply of gus in this village where there is a church?]
Walter	[I will borrow a car at the Embassy and will change the number plate while we use the car during these operations.]
Carl	[You mean to have made the operations look as the work of Particans.]
Albert	[Who is to take Duke to where this car is parked?]
Walter	[I understand on that day Hans von Dinklage is scheduled to arrive from Paris.]
Albert	[Is Duke taking the Duchess?]
Walter	[That's not what I know, but probably not. We need to take her out on a separate occasion.]
Carl	[So, all what we have to do is to take Duke out?]
Walter	[Ambassador Hyumne was saying that he asked one other person who is a Japanese to help taking Duchess Wallis. This person is to arrive here in no time but as yet I haven't seen him.]
Carl	[So, what you mean is that we are to act separately as we are to take the duchess out, too.]
Walter	[Carl, Will you take the role of taking Duchess out cooperating with the Japanese.]
Carl	[Roger.]
Waiter	[This is from your companion. He said he would be a

	bit late in coming.]
Albert	[What is it?]
Waiter	[This is carpaccio of bluefin tuna lean meat.]
Walter	[Looks delicious.]
Albert	[I will see how it tastes.]
Carl	[You must have been sick and tired of melon wound by jamon cerrano?]
Walter	[The black pork, jamon iberico and cerrano of white pork, all what has been served is eiher one of the two. No wonder we are tired of taking the basically pork only.]
Albert	[Why don't you just say, yes, go ahead and take it?]
Walter	[Yes, go ahead and take it.]
Carl	[. . .]
Albert	[Wow, this is tasty.]
Carl	[Are you getting numbed slowly now?]
Albert	[Ugh!]
Carl	[So the answer is NO!]
Albert	[Oh, this is good enough to numb!]

While they were excited at that delicious dish, another cuisine for four servings was brought about. This second dish was worth looking at. It was a big salt baked black snapper of the size of so-to-called "Menoshita Hassun" meaning 8-sun (1 sun equals to 3.03cm) measured from underneath the eyes (which actual measurement means about 24cm measuring from the edge of the eyes on the back side of the fish to the wingtop joint of it).

Waiter	[This is a black snapper grilled whole.]
Walter	[We did not order this either!!]

Then, at that moment, one man came out and took the seat among them folding an apron that he had been wearing.

Onimaru	[This snapper just delivered from Lisbon.]
Walter	[Oh, this is from you!]
Onimaru	[I came to the kitchen through the door of the backyard and cooked for you. How do you like my seafood cuisine?]
Walter	[You must have been asked by Ambassador Hyune to do this cooking.]
Onimaru	[Here, I have the blueprint design of the mansion in Lisbon. I also have information of the number of guards there. It will be next to impossible to take the couple out directly from there. But there is a possibility of success if we induce them to go out separately. All depends on the condition that Duchess would participate to show up at the luncheon that is going to be held at Italian Embassy that day.]
Walter	[How many guards will be when they go out?]
Onimaru	[The code-named Rosina whom you know has a free access to the mansion as the wife of the doctor. When they go for an outing, 3 guards for Duke and 1 for Duchess are to be with them respectively. In the mansion, two other guards are stationed at the entrance and the house which stands in front of the

backdoor of the mansion has been rented by the Portuguish Police.]

Walter   [Rosina, I see. Will Duke be called back to London?]
Onimaru   [Rosina seems to put her and her busband's name on the waiting list of a vessel sailing for London.]
Walter   [So, U boat will play the last means.]
Onimaru   [Duke is planned to be aboard a destroyer so there's absolutely no possibility!]
Walter   [If we miss this chance, no more such chance will come.]
Onimaru   [Well, let's leave the details to be discussed later and have the dishes for this moment!]
Walter   [Okay, let's.]

  That night, they altogether returned to the hideout and a detailed explanation was made about the brueprint of the mansion in Lisbon. To go to the living room or the bed room, stairs must be used from the ground floor. Onimaru explained that preventing guards rushing into the mansion from the back door, to quietly take Duke and Duchess and the pair of Scottish Terrier is quite difficult. The arrangements were agreed on as follows. On the appointed day, Walter and Albert were to wait at the hunting place of the Spanish side and to execute the plan of taking Duke out, and as soon as Carl and Ginji Onimaru receive the news of the plan of taking Duke out could be done successfully, they were to take Duchess out from the luncheon party at Italian Embassy.

In the afternoon on the same day, the telephone on the desk of Cardinal Salvatore Borjia rang out. The caller was Caudillo Franco, the leader of Spain.

Franco	[Your Eminence, Can you spare a few minutes to talk with me?]
Borgia	[If you with to talk about Exocists, I am always ready to listen to you.]
Franco	[Do you know SS are plotting out to take Duke and Duchess Windsor to Spain and to crown Duke as Emperor of The Third Reich?]
Borgia	[Oh, Your excellency has big ears.]
Franco	[They seem to understand that the Portiguish Police will not dare to chase them beyond the border, but seem not to realize that the nobles can move not bound by the border. What I mean is if the active involvement of Germans is known, there is a fear that this case might be reported to U.K. as Germany supporting Spain.]
Borgia	[How many Germans?]
France	[three. And one other who works to take Duchess out.]
Borgia	[You wish to exorcise evil spirits?]
France	[Five Garland rifles can be submitted by us. We confiscated them from the Popular Front. I wish you to help us by sending armed monks. Please guide Duke to a castle of the Borgias and exorcise those Germans.]
Borgia	[Do you intend to crown Duke by the hand of Spain?]
Franco	[Until we can see the result of the tactics between

	U.K. and Germany, we will treat them as our guests. If Germany's winning percentage is high, we will hand him over to them as Emperor of The Third Reich so we can demand gratitude from Germany. If U.K.'s percentage is high, we will not attack Gibraltar so can get gratitude from U.K.]
Borgia	[Your Excellency is quite a hard one to deal with. If now were the Reneissance time, you would have been throned as Pope.]
France	[If now were the time of Reneissance, this world would have been your clan's. Sericously, will you accept my request?]
Borgia	[If all is executed within Spain, I will accept your request.]
France	[How do you plan to take Duchess out?]
Borgia	[I will let a man called Kraken guide her to Spain subject to confirmation of the securance of Duke.]
Franco	[That codename sounds like a goblin.]
Borgia	[My clan's job is exorcism, you know.]
Franco	[What is the characteristics of the man Kraken?]
Borgia	[His pocket watch's underhand trikery. At 1200 hours, a marmaid shows up. When this marmaid is dried by the flame of a red color candle, the fish that is covering the lower body of her drops off and she goes all naked. Then at the same moment a big octopus appears and puts out its feeler and rape her lower body.]
Franco	[I wish such a watch made for me. Do you know

Borgia	where I can place an order for it?]
Borgia	[As I remember it, Patek Phillippe seems to have ordered…some craftsman called by such name as Atolini or so, but I am not at all sure about it.]
Franco	[Oh, Your Eminence is the God's exorcist, indeed. There seems nothing you do not know. Isn't that watch the one that everyone may wish to try use it if chance to get one comes.]
Borgia	[For use at the church, I suggest you to use it together with indulgencies.]
Franco	[You are an ancestrally good business man, aren't you.]
Borgia	[Certainly, as I am a servant of God.]

Then, the telephone was hung up.

On the morning when the hunting was programmed, Hans von Dincklage was also supposed to join and to persuade Duke of Windsor to come with them to talk about the crowning Duke as the Emperor of The Third Reich.

On that day in the early morning when it was still dark, the telephone in the branch manager's office of the Jumonji Trading Company in Lisbon rang.

Onimaru	[Hello, This is Jyumonji Trading.]
Roxy	[No egg has been laid.]
Onimaru	[Rosina, No movement in the parking area, is this what you mean?]
Roxy	[Certainly.]

This was a cipher between Onimaru and Roxy who lived in front of the parking area which was located in the backyard, not to have Roxy's husband, Robert, aware of the contents of her telephone talk with Onimaru. Onimaru called Walter in Madrid right away.

Onimaru [After all, Duke did not move. I mean he did not agree to join the hunting proposal by Miguel, the noble of Spain.]
Walter [Is there any place where we could hide ourselves?]
Onimaru [Hotel USA Lisbon should still be a safe place to stay at, even if two more members join us.]
Walter [I will be there in the evening of this Sunday.]
Onimaru [Shall I meet you at the station?]
Walter [No, thanks. I will arrive at the hotel on my own.]

Thus, Walter drove himself to Lisbon aimlessly, as it was necessary for him to carry weapons and to escape from the eyes of American pressmen.

On Monday, July 29, Onimaru kept Roxy who went out to buy sugar waiting for him at a separate room in Jyumonji Trading Company. He gave her a pack of sugar of Taiwan made. There, appeared Walter.

Walter [Have you been keeping well, Rosina?]
Roxy [I have abandoned that name.]
Walter [Here are 1,000 pound notes. Please use these as a temporary fund.]
Roxy [Okay, then what do you want me to do?]

Walter	[Tomorrow morning I will throw a pebble to the window of the kitchen, so, can you pay someone off for him to take the bolt off the gate?]
Roxy	[You know such request is difficult for me to comply to as I'm a new comer at the Duke's. In addition, at the house in front of the back gate there always are police people and U.K. related people.]
Walter	[I see⋯then what about sending a big volume of flowers making some plausible reason, and get an access to the living room of the Duke's mansion and take Duke and Duchess out?]
Roxy	[What sort of reason do you have in your mind to send flowers?]
Walter	[Let me think about it for a while more.]
Roxy	[Then, I cannot receive this envelope. Sugar is enough.]
Walter	[Please don't say something like that. A newly married couple needs fund, don't they. Take this envelope. In any case, this money is useless if I keep it.]
Roxy	[If any new movement happens I will contact Jyumonji Trading.]

Having said so, she went away taking the pack of sugar and the brown envelope without examining the contents in it.

On the following day, 30th, in the evening, telephone call came from Roxy.

Onimaru	[Hello, Jyumonji Trading.]
Roxy	[What I have gathered from the talk of Sir Walter Monckton who came here for the afternoon tea, Duke

and Duchess are going to Bahamas on August 1 by the steam ship Exscalibur of American Export Line, where Duke seems to take up the post of the governer-general of the Bahamas.]

Onimaru [When does the vessel sail out?]

Roxy [The vessel in the afternoon.]

Onimaru [Is Rosina going together?]

Roxy [U.K.government is intending to replace all employees with new ones.]

Onimaru [Well, U.K. looks like intending not to have Germany seizure an American vessel. Or, reasonably thinking, U.K. doesn't want a battle by using their Destroyer. Isn't this so Churchill like.]

Schellenberg who was listening this conversation standing besides him picked the phone away from Onimaru and talked to her.

Walter [Try to do the packing of the vessel trunks as slowly as possible. If we can delay the sailing time of the vessel we may be able to find some measures.]

Roxy [As everyone is reluctant to part from Duke and Duchess, I think that will be possibly done.]

On the following morning, a messenger sent by U.K.Embassy gathered all employees in the hall and announced a dismissal notice to all of them effective as of the next day. All of the employees were deeply disappointed and many were sobbing and blew their noses on their handkerchieves so the place buzzed with excitement. In such atmosphere, packing was started. Roxy helped them to pack the necessary goods into ten and more vessel trunks but all the dismissed employees were totally out of mind and packing work did not progress at all.

Time was not generous enough to wait for them. The day August 1 came quickly. Taking a pair of dogs, the Duke and Duchess went out by car just after the noontime to attend the last afternoon tea party at U.K. Embassy. Schellenberg parked his car near the peer and ordered the expert marksman, Albert, he was to wait in disguise in the shade of cargoes there. Albert wearing a hunting cap was holding an M1 Garland rifle. This rifle was what the army of Franco seized at time of Spanish Civil War. Even if the situation developed to the worst phase of a gunfight, this rifle was provided with him to make the whole issue look to be arisen by the survivors of Spanish Popular Front. Nearby the gangway of the quay, Onimaru wearing a Panama hat and fanning himself occasionally and Carl the gunfighter wearing a hunting cap were pretending negotiating some business deal. In the place from where an unbroken view of those allocated people could be gained, people who had been to the Catholic funeral celemony was getting off the bus marked with a crest showing a figure of red bull on a shield but no one paid any attention to them. They were the members under Cardinal Borgia.

When the time came, a truck arrived and off the truck about ten Portuguese guards fixing beyonets stood in a rowline. And there, a black Bentley was being driven in. When the rear side door was opened, Duke came off in the first place, then the two dogs and lastly Ducess having respectfully taken her hand by Duke came out.

Taking the salute of all people there, they stepped up the gangway. But Schellenberg did not move at all. Albert was waiting for Schellenberg's instruction holding his breath. At the top of the gangway, the captain of the vessel in white uniform was greeting Duke and Duchess.

Captain [Welcome to Excalibur. I am the captain Richard Harrison. Please feel at home here and relax.]

Edward [Thank you. This is my wife Wallis.]:

Captain [Your Royal Highness is the pride of America. Do enjoy your voyage.]

Wallis [Thank you. It is after quite a long while that now I can hear the accent of my hometown. Are you from Boltimore?]

Captain [My mother is from there. Is that the reason why you keep Scotish terriers?]

Wallis [Hey, don't lick the captain's shoes!]

With their smiles and affatable behaviors they kept the people around them in friendly atmosphere and then they disappeared into the vessel. There remained one problem. The luggeges of Duke and Duchess did not arrive as yet. Schellenberg rang U.K.Embassy using a public telephone stand nearby. A few minutes afterwards, a bus arrived from the Police and about 20 policemen entered the vessel. A kid taking a piece of paper came to Carl.

Onimaru [What is written?]

Carl [When a bombing mess takes place, we are instructed to take Duke and Duchess out from the vessel and when they come off the vessel,put them on a car and

	leave here.]
Onimaru	[delayed arrival of luggages and the rise of bombing mess in the absence of luggegges…a very well considered plot.]
Carl	[What are you talking about?]
Onimaru	[It means the necessities of Duke and Duchess are still in our hands so it is okay for us to take them away.]
Carl	[I see. But what will happen if they don't come off the vessel?]
Onimaru	[then it will mean this plot has ended in failure.]

Consequently, what actually happened was that inspection of luggages was finished and the loading work of the trunks of Duke and Duchess was safely started. The commercial luggages that were additionally loaded in Lisbon were very few so no mess and confusion occurred. Figures of Duke and Duchess waiving their hands were getting smaller and smaller as the vessel kept sailing out offshore.

24. Cancellation of Operation Sea Lion

Since July, 1940, the German air force was rolling out every day in order to secure the mastery of the air in U.K. In late September, Luc and Sophie, finishing their long vacation, came back from Luc's hometown in Nice. At that time Paris was under occupation of Germany but kept its calmness. Difference observed then from before the occupation was that all major buildings that Germans occupied were guarded by German soldiers and that some places were put under traffic restriction control. While Luc unloaded the trunks of his car, Rudolf Brandt wearing the SS officer's uniform came around taking two soldiers with him.

Brandt   [Hi, Luc, how was your vacation?]
Luc   [Yah, I did enjoy it like all the past vacations. By the way, are you in charge of this area?]
Brandt   [I am working as secretary to Your Excellency Empire Leader. Will you come with me to his place?]
Luc   [Has he been in Paris now?]
Brandt   [Yes, The superior of the Leader, too.]

Then Luc was pushed into a car and taken to Hotel du Crillion. When he was shown to the most gourgeous room that looked out Place de la Concorde, there he found Himmler sitting. Brandt politely raised his right arm and saluted to him.

Brandt   [Sieg Heil! I took the astrologist of the Borgias here.]
Himmler   [Well done. You may be excused.]
Luc   [What can I do for you today?]

Himmler suddenly stood up and offered Luc to sit down on the sofa in front of the fireplace, and sat next to Luc facing a coffee table. Brandt knew well that this sort of gesture Himmler showed was to mean his friendship so he had coffee made ready quickly and have it delivered to that coffee table.

Himmler [Luc, I understand when your ancestor declined servicing Catherine de Medici, he appointed Nostradamus as his successor. Incidentally, regarding the difference between the Scottish Queen's Book and the French one was there any evidence of France having exchanged information with U.K.?]

Luc [All what can be done is to speculate if with political correspondence.]

Himmler [I don't really get it what you mean.]

Luc [Suppose U.K. had deciphered the relation of the development of French Revolution and Napoleon's rise and fall, how did U.K. treat this matter, is what I mean.]

Himmler [U.K. would not choose to fight in face with Napoleon when he was on his rise.]

Luc [If U.K. could have deciphered when Napoleon would fall, U.K. could have made good preparation.]

Himmler [Will this time be the same way?]

Luc [Even if we could decipher the scribblings of Catherine's Book, we couldn't do this with Mary's Book. But we may make a good guess watching the movement of the opponent.]

Himmler	[Are you of opinion that U.K.at this time will not surrender to Germany?]
Luc	[Comparing the horoscopes of leaders of both sides, suppose Churchill is aware that for this time being patience is the most powerful weapon against Germany?]
Himmler	[Churchill will not made surrendered by the German air force, is it what you mean?]
Luc	[Reason why the horoscope of Marshal Goring is lacking of power is because German air force does not possess torpedo bombers and torpedoes.]
Himmler	[German is fundamentally a land power country. Air force needs close above-ground support in the first place. But apart from this, what the horoscope of Marshal Goring means is that our air force totally lacks a winning chance whatsoever the reason is.]
Brandt	[Dinner is ready. Dupty leader is waiting for you.]
Himmler	[Luc, Sorry for this very sudden invitation but won't you stay and join us for dinner. Take it easy as His Excellency will not care about it if you are not formally dressed…If at all possible, we should have asked your wife, too, with both of you formally dressed.]

Thus, Himmler and Luc were led by Brandt and guided to a small room on the same floor as they were. They passed each other of two men of South Asian look at the doorway coming out of the room.

Himmler [Your Excellency Dupty Leader, I have taken the said person.]

Hess [Be seated quickly.]

Himmler and Luc were shown to each respective seat, where Hess could easily face each of them. Waiter asked Luc what drink they would like. Luc requested some cold tea as he knew they didn't like alchoholic beverage. Then they started taking the served dishes as they were placed on their table.

Hess [Are you a vegetalian like me?]

Luc [Not precisely. I just do not take much meat.]

Hess [Now, to start with, I heard from some researchers that the word Hister which appears in Les Centuries would mean His Excellency Leader, but they do not talk about any bad news against NSDAP. Have you ever deciphered to arrive at any new conclusion?]

Luc [At two places in Les Centuries 9, there appears the word the third tiers for twice. If this word is deciphered as the third reich and the king as the master, this part has a possibility to imply some bad meaning. Those who may have noticed this part may keep silence being afraid of taking offence of Your Excellency.]

Hess [Never mind, tell me all in details.]

Himmler [I will personally guarantee your status, so take it easy and tell us.]

9-5

Tiers doigt du pied au premier semblera

A vn nouueau monarque de bas haut,

Qui Pyse & Luques Tyran occupera
Du precedent corriger le deffaut

Luc	[9-5 The toes and finger tips of the third reich looks alike the first Rome The new master who rose to the high position from the canaille Will seize the brilliance by peace and tanks To rectify what the predecessors could not achieve]
Hess	[I don't think this does not have any much bad meaning, but please explain your deciphering.]
Luc	[At the third reich, Passo Romano and Salute Romano have been exercised. As regards the way to raise hands at time of giving a salute, what is that style based on?]
Hess	[The right arm of eqestrian statue of Marcus Aurelius which is towering on Capitoline Hill was referred to. I understand Mussolini used as a reference the remaining marble statue, but the right arm which used to be set at the same angle as the equestrian statue was lost because the rectangular timber at the joint of the arm and the body got thinned as time passed by and dropped off. He did not take this fact in his consideration when he fixed the way of raising the hand.]
Luc	[The word Pyse that appears on the third line means peace and the word Luques a castle as a Chess piece, but the original meaning is a Roman chariot or can be Brilliance as another meaning.]
Hess	[I understand. Then what about the other third reich?]

Luc	[9-17 Le tiers premier pis que ne fit Neron Vuidez vaillant que sang humain respandre: Re'difera le forneron, Siecle d'or mort, nouueau Roy grand esclandre. The Third Reich is the top commiter of Nero's evil deed This deed shall derive people of their fortune and human blood will be spread Economy may be reconstructed but The century of the gold will be led to death by a great scandal of the new ruler]
Hess	[It is a fact that Germany is confiscating Jew's forturnes. Himmler, are you taking any countermeasure to solve this problem?]
Himmler	[Regarding the negotiation with Vichy France, we have not received any answer as yet. Therefore, the Madagascar resettlement plan of jews is kept shopworn. To combat with this problem, we are now having construction of Getto in Warsaw accelerated.]
Hess	[No one will desire to face a big scandal that will be recorded in the history.]
Luc	[We don't hope that will happen either, but the fearful part of this statement of Les Centuries writes in case some evil plan that equals to a big scandal is exercised, the century of death will arrive, so, I'm not surprised if no one has dared to report this desiphering without obtaining guarantee of their position.]
Hess	[Rest assured we have set a previllege of tolerance to pythons.]
Himmler	[Don't tell this to Goebbels, as he will immediately report it to the Leader and in addition, you will be

	exposed to the troublesome jerousy of those surrounders of the Leader.I remember his reaction was like that when he saw the propaganda film Olympia which Leni Riefenstahl produced.]
Hess	[Luc, regarding the matter which I had Schellenberg told you about the other day, tell me how you feel about it just as is.]

By this time already, Italy had invaded the West Egyptian Boader having made a sortie from Libya. As they were unable to secure the fully stretched supply line, they were resorting to the strategic withdrawal. At the Italian side such information as if Italy were smoothly advancing the army towards victory was being aired on radio. As a matter of course, the German side had taken into their consideration of the possible difficulty of supply of necessary goods across the desert, so they did not take the report by Italy seriously.

Luc	[According to the findings made by the horoscope of Marshal Graziani of Italy and General Wavell of U.K., the latter is more lucky-starred.]
Hess	[What is the horoscope telling as regards who should be ordered to take the post of commander of the reinforcements?]
Luc	[It is General Rommel.]
Hess	[The two men who left my office crossing with you are Subhas Chandra Bose, the Indian, and his astrologist Raja Mitra.Their decipherings correspond with yours.

	They proposed to organize SS Indian Division using the captured surrenders of the Indian division of North African Campaign. Do you think it is possible or not?]
Luc	[Deducting those war dead in the battle, I think there is a possibility.]
Himmler	[Suppose we add Indian soldiers to SS, how many astrologists will be among them, do you think?]
Luc	[Is Your Excellency Empire Leader intending to form an advisory group of astrologists?]
Himmler	[I may need an Aryan psychic advisory group.]
Hess	[Will safety of the Third Reich be broken from the south?]
Luc	[If SS let Japan as the allied friendly power attack India and can seal the sea, the SS main force in North Africa can be well protected, but my prophecy reading is coming out that Japan will not move at this stage.]
Hess	[At the moment in Berlin, we are proceeding to negotiate the three-country alliance with Japan and Italy, but I wonder when Japan will make a movement towards the completion of this alliance?]
Luc	[I do not think Japan will move while it is under the control of Prime Minister Konoe.]
Hess	[A cease-fire between Germany and U.K. seems to be necessary.]
Himmler	[Is Your Excellency considering to make a cease-fire possible by requesting the other Queens Book?]
Hess	[Well, It may not go so easily as when Austria

	submitted lance of Longinus.]
Himmler	[It was a very stupid action that they easily submit the supernatural symbol of rulership of Europe.]
Hess	[If at the side of Churchill some astrologists exist,Churchill will not choose to surrender. Isn't it a problem. By the way Luc, you were referring to the word Barbarossa in past, were'nt you. If, by any chance, I mean one in a million chances…if Germany makes a war against a country who has a huge army power, which day of which month would be most suited for starting such attack and how should the campquarters be arranged..can you decipher such instance?]
Luc	[That is the matter which Schllenberg referred to you last week, isn't it. My deciphering reads that May next year would be the best timing in consideration of the leaders' fortune and horoscope of the main generals.]
Hess	[Do you have any concern about this question?]

1-43

Avant qu'advienne le changement d'empire,
Il adviendra un cas bien merveilleux:
Le champ mue, le pillier de porphire
Mis, translate sus le rocher noilleux.

Lec	[The deciphering of Les Centuries 1-43. Before a change arises in the Empire A strikingly surprising

	happening will take place The plan of battle shall be renewed, and pillers painted in camouflage Will be transferred onto the rugged rock and fixed there The third line above can be interpreted as that the plain will move, and if the latter half of it is meant for a cannon in camouflage, it will be read that the cannon in camouflage shall be placed on the armored vehicles. In other words, it can read that such big troop of armored vehicles as to shake the vast plain will take place. The important part is the first line which states the change of the Empire. This Empire cannot be France as it is not crowned by the adjective 'great'. So, it has a possibility that this means the Third Reich. I'm afraid if the meaning of 'change' is deliverately hidden in this word?]
Hess	[What you wish to say may be that there is a possibility of the Third Reich will vanish away from the history, do you?]
Luc	[If Germany wish to win the war, the 3 million must be equally divided between the three commanders each one million.]
Himmler	[The number of soldiers that belong to the 40 divisons is far too less than that figure, therefore I think it may be referring to the next world war.]

Hess kicked the leg of Himmler under the table and let him shut his mouth. Himmler did not yet know about the existance of Barbarossa, but Hess who has a free access to the study of Hitler knew about the outline of the Chief Officer's plan. As regards tanks and stukas, in an endeavor to speed up the mass production of these, production of large lot of parts was secretly proceeded.

Hess   [Luc, please continue.]
Luc   [Staring from north, the numbers must be allocated as 1.5 million, 1 million, and half million.]
Hess   [And the reason?]
Luc   [Goods that America which has a huge power of production will supply will be delivered by sea. They will supply ball bearings or the like which will be needed to produce more trucks, tanks and aeroplanes to fill the lack of those which were destroyed at the beginning of the battle. Regarding the southern area, occupation of Greece will enable to block up the sea transporting route. Also, Moscow needs to be occupied as it is a strategic point to fasten the railways in a radial patternlike.]
Himmler   [That strategy may not guarantee the extension to Ukraine to protect its ethnic right of existence?]
Hess   [Unless we win the war, all matters like that will fail to be guaranteed. Luc, your opinion is quite interesting. Did you say this as results of your astrological analysis?]
Luc   [All depends if I have a power to imagine a different spatiotemporal pattern as a shaman does and to decipher that pattern. Like Kaemon Takashima, not only just to decide on which general to choose, but

	also help him guide as to the specific stratery such as from which direction to attack the enemy.]
Himmler	[If I remember it correctly, the person you just mentioned is the one who nominated the name of the assassin of the Japanese politician Hirobumi Ito. I guess those Indians also have a good power of making prediction.]
Hess	[It will be possible to assign Indian or Tibetan mediums to SS headquarters. As Defence Forces will not like such an idea.]
Himmler	[I will arrange this matter right away.]
Hess	[I will leave the arrangement of matters relating mysticism to your good hand.]
Himmler	[It will work usefully if we can assign mediums to armed SS theater headquarters per army group.]

As Himmler was told nothing by Chief of Staff, he was taking in good mood harb tea served in a cup, but Hess looked rather disheartened. The part in Les Centuries 1-43 shown as the plain to move can be deciphered as the military operation strategy can be changed in the military terms. He cannot help praising Luc's ability of his very sharp deciphering which is befitting to the descendant of Luca Gaurico who appointed Nostradamus as his successor. Luc is too clever a toy for Himmler.

If we are to verify the history, the huge productivity of America did function as backbone of the military strength of U.K. and Soviet so that cutting off logistics to the ports on the side of Soviet's Arctic

Ocean at the point no further beyond Leningrad was made impossible. America-made trucks were supplied in large quantity from the north side of Soviet to support its logistics. In addition, supplies in large quantities of fighters and airplanes and also bearings that are needed for production of tanks were all made in America. The strategic spots of railways in Moscow are highlighted by military researchers, but even those professional military researchers do not know much about the logistics that support military productivity. This fact would mean that the era when only servicepersons were assigned to develop strategy was over at that point. War is merely one single means of many to perform the ultimate aim of international politics.

The dinner was over. Louise the subordinate of Schellenberg sent Luc back to his home.

Louise	[Is your wife doing well as usual?]
Luc	[Yes, thanks. By the way she told me a rumor that recently Black Caruso seems to be completely struck by a woman of the name of Catalina.]
Louise	[She keeps infesting at Ox-on-the-Roof. She is an artist from Sicily by the name of Cataria Gambino.]
Luc	[Do you think she is a talented painter?]
Louise	[That she is a good painter does not always mean she possesses the originality as an artist, and also, even if she has it, if her art doesn't get well along with the ongoing historical background she would not be able to escape from her life in poverty.]

Luc	[As I am not asked to tell her fortune, it's none of my business, but I can say this love story won't come to a happy end.]
Louise	[Did you read their compatibility?]
Luc	[Not the slightest divination sign is showing for Black Caruso getting married. This means their relationship will come to cease soon.]
Louise	[That your family has been engaged in the advising work of one same family tree for hundreds of years, can you come to tell even such a thing so easily?]
Luc	[You, too, will go somewhere in the east.]
Louise	[Oh, You know something about me, too.]
Luc	[Germany will do something of great magnitude towards east.]
Louise	[When do you know that will happen?]
Luc	[I don't think it will wait for this summer.]
Louise	[I guess you mean the result will be bad if the action is delayed. I somewhat feel what is in your mind.]

While talking, the car arrived at the front gate of Luc's house.

Now, after parting with them, Hess returned to Germany by plane during that same day and what he did for the first thing on return was to have his secretaries Alfred Leitgen and Karlheinz Pintsch make reservation with Wilhelm Stor of the flight training using Messerschmitt. The flight training that Hess received was being done by usig Messerschmitt Bf108 and Bf110. Items of the drill that Hess received were take-off and landing, including radio compus (a drill to fly on the directional radio waves), the separation of drop tank and parachute drop training at time of emergency.

25. Invation Strategy Against Soviet Russia

When summer came, based on 『Invation Plan during the summer time』, German Headquarters of Staff Officers established a more concrete plan for invation into Soviet territory moving 3 million army soldiers. When December, 1940 approached the staff started visiting the Hitler's official residence every day. As a matter of course, Hess knows the whole plan in detail far better than anyone else.

An aggressive armored division and an airforce troops of ground support were formed and according to the established plan, by the time winter came Moscow was to fall down and to be under the control of Germany. To the three separate troops the equal size fighting force together with one million soldiers were allocated and each general of the three troops was given the even chance of distinguishing each one on the field of battle. Hess, who was asking for advice from a plural number of fortune tellers, did not feel easy of the plan which consisted of just the mechanical way of portioning out the figures.

On that particular day, the war planning meeting was being opened. On the huge table of the meeting room, another huge map that covered from Poland through to the neighborhood of Moscow was spread out. The troops were given each one million soldiers of Army Group North, Army Group Central and Army Group South in the order starting from north. The guideline set in the first place was that dive bombers were to take off two hours prior to the sortie of the army armored division and to start bombing the Soviet airfield. As the first priority, the policy not to allow Soviet's support by their fighters for Russian army at the operation zone was decided. Then, following this bombing, the dive bombers were to destroy Soviet armored division from the sky.

Himmler who then came to know the whole scheme of the strategy showed a keen interest in the plan of enlarging the survival area of the German race. Being the graduate of Agricultural Department of the university, he was concerned about the fertile black soil zone so his interest was forcussed the ways and means as to how efficiently different races or alien elements were to be removed. It goes without saying that to establish a scheme to purify the land removing those undesirable elements without getting annoyed by his conscience troubles has an essential importance. In order to secure his own voice to keep it influential, Himmler requested Hitler to keep the firing power of each armored SS division not to be less than that of the defence forces, or more exactly saying, to make the SS divisions to have more elete cadre. Regarding the strategy to follow up a speedy preparation of colonization of Ukrine, Himmler left the authority to exercise this project to Hydrich who was called the Brond Hair Beast.

On December 18, 1940, Hitler made his decision and the command No. 21 to Defence Forces, namely, Operation Barbarossa was shifting on to the imminent stage to be commanded at any time.

Hess had all his prophets gather and demanded them to tell the timing of horoscope when the lucky star of Hitler and his German side main commanders will surpass the star of Stalin and the commanders of the Soviet side. Toward the best month of May, the production lines of the war supplies were put in full operation. Nevertheless, Hess could not ignore Luc's and several other prophets' words which kept staying in his mind.

Hess tried to place Tarrot cards by himself many times and also read the horoscope of Hitler. Results coming out of his efforts using Tarrot cards or reading Hitler's horoscope came out as same as when he requested Elsbeth Ebertin years ago pointing out that the year 1945 would be the year of bad luck to Hitler. That several staff officers were objecting the practice of the two-front war for the reason that it would mean the second advent of WW1 was also disturbing him.

Hess [Fred, Will you fly to France?]

Fred [You have something to worry about. By whom do you wish to prophet your worries?]

Hess [Please be most cautious not to have your movement noticed by Black Caruso. Firstly, ask Ave Maria to tell the current movement of time in her Japanese way like Kaemon Takashima did. Secondly, have La Voisin in Lyon prophet by horoscope and Tarot Carta.]

Fred [Kaemon Takashima? Is he the man that serialized his guidance on the newspaper as to from which direction Japan ought to attack Russia at time of the Russo-Japanese war?]

Hess [As you must know it, there have been not too many people who predicted the means to win the war. If we can use such methods, we can at least find out whether the war plan that has been approved this

Fred	[Then, if the answer comes out to be negative?]
Hess	[Stoppage of the war against U.K. will become mandatory.]
Fred	[If we cannot reconfirm what the astrologist of the Borgia predicted the other day, then we shall have no problem, shan't we?]
Hess	[If those parts as bearings that are coming from America cannot be delivered to the factories in Soviet, there is a fair cance of success on our side. Without those bearings, tanks and fighters that are sleeping in the Soviet's factories will no longer be made functional.]
Fred	[If our Defence Force has a problem to evenly allocate the theater of war, I think if we allocate the armed SS .6 million, .3million and zero starting from the north it will solve the problem.]
Hess	[It will be difficult to persuade Himmler who is blinded by greed to get the black soil area of Ukraine.]
Fred	[Do I not need to visit the man Luc?]
Hess	[I'm more worried about the leak of our action via Black Caruso through to Vatican, so act very carefully not to be noticed by them.]
Fred	[I understand.]

Fred flew to Paris by air in his business suit and shopped Noel color napkins for the Christmas party and some small size ornaments at Rue de Paradis before he was going to meet Fthe fortune tellers. And there, he happened to see Borgia carrying shopping bags in both hands and following a woman but he could narrowly escape from their sight. Perhaps they did not recognize him as he was not in his usual army uniform. Getting worried about time, he hurried up to Ave Maria. Maria was ready to receive him in her usual manner.

Maria	[Are you here today for my advice about the war?]
Fred	[We learnt and understood that Kaemon Takashima led the loosing Japan to victory during the Russo-Japanese war.]
Maria	[The best timing would be mid May. All strategic materials will be supplied from north. America-made trucks will become troublesome if sent to Soviet. If ports facing Arctic Ocean and Bosporus Strait are seized, no tanks nor fighters will become possible to be produced. One point that must be noted is the adverse party will show off something that will induce the German side to wish to cling to Ukraine or further north. Therefore, not to yield to such temptation will become necessary.]
Fred	[In case the timing is missed?]
Maria	[The peak point of the horoscope power will be idly wasted. The time thus wasted will never be back again. You will realize you can never match up with Stalin's horoscope.]
Fred	[I will surely convey your message to His Excellency.]

Next, Fred met La Voisin whom he had Schellenberg taken to Paris at Ox-on-the-Roof. When he came into that cabaret-bar, she had just finished lunch and was taking tea together with a woman who was accompanied with her.

Fred	[I understand you have already heard from Walter the purpose of this meeting.]
Catherine	[This young woman is a daughter of my cousin. As she can read the current tide better than I do, I took her with me here. Her name is the same as mine but as she is an Italian, she is to be called Catalina Gambino. She is normally an artist, but maybe she is more popular as a designer of Tarot Carta.]
Catalina	[The client shows the sign of longevity. He can go to the north. He will be living in a large castle like building till he reaches his ninetieth.]
Fred	[We are not asking for the fortune of the individual. We wish to learn how the war develops.]
Catalina	[You must start the war not missing the timing of mid May. Also seal the port in the north. As regards south end, you had better stop the troops at or before Kiev. Firstly fall Moscow.]
Fred	[Surprising you, too, can see that far.]
Catalina	[You are asking other fortune tellers to tell the fortune, aren't you.]
Fred	[My master reads fortunes by himself using Tarot Carta. Only when he cannot read it thoroughly, he asks for help from professionals.]
Catalina	[But your adverse side will no doubt try to counterplot our psychic reading. I do not think you can stay optimistic.]

Fred	[Even in the communist bloc?]
Catalina	[I'm afraid, Yes. Remnants of nobility or their family pythons are still there. Russia could withstand the attack from the west world.]
Fred	[Well, surely the Napoleonic army also invaded from west…]
Catalina	[As Russia is the district where Orthodox Church is predominating, they would be able to analize the intention of the menace approaching from west. This analization is difficult to be done by the eastern side as they do not share the same sense of values or logics as the western side. Reason why they could not compete to the attack by the troops that invaded crossing frozen Volga can be attributed to their inability to decipher the sense of values of the Mongolian troops.]
Fred	[So you mean there will be a possibility that our tactics will be read by them?]
Cataline	[At first they may not be able to decipher the exact jump-off day of the attack or its time, but they will soon or later come to realize what pattern you are following. Only if they know who your fortune tellers are, they may come to understand your behaviors to deal with what you have to do.]
Fred	[Was the reason of the cause of Russians' defeat at the Russo-Japanese war that Russia could not decipher the Japanese behavioral pattern?]
Catalina	[Admiral Togo's strength of the game led him not to take the measure of dividing the inferior fleet into two

groups at Tsushima and Tsugaru. Kaemon Takashima is the person that saw through this strength of the game of Admiral Togo.]

Thus, Catalina finished her talk. Finishing the meeting when Catalina and Catherine went out from Ox-on-the-Roof, Borgia who was smitten by Catalina found her. Borgia was being called for by Maurice, the owner of Ox-on-the-Roof for a claim against the cutlery he purchased. A few month ago Borgia introduced an uncle of Catalina for a transaction of the uncle suppling cutleries for use at the cabaret-bar. Seemingly, there were some quality problems of the cutlery the uncle delivered to Maurice.

Maurice [Regarding the three dozen Laguiole knives I bought from your acquentance Mr. Gambino, during the past three months time, the bee shaped decoration on five knives came off. I tried to contact Mr. Gambino and called his office but no answer at all. As you told me you can make the price half and can gurantee the quality, I guess you ought to mend these five knives.]

Borgia [Yes, I will have these mended free of charge as the warranty period has not expired. But these are not bees but flies.]

Maurice [Flies? Why flies?]

Borgia [Don't you call in French the part you press a knife with your finger a fly?]

Maurice [Ah, you're right. Okay, I will call it fly but for the use at a restaurant, to name it a fly sounds disreputable. Call it a bee at least at this place.]

Borgia	[Alright, I will duly receive these five knives and five flies⋯No, bees.]
Maurice	[Please try to finish reparing them prior to Noel.]
Borgia	[Yes, leave it to me.]
Maurice	[Are you able to contact Mr. Gambino?]
Borgia	[As I know his niece, as long as he is in Paris, repair can be done no problem.]
Maurice	[That is a good news.]

In fact honestly, this knife was not a genuine Laguiole. It was a product very alike Laguiole but was produced in Sicily by the name of Laquioro which was registering gold fly as its trademark. Thickness of the blade is not 1.5mm but was actually 1.45mm but was rounded off to indicate as 1.5mm. Because of his desire to sell Italian products, he kept shutting his month about this fact.

While he was wrapping the faulty knives quickly, his eyes caught Fred coming out of the small room where Catalina had been. This man called Fred was in a business suit but Borgia noticed he was Alfred, the secretary to Hess. Knowing that Catalina was telling fortunes, he came to intuit that Germany must be planning something big. But his prudence told him not to dare to ask Catalina straightforward such a thing that was against business ethics as the details of the fortune telling request made by the German side.

26. Challenging The Third Reich's Doom

In March, 1941, Soviet's military mission visited Germany. Purpose of this Soviet's visit was asking for the Germany's advice regarding production of tanks. Schellenberg was one of the members by the side of SS to receive this mission. After the mission went back to their home country, Hess started to collect information about the visit of this mission from Himmler.

Hess [How was the Russians' attitude when they were here the other day?]

Himmler [They were keen to observe the weight and shape of the German tanks rather than to check the armoring of the tanks and singing the praises of those, went back.]

Hess [Didn't they mention anything like an advice about our tanks?]

Himmler [Schellenberg reported he felt they were convinced of superiority of their light tanks.]

Hess [So that is what he intercepted, isn't it.]

Himmler [You are right.]

Hess [Suppose their new type tank is a powerful one, what countermeasure do you think of ?]

Himmler [Well, this is the turn of His Majesty the Marshal who is only concerned about the number of stars on his shoulder. Now is Jericho Trumpet of his proud Stuka's time.]

Hess [I hope weather will maintain to enable flying at all

	times.]
Himmler	[Fine days are many in the summer time so you wouldn't have to be worried.]
Hess	[All depends if we can fall Moscow in four to five months time starting on May 15.]

From the geopolitical viewpoint, Hess' uneasy feelings about this instance seem to grow up to be a reality. The horoscope of German commander tells that the best period of time will not be long enough. Before it becomes necessary to replace the commander, the current situation must be settled, otherwise, Germany would be getting cornered to the worst consequence. In any case, two-front war was an undesirable strategy, but having Japan participate in war and force Soviet to exercise two-front war would not be possible either. In the current 21st century, all information is disclosed so that it is well known that the damage on the side of Soviet at Nomonhan Incident was greater than that on the side of Japan, however, at this point of the history propaganda spread by the communists still had a substantial influence so that Japan could not grasp precisely what had happened. This became the reason why Japan changed its strategies and decided to go down to the south for procurement of resources.

On April 13 when Japan-USSR Neutrality Pact was signed, Hess' uneasiness was further increased. With this Pact possibility of Japan becoming a threat to Soviet from its back was extremely minimized. Still, the possibility of Japan arbitralily disregarding this pact and making an attack to Soviet was not totally negative, but suppose the propaganda of victory of Soviet at Nomonhan Incident was widely believed as a truth, that this possibility of Japan's attack to

USSR had become indefinitely near zero was also a validly established fact. At every occasion when Hess met the commanders of Defence Force, he showed them that huge figure of 85 million tons of America's annual production volume of crude steel and tried to tacitly urge them to re-arrange the troop strength. If this huge production of crude steel made it possible to supplythis material to Soviet free of charge, the supply would arrive at harvors of Soviet facing Arctic Ocean because Bosphorus Strait of Greece and Romania both of which were located on the south side had been seized by Germany.

Though it could be taken for granted that the stationing position of the three army groups be held firm as was in view of the fact that Hitler had already granted his agreement to the overall framework of the strategic plan, the new strategy to fall Moscow and to seal the north-end harbor by shifting the main war potential to the north could prove its validity only when the total war became extended for a long time of period. The supply of the materials by rail from the side of Pacific Ocean could be well stopped by brockade at sea by Japan. However, one thing that should be noted was Japan had concluded a treaty with Soviet as Soviet-Japanese Neutrality Pact, which was practically contradictive in view of the cooperative relationship between Germany and Japan. However, this may be understood as Japan's strategy in the belief that a four-country alliance of Japan, Germany, Italy and Soviet would be formed. In Hess' viewpoint, such a possibility must be nil.

On May 6, Soviet changed its line-up and Starlin became a new prime minister of Soviet concurrently taking the post of dupty prime minister, with Molotov as the foreign minister. While Hess had been feeling the necessity of changing the flow of destiny, the change of world situation alerted him to take a typewriter into his office. Taking a few hours, he finished typing, so he put the letter he had written into an envelope and sealed the flap of the envelope dripping wax on it. He however did not address the envelope and put it back into the drawer of his desk.

In the afternoon of Saturday, May 10, Hess was dressed in the leather flight suit of airforce captain, and handed that letter now addressed to Hitler on to one of his secretaries called Pintsch.

Pintsch [Rest assured I will hand this envelope to the Leader by noon tomorrow.]
Hess [Thanks. Then, as discussed, ask the air force to transmit a radio guidance wave to the direction of the north northwest 335° from the location of the airforce office.]
Pintsch [Right before the time you appointed I will contact the airforce and tell them your order.]

Thus, at 1745 hrs, Hess rode on a Messerschmitt Bf110 and flew away leaving the roaring of the twin engine plane. The plane quickly became a dot amongst clouds and soon vanished away. He did not know Goering had already ordered the search of Hess and search planes had been despatched. However, because it was already late afternoon and was getting dark, and also the plane functionarity at that time was not competent enough to get Hess' plane in their sights, they lost track of Hess. At 2058hrs, Hess changed the flying course to 245° to west-southwest.

After a while Hess came to recognize the coastline nearby Bamburg of Northeast England. The town lights were observed alongside the coastline. As that night's age of the moon was 13.58, visual confirmation was comparably easy. Taking a map from his baggage, he tried to find the steeple of a church in groups of buildings that looked like a town or a village, carefully comparing the location of those buildings against the uneven coastline. He compared the port, and the location of a church and the roads that were shining in white color reflecting moonlight, then he flew back to the off-shore for a few munites, then again came back and repeated the confirming work of the relative positions. He continued this repeticous action many times and prudently kept tracing the coastline that led to Scotland. On the U.K. side, the sight of his plane was noticed so they had two spitfires taken off to chase Hess' plane in the first place and another later to be added for the search. Despite their search, they missed Hess' plane out to nowhere.

As no radar for the enemy detection purposes was equipped with the fighters at that time, the only searching means was to check with eyes. Therefore, detection without knowing Hess' flying up to the north in zigzags did not work as the spitfires simply searched Hess on the straight route to north from the last point that he was caught by the radar equipped on the ground. Consequently, the searching spitfires quickly passed Hess who was taking a lot longer flying time doing the zigzag flying. At 2208hrs After Hess'

Messershumitt dropped its fuel tank onto the sea, he continued to do the zigzag flying furthermore while checking the terrain features against the map description. When he arrived near Glasgow, he lifted the plane up to the height of 6,000 feet(1,800m) so he escaped from the plane at 2306hrs in parachuit. After three minutes Mesershumitt crashed at 19 kilometers west of Dungavel House.

A farmer called David McLane who got aware of the sound of the fall and explosion of an aeroplane saw a white color parachuit in the moonlight and ran to it and found Hess, bearing with the pain of sprained left ankle, struggling with the soft fabric of parachuit which was clinging to his body by the wind.

David [Are you a German soldier?]

Hess [I am Captain Alfred Horn. I wish to meet Duke Hamilton. Won't you give me your hands for now.]

David [All right, but why have you flown to such a place as here?]

Hess [Because I have to meet Duke Hamilton and talk with him.]

David [I will anyway take you to the army facilities so you can tell what you want. I myself neither know Duke Hamilton nor have met him.]

As it very already midnight, he was just taken to Maryhill Barracks, the army facilities of Glasgow and put away there.

The following day was a Sunday, but Wing Commander Hamilton came over there to meet Hess from the Turnhouse military base near Edinburgh. He never knew a man called Alfred Horn, but as this man had appointed him to meet, he decided to meet this man in person. Entering through the iron door where two guarding soldiers were standing, he found a man with thick eyeblows sitting on one side of the long table. He thought he would take a seat at the opposite side of the table and walked near to a chair there, when the man with thick eyeblows issued a voice.

Hess [Long time no see. I am Rudolf Hess.]

Hamilton [Oh, my! Are you really Rudolf?]

Hess [You look not changed at all.]

Hamilton [You, NSDAP Dupty Leader, are personally visiting me, does it mean something serious to talk about with me?]

Hess [U.K. is one of quite few Germanic nations just as same as Germany. We are the same Germanic nations so we cannot afford to spend our valuable time using each other's power to diminish which is only to contribute communists develop their power.]

Hamilton [I understand what you are trying to mean. But I am not a diplomat nor a prime minister. I am a mere lieutenant coronel of U.K. Airforce. I'm afraid all what I can do for you is to make a contact to our Prime Minister Charchill and let him know you are here.]

Hess [I do appreciate it.]

Hamilton [I haven't been to Berlin since the last Olympics, but I think now is the time of lilac to bloom beautifully.]

In this way the two men changed the topics to talk about the nostalgic past.

Having finished the meeting with Hess and transferred him to Buchanan Castle in that afternoon, Duke Hamilton placed a call to Prime Minister Churchill. Actually, he had a close relationship with Churchill.

Hamilton [Your Excellency, Late last night one German fighter broke through our air defence network.]
Churchill [Ha-ha, Did our airforce shoot it down?]
Hamilton [It was NSDAP Dupty Leader Rudolf Hess that landed by parachute. He proposed U.K.-Germany cease-fire.]
Churchill [It's not see coming:It's NAZI coming!]
Hamilton [Do you wish to meet him?]
Churchill [I will have Ivone Kirkpatrick go see him. Please show Ivon to him.]

The position that Ivon was seizing at that moment was Director of the Foreign Division of the Ministry of Information (MOI). After this issue, he was made Manager of BBC Europe in October.

At this time on May 11, the movement at the German side was such that Captain Pintsch dressed in SS army uniform who received the letter that Hess had written came over around the noon to Berghof in Obersalzberg where Hitler's villa was located. The guards who remember the registration number on Hess' car let the car go through the gate with no question, receiving him with Nazi salute. Parking the car besides the stone-made grand staircase, Pintsch quickly ran the staircase up with short steps and entered while the guard held the door open. Weather in May in that area near Alps was still cool even a little past the mid noon time.

At one step inside of the gate door, he raised his right arm and gave a salute and told he was going to meet Hitler, and he was led to the grand hall without any further question. The hall was constructed with a big white wall and strong looking coffered ceiling made of Swiss pinewood from where a bronze and gold chandelier and in the round shape center of it thirty candle shaped lamps were being lit. Three steps up from there on the place in front of the fire place there was a big sofa that can easily provide seven people with seats. He sat down at the end of the right corner of the sofa and was told to wait for a while. In the fire place, one thick stem of white birch was quietly flaming. A large framed picture on the right wall was decorated with an oil painting showing a fully naked Vinus lying with her head down on the left side, extending her hand to Cupid running towards Vinus from the righthand side. In that state, he was kept waiting for nearly three hours, then finally Hitler showed up in front of him. He opened the wax sealed letter from Hess by a paperknife and a little while after having read it once, he eventually let out his voice.

Hitler [Then, where is Hess at this moment?]
Pintsch [My master has not contacted me since he took off.]
Hitler [Is BBC broadcasting any news about him?]
Pintsch [No, no news have been broadcast.]
Hitler [All depends on Charchill's reaction to this matter. How this will influence the diplomatic intercourse will have to be considered.]
Pintsch [Are you talking about the case when this exercise has failed?]
Hitler [I'm afraid the U.K.side will come to grasp some information about Barbarossa.]

Hitler drew the telephone on the side table near to him and started ringing several numbers.

Hitler [Do you see who am I? A problem that could develop into a diplomatic issue is now going to happen. As the situation is unpredictable, you come to Berghof. Yes, be here during the morning tomorrow.]

Pintsch [Anything I can do about this matter now?]

Hitler [You are to stay at the guest house and explain what happened to Ribbentrop who is coming tomorrow here. We are to discuss to analize the possibility of conclusion of peace agreement with U.K. Whatever the result comes out, that we try to coup with this situation is necessary.]

Around the noon time on the following day, Foreign Minister Ribbentrop came over there. His opinion about this issue is such that if this plot can be successful, Germany is to construct annihilation front of communist block against Soviet and in that case U.K.is supposed to take a role of supplying resources needed, but in case of this came to be a failure, it would give such impression that Germany might give such an impression as if Germany betrayed the peace agreement by Italy and Japan with Germany and consequently failed.

When they were about to arrive at the above conclusion, Martin Bormann suggested an excellent idea. It was to fabricate Hess' having gone insane. Reflecting this idea, the 8pm radio spread the news that Hess took sick and in defiance of Hitler he rode on an aircraft and had not since come back.

Past midnight time on 13th, Aivon Kirkpatrick, the Ministry of Information met Hess shown by Duke Hamilton.

Hamilton [Won't you explain the purpose of your having flown here this time?]
Hess [Germany wants to cease-fire and make peace with U.K.]
Aivon [For what reason?]
Hess [In the European Continent, danger of communism is speading nowadays.]
Aivon [You must know that you can just ask Churchill for peace without any consideration.]
Hess [On the whole area of west Europe we will evacuate all occupation zone in the west side of Europe. However, we wish you to admit our broadening the front against Soviet so we can protect ourselves from communism.]
Aivon [What will happen to the position of Poland?]
Hess [As half of Poland had been seized by Soviet already, if the danger of this area affected by communism is removed, there is a possibility to come out of the right of self government getting granted.]
Aivon [Any other concession that you may be able to offer to the U.K.side?]
Hess [We have an idea to receive Duke of Windsor as the emperor of The Third Reich, and should he fail to develop a family, an alternative idea we have is to receive the King of U.K. as Emperor of The Third Reich. To raise an actually existing example, Austria

	and Hungery were taking the double Empire system.]
Aivon	[Do you mean you intend to add the Union Jack into the design of German flag?]
Hess	[I presume it would be possible to put the Union Jack in one of the four crisscross spaces of the German naval ensign.]
Aivon	[Regarding your emphasizing the need to protect communism, do you really believe that Soviet has that much capability to attack the British Empire?]
Hess	[Yes, I do. Such statement is written in Les Centuries. Do you know it?]
Aivon	[Ha..Nostradamus you mean?]
Hamilton	[Are you saying there is something that looks like to be real?]
Hess	[On 5-26, it is written that the troops of the Slavs are to cross the sea.]
Aivon	[Nevertheless could it mean a dispatch of troops as far as to West Europe⋯]
Hess	[In 5-54, there is a statement that their troops would come out from beyond the Black Sea to fight against France. Also, in 6-80, it is stated that the Asian magnate will lead big troops of both navy and army.]
Aivon	[Just because of that it doesn't necessarily mean the involvement of U.K.]
Hess	[10-86 and 87 say The King of Europe will advance near to Nice taking the nation of the north. And there is no guarantee that the big empire may not be U.K.]
Aivon	[Is there any possibility that such can be the Third

Hess	Reich?]
Hess	[In 1-54, a person who carries a big sickle is to raise two revolutions. The perishment of Romanov Dynasty was in fact brought about by the communists. Don't you think there will be a big possibility that Windsor Dynasty could become the target?]
Aivon	[There are other royal families in Europe than Windsor.]
Hess	[But it was the Windsor Dynasty only that is mastering the seven seas. It does not involve Spain or Portugal.]
Aivon	[Do you really think that U.K. is in danger?]
Hess	[If I can have a chance to review the book that exists in your country, I may be able to point out that answer.]
Aivon	[What at all do you with to take a look at?]
Hess	[Mary who was the qeen of Scotland got married with Francois the French crown prince in 1558. She was in a position to directly ask questions to Nostradamus and obtain answers from him.]
Aivon	[And what's the problem about the answers?]
Hess	[There is a possibility that book has some remarking writings.]
Aivon	[I understand the original book of Catherine exists in France?]
Hess	[Her writings mus be compared against that of Mary's book.]
Aivon	[Why?]

Hess	[Because by so doing the questions and answers exchanged with Nostradamus can be read at one time together and understood.]
Hamilton	[You must have read the Catherine book.]
Hess	[You're right. The book that Mary brought into U.K. was one other Queen's Book. In the copies of the first edition, these two copies are the very special ones.]
Aivon	[I now see what you are talking about, but suppose Charchill could borrow the book from the Royal Family, if he could not convince himself I don't think he would release you. Should you truly foresee the future precisely, he would all the more wish to keep you.]
Hess	[I cannot get why?]
Aivon	[Because no leader wants to have the destiny of his country managed by another country.]
Hess	[That Germany can fully fight against communists will benefit U.K., won't it?]
Aivon	[We of course are willing to consider peace and cease-fire, but I wonder that all what you have just pointed out would not necessarily mean WW2.]
Hess	[No, surely I will not deny all is meant to happen as WW2. Some may happen in WW3.]
Aivon	[May we take your proposal as a whole means that you wish to make peace between your country and ours?]
Hess	[Yes, exactly.]
Aivon	[I will contact Charchill and discuss this matter with

him.]

Accordingly, the four-hour meeting before dawn came to the end. Ivon called Charchill on the telephone.

Charchill [Aivon, Did you collect what Hess has in his mind?]

Aivon [What he proposes is that he wants us to back up Germany to enable it to fight a full-scale war against Soviet on the condition that Germany will vacate all the German occupied territories of the west war front to U.K. He emphasizes that the reason of the war is to prevent communists from raising a revolution in U.K. He added another condition that is, depending on the situation, Germany will crown the king of U.K. as the Emperor of their Third Reich.]

Charchill [I now see that coming!]

Aivon [Our conclusion is completely different from what Germany is saying, namely due to his sickness, but then what information shall we have BBC tell on the radio against the last night's Berlin broadcasting?]

Charchill [Make it very simple and just to tell Hess' landing here, and perhaps it may be an idea to imply a possibility of defection. Anyway, I will leave the expression to your hand so have some excuse that can earn time cast on the radio. All depends if we can negotiate his conditions somewhere like in Switzerland. By the way, did you confirm that Hess possesses Full Powers signed by Hitler?]

Aivon [Understood. As Hess looked like exhausted, let him rest till the noontime. I could not confirm if he had the

	Full Powers or not.]
Charchill	[Okay, I see. It seems we also will have to ask for the opinion of a doctor who can presumably diagnoses Hess' state of mind. Without Full Powers such negotiation itself may loose its significance.]

Cutting the line off, Aivon called his close advisor deciding to have him locate a psychotherapist who is also familiar with Les Centuries. As a matter of course, it will be necessary to choose from the member list of U.K. Society for Psychical Research an expert doctor who also is good at foreign languages. Robert Grant is a doctor who was chosen deemed as the most suitable. Stewart Menzies, the M16 Chief Director immediately called Robert.

Menzies	[Dr. Grant, If you look over this shorthand version of the report from Aivon, are you able to diagnose Hess as sane?]
Robert	[I am not sure whether his deciphering of Les Centuries is authentically correct or not…but I can say he is sane by and large. I think he is valuing the production ability of America in the right way, and it seems he also understands that Germany is not capable enough to carry out two-front war. In this meaning, Hess may be much saner than that unreasonably optimistic Marchal Goring or Himmler, the head of the occult group.]
Menzies	[It is a certain fact that subjects raised in the speech of Goebbels later bring out clearly the grounds on which those subjects are built, but, nevertheless, there

	remains some unexplainable madness in those grounds.]
Robert	[Tell me what is the real reason why I was called out here?]
Menzies	[You are expected to reveal the contents of Les Centuries which Hess has deciphered. I guess what Charchill wishes to know the most will be the true intention of Hitler, and in case Hilter dies the will of the highclass officers left after Hitler's death.]
Robert	[How long is the time left?]
Menzies	[The longest would be tomorrow; whether we can have the peace negotiation progress or not by tomorrow.]

On the morning of 13th, At the German side, the high class officers were gathered at Berghof where Hitler's villa was located.

There was an important subject for discussion as to how to adjust the ranking order or the organization system without Hess and also as to how to deal with the possibility of peace negotiation with U.K. which Hess was trying to work out risking his life.

Right before the start of the meeting, Goring was whispered by Himmler not to promote Martin Bormann, Hitler's secretary, to the position of the Dupty Leader of NSDAP.

Hitler	[I guess all of you have already been aware of this fact that Hess flew to U.K. I understand that Hess' intention is to negotiate Germany and U.K. peace reconciliation, but this action of his may not be welcome by Japan nor Italy.]

Goring [I ordered to fly a search plane as soon as the request of radar guidance came to my hand. However, they failed to catch Hess' plane. They believed Hess could never make it because of the U.K. powerful radar network system. However, this morning's BBC news reports Hess is now in U.K. I believe this news. Now, we have to think what reaction U.K. will show. Would this situation mean a chance to us or not?]

Jodl [There are two possibilities. That we do not have to exercise a two-front war woud mean we are not to repeat the mistake of WW1, or, there still remains a possibility that Charchill would stand for Soviet and make Starlin over-reacted.]

Hitler [The originally set initiating date of Operation Barbarossa was May 15, but in view of this situation, it will have to be postponed.]

Himmler [To crop wheat past the harvest season of barley does have a significant meaning. By doing so, farmers find it easier to compare the volume of crops per unit of land with the quality of soil there. Regarding the selection of land where Germans are to be settled in…]

Jodl [Well, as a habitual exercise of Russians, they may exercise the same scorched earth strategy as they did it against Napoleon.]

Goring [Out of our air force we will be able to send more reinforcement from west, but all depends on whether Charchill will agree to peace or not.]

Hitler	[For now, we will try to treat whatever is easy to be decided on. We will keep the Hess position open and will not nominate any new one to replace him. Regarding my secretariat department, I am thinking about Bormann as chief cabinet secretary. What do you think?]
Keitel	[The clever Leader really has a sharp eye.]
Hitler	[Bormann, Tell me what your viewpoint will be to settle this present issue?]
Bormann	[If we receive some contact through Switzerland or Spain, that would mean Churchill would agree to peace. If no contact, then, though regretfully, we will have to decide to broadcast that Hess has gone mad. If this is accepted, the attacking plan against Soviet will become a false news.]
Hitler	[Unless we hear any contact to our embassy by midnight tonight, be prepared to make a broadcasting in the morning on 14th to release the news of Hess having gone mad.]
Boebbels	[I understand.]

On 16th when Hess was confined in Tower of London, Menzies had Robert meet Hess for the purpose of finding out whether the German announcement of Hess' insanity is a fact or not.

Robert	[Mr. Hess, I am Robert. I am interested in what you talked to Aivon.]
Hess	[Do you mean the cease-fire negotiation?]
Robert	[Do you consider that the single cease-fire against U.K.is a simple matter of economy power or army

	force power allotment? As you risked your life to fly over here, you must have some established reason for this action of yours.]
Hess	[What I know for sure is that no one can be sure to such presumption as The Third Reich will be able to keep the thousand year thread of life. Already now military expenditures have unmanageably swellen so that if German keeps winning wars, the economy may come to be broke. While we were aiming at acquiring the resume, I did believe Hitler is the same person as recorded as Hister in Les Centuries. However, as there is a statement in Les Centuries that makes us believe to be referring to WW3, there will definitely be a risk of a destructive financial failure to finish The Third Reich. My only wish is to avoid this risk.]
Robert	[Is what you have just said why you need this?]

Saying so, he took out one Les Centuries first edition from his well-used dark brown bag.

Hess	[My, this is…]
Robert	[I see you can understand what this is just looking at the front cover.]
Hess	[Queen's Book, isn't it.]
Robert	[Yes, Charchill borrowed it via Duke of Westminster.]
Hess	[Am I allowed to check the inside?]
Robert	[Charchill also recognized well the threat by communism, so he tried to esteem your efforts to make a single cease-fire agreement. But unfortunately, before his decision is announced at the parliament, the

	broadcasting report by Goebbels came out so peace is gone. This means the possibility of what you are now going to decipher being reflected on the history in future is now unlimitedly near zero. In this situation, are you prepared to agree that you will present what you have deciphered to the U.K. Government?]
Hess	[That is a great regret. Do you have any other condition to propose to me?]
Robert	[I wish to ask you who told you the existence of Queen's Books.]
Hess	[That is Luca Gaurico, the family tree fortune teller of the Borgias.]
Robert	[Is the other Queen's Book at the Borgias?]
Hess	[The Catherine's Book is an official asset of France after the downfall of the Bourbons.]
Robert	[The Mary's Book is allowed for your review only while you are here at Tower of London, so I suggest you not to loose time and do a quick copying work here. Do you understand me?]
Hess	[How many days are allowed to me?]
Robert	[I understand you will be transferred from here on 20th. This means this book will be taken back on 20th and returned to the Royal Property Vault as one of the forbidden books.]
Hess	[So, I am the only one that is allowed to read this book.]
Robert	[Yes, you're right. It is Churchill's classy move.]
Hess	[I do appreciate it. Then I will agree to that my

	deciphering be reflected to the policies of the high-class officers of the U.K. Government.]
Robert	[Bear it very sure in your mind that you will not add any single writing on the book.]
Hess	[Well noted.]

Then, taking some time as Hess found any additional writing he kept copying these into his notebook.

27. Actuation of Operation Barbarossa

On Sunday, June 8, 1941, Borgia arrived at the house of Catalina Gambino riding on a polished-up car. She appeared hanging a rattan basket in her hand. She had just been to the church services. He opened the door of the assistant's seat for her and let the car run a bit more prudently than usual. Opening the car window fully down and also the roof of the car, they could enjoy pleasant wind of June in Paris. They ran for a while to south and arrived at Palace of Fontainebleau. They parked the car there and looked around.

This Palace is coordinating the middle way of the art style of Italian Reneissance and Baroque with the stylish and light feel French style. Borgia proudly commentated on the Italian influence on to France and she seemed happily listening to him. To Catalina who was from Sicily, Italy was more congenial than France. In the early afternoon, they sat on a bench beneath the shade of a short tree at the side of the flower bed and Borgia tried to remove the cork screw of a bottle of champagne.

Borgia [My God, the fly on Laguioro dropped off.]
Catalina [That is the cutlery that my uncle is handling, isn't it? That missing fly must go out to search food.]
Borgia [Then, coming back it tells where food is to its mates.]

He stood up to come nearer to her to kiss her, but she stopped him with her first finger.

Cataline [Only when destiny permits it.]
Borgia [Destiny is the thing that can be opened by a person's

	will.]
Cataline	[No, it is what is predominated by Gods or spirits that are beyond human understanding.]
Borgia	[Is that what you believe? I don't.]
Cataline	[Oh, you are always an impious person. I am not. I do believe it.]

In this way, that day came to the end for Borgia without telling her anything more.

He felt that the moon at that night was still the stage of the thirteenth night of the lunar month so he felt the right timing had not arrived In the evening of June 9, Borgia visited Catalina at her house and found a car of SS officer parked there and the atmosphere there was different from usual. When he came at the entrance connecting the staircase of the apartment, he saw Louise whom he had met before and who was the subordinate of Schellenberg came out dressed in the uniform of SS lieutenant general. She was holding a Luger P08 which is different from usual time.

Louise	[Mr. Borgia, do you have the key of the room of Catalina?]
Borgia	[No, I haven't received it from her as yet.]
Louise	[Aren't you slow this time which is unusual.]
Borgia	[Wait.]

He found the key under the potted plant at the side of the entrance.

Borgia	[Let's open the door with it. By the way, what for is it?]

Louise	[Hitler ordered to arrest all fortune tellers who have Hess as their customer.]
Borgia	[Her, too?]
Louise	[No one can just say 'I didn't know it'.]

Borgia came into the room and found she had already left taking her belongings. On the large miror in the washroom a farewell note was written with a rouge.

Forget me all. Thank you so much!!

Louise　　[Oh, we are too late.]

Having said so she promptly turned around and went out taking the two soldiers. After they were gone, Borgia was left alone totally dazed.

Borgia in the room where no one else was but he, found a record of Caruso. It was a record which was given to her together with a gramophone as Christmas gift. He put the stylus on the record and the crushing out voice of Enrico Caruso singing 『Core 'Ngrato (Short-lived Love)』 which echoed throughout the room. This song has another name of 『Catari Catari』 and is a great song composed by Salvatore Cardillo:Feb./20/1874toFeb./5/1947.

The songwriter deceased in 1940, but because the copywrite is held effective for 70 years after the death of the composer, I solicit the readers' understanding as to the fact that I am not in a position to copy the lyric here, since the lyric and the music are inseparably related.

Around when the arresting drama of the fortune tellers under exclusive contract to Hess was started, huge volume of munitions started to be piled up at the east war front carried by many cargo cabins by rail. These goods were mainly shells, fuel or foods but when time of a week before came soldiers who finished their vacation also started to go back to the east war front. In this situation, the U.K. Goverment started to throw a veiled reference to the ambassador of Soviet stationed in London that U.K. was analizing this phenomemon as a sign of Germany making a war against Soviet.

On the otherhand, Starlin did not take this rumor seriously, suspecting it would be a plot to purposely disturb the relationship between Germany and Soviet. To the U.K. Government that stands for Poland, Germany and Soviet are the countries forming an alliance for invasion into Poland. As imagined by U.K., Starlin at that time was too busy to adjust the struggle for power inside the communist resime, so that the new arrangement of the German army stationed in the former territory of Poland or the selection of human resources of commanders stationed there tended to be neglected. This fact led to diminish the functionability of German army of establishing sufficient guard against the enemy coming from outside of Poland.

On June 20, Mihail Gerasimov who had already obtained unearthing permission from Stalin of Gur-e-Amir was at the mausoleum under the ground in Samarkand. This mausoleum was a beige color stone made dome of about 37 meter high and the inside and outside walls of the dome was decorated by mosaic tiles of deep and light blue geometric pattern. Inside the dome in front of the altar a decorated stone coffin was placed and right below the decorated coffin another coffin was sitting which was made by curving greenish black nephrite (soft jade). The body inside this coffin was that of Timur who deceased in 1405. A native underworker helping the excavation work read the letters written on the coffin.

This underworker who deciphered these letters told Gerasimov that it was a curse, but to Gerasimov, facing the dead was his profession, so he did not take the underworker's word serisouly. Therefore, he opened the lid of the coffin without hesitation and found the body. He quickly measured the height of the dead body and started to record figures. The body length of 173cm was quite high for a person lived in the fifteenth century, and he also noticed that the body's right leg was clippled as the legend had been telling. He also confirmed that the body was with red beard. However, he failed to find any gourgerous crown that should usually be with rulers, nor did he find any armors. He wondered that Stalin would be disappointed and checked the body further and found a dusty sheepleather bag placed in the midst of the body's chest. In there, there contained a red cabochon-cut stone of about 15mm diameter.

He handed this jewelry to Lavrentij Berija who was directly reporting to Stalin. This is what Stalin demanded in place of giving Gerasimov his permission to unearth Guar-e-Amer. Stalin's hopeful expectation was that the height of Timur must be shorter than 163cm which is the height of Stalin. Stalin also expected that the Barlas ruby which was used as a talisman to lead the army to be a genuine ruby. Berija hurriedly flew to Moscow taking this bag containing the jewelry and took it to Kremlin on the following morning. He walked on the red carpet to the Stalin's office in haste.

The office door of Stalin was guarded by two sentinels. Berija asked them to open the door and entered and found Stalin and The Foreign Minister Molotov and the Jewish doctor Casper Rubinstein were altogether sitting on the sofa placed facing a large desk, taking tea putting strawberry jam in it.

Stalin [Show me the content of the leather bag.]
Berija [Here it is.]
Molotov [Fairly big size loose, isn't it.]
Casper [Surely it is of Cabochon-cut as we thought it would be.]
Stalin [And, what about the quality?]

Molotov picked that small red stone up and put it on the Pravda issued by the Communist Party of the Soviet Union while Stalin was gazing it. All people there, with Stalin first, then, Molotov, Berija and Casper in that order examined and confirmed how the stone was reflecting the letters on Pravda.

Stalin [To my regret, you won the game, Casper. Take it with you as promised.]
Molotov [Yes, you're right. The stone has this much size but letters can be seen not doubled.]
Berija [Which means single reflaction.]
Casper [As I said in the first place, most of the ancient Barlasrubies are not really rubies but so-to-called spinel in the modern age. Until 1880 when the difference of the reflactive index became able to be analyzed, ruby and spinel could not be subtended.]

In fact, ruby looks doubled when a large size loose was put on a string of hair or on newspaper because of its nature of double reflection. Therefore, if the stone does not show the double reflection, it means it has the nature of single reflection.

Berija [The height of Timur is 173cm which is fairly tall for an Asian person in the 15th century. I also heard he was growing a red beard. In his coffin the words were written as 『Against any one who dares to uncover my grave I will release a far more fearful invader than myself.』]

Stalin [Well, well, result of this time's unearthing work does not sound comfortable to us.]

Casper [Now is the 20th century of science. Era of Marxian Science. Curse is nothing but superstition.]

Molotov [Casper was a realist who never had any imagination power.]

Stalin [How are you intending to spend your life after retirement?]

Casper [I am taking several oil paintings and this spinel and perhaps may go to my son's and his wife's place. My son is a doctor in Stalingrad.]

Stalin [Keep well and live long.]

Casper [I thank you for your goodness to me while I was in service.]

Stalin [Exactly likewise.]

Morotov [Please take good care of yourself.]

Finishing the farewell greetings to Stalin and the others, Casper, putting the flamingly red spinel back to the dusty leather bag and pushed it into his briefcase which contained such as stethoscope, hastily stood up. At the doorway, he turned back and bowed to Stalin, and after waiting for Stalin to raise his right hand lightly, he left the place.

Berija [As I remember it, I think Casper possesses French oil paintings of the 19th century, doesn't he.]

Molotov [Of which about eight paintings are what he obtained winning the bet with Stalin like what happened this time again.]

Stalin [His discerning eye and his peremptory attitude to take away the thing he won could be attributed to his Jewish blood.]

Molotov [His sir name originally means red color stone, so this bet was on the backfoot of our Master Stalin.]

As that day was a Saturday, the meeting was finished before the noon time.

On the otherhand, at this same time, 3 million of German Defence Army and armed SS soldiers were being spread over the area of 5 kilo meters off the border line to the new east-side area. As the age of the moon that night was 25.92, those troops further advanced another 2 kilo meters before the sunset and took a nap there.

Hitler in his usual habit put a tripod on the balcony when the midnight time came, and photographed the night sky by his Leica. A collection of more than 200 photos which Hitler had taken before he started taking some important actions were seized in the postwar days. Those photos were all taken by himself and, with his handwritten notes added on those, these were contained per the date of the photographing in separate envelopes. According to what Schellenberg wrote, Hitler seemed to have told Schellenberg such as 「One (Goring) is always concerned about the number of stars on his shoulder and the other (Hess) is about the stars in the sky」, but this writing of Schellenberg would mean that he did not know Hitler himself are also concerned about the stars in the sky.

At 0100hrs of Sunday, June 22, a preliminary alert was issued by the Soviet troops but this alert was accompanied with the inhibition not to make any kind of provocative acts against the German troops. This inhibition was meant for avoiding the start of the war as normally when the army soldiers arrived in the area within 4 kilo meters from the border line a battle was to be started within one hour's time. At this time, too, the first action taker was the German Air Force. At 0315hrs bombers guarded by fighters started invading Poland and precisely targeted and destroyed airports in the former Poland resime. On receiving the alert, the Soviet Russian Air Force had taken their fighters out to the aircraft parking apron so that the Soviet Russian fighters were damaged and destroyed by the scattering pieces of iron of German bombs. The body of the Soviet Russian fighters which was riddled by those iron pieces meant the fighters could no longer fly.

Following this, heavy bombing was performed on the major airbases from Kronstadt, which is the sea port of Baltic Fleet, over to The Crimean Peninsula, in order to stop the following air support. At dawn, invation by the Panzer Division, that had been guarding the German east war front, started. The Soviet land forces which lost the mastery of the air had to get scared by trumpet of Jericho issued by Stuka dive bomber in addition to bombing coming from the war front. In other words, Soviet tank soldiers had to go ahead to fight against the German Army and at the same time must turn back when they heard this siren from their back and must jump off the tank to escape from the death.

The main striking force of WW 1 was limited to foot soldiers and cavalry soldiers. Fighters and tanks were still at the stage of demonstration purposes only. At WW2, on the ground war, armed troops and dive-bombing made the difference in the war. On the ocean, the aircraft carriers and torpede bombers fiercely collided and on the supply line, destroyal of trading line by submarines which fought against the sentry aerocrafts. Here, the writer's viewpoint is the core of the attacking power of aircraft carriers was exclusively meant for the attack to the torpedo bombers and not to the fighters that guarded bombers. It was the torpedo bomber that played the most important role to sink the major force of the enemy's fleet into the sea, though the writer presumes that at WW3 the battle tactics will shift from the battle of electronic weapons to thermoneuclear wars.

Incidentally, the Nazis German troops at WW2 were constructed by the armed SS that are consisiting of NSDAP private army together with German Defence Army as the regular army and, in addition, the volunteer army coming from the fascism orientated countries. Because of this reason these troops were called Nazis

German troops, however in the writer's opinion, these troops had better be called as NS German troops or else, The Third Reich troops in view of the historical ground. Concluding, now we have entered the era when we are to objectively appraise the history.

On 22nd when the war was started, till around the noon time of that day, at the war fronts the fall of Soviet was becoming obvious. Needless to add, while by dawn after Soviet bases started to be attacked, Stalin showed up at his office in Kremlin, but he was unable to make any decision as the information gathered were excessively intricated.

Molotov   [Fascists are invading into our country. What countermeasure do you instruct us to take?]

Stalin   [Hitler is supposed to press down the warlike generals, Isn't he?]

Molotov   [No, I don't think so. As long as we judge from the broadcasting announcement of this morning by Goebbels, minister in charge of propaganda, there is no alternative but to take it as a well planned invation. He has clearly told on the radio that this invation is being executed in the size which is ever the largest in the history. He is also declaring the divine protection of god is at the side of The Third Reich. This is annoying.]

Stalin grasped the frame of a photo which was showing he and Hitler shaking hands, and slapped it onto the floor. He did not reply to any question that Molotov made to him at all. He just sat on the desk and tore out his hair. Then he gestured by his hands for Molotov to clear his office to him alone.

To Molotov who returned from Stalin's office many reports had been transferred. Molotov pushed the set of sofas in his office away to a corner of his room and have a huge size map of Soviet's west war front spread on the floor space made by removal of the sofas. He also had the pieces to show The Red Army and also Black Nazis German pieces. Around the noon time when Molotov returned to his office finishing the radio announcement to the Soviet people, the pieces had been somehow arranged on the map to show the situation of the whole war fronts. Keeping his office to himself he decided to meet just one person that was Berija.

Molotov	[Take an overall look of the situation shown on this spread map. I wish to hear your straight opinion as a non-serviceperson.]
Berija	[Does Stalin know about this overview?]
Molotov	[He knows all the information available⋯but he becomes totally absent-minded since this morning and never issues any single word. What's worse is he locked his office out and won't see anyone.]
Berija	[Don't you think the number of the Black fascists too many?]
Molotov	[This number of their divisions which we gathered should be correct.]
Berija	[The description here of the red army airforce fighting

	strength should be at least 12,000…]
Molotov	[Very regretfully, by the time of the Nazi second attack, about 3,000 fighters seems to have been destroyed. Unless we move the fighters from the eastern side, our red army will have to face the enemy without any mastery of the air.]
Berija	[What about this SS? Isn't it easy to be destroyed as they are not regular forces?]
Molotov	[They are the private soldiers of the party that Himmler leads. Unfortunately, they are forming an elete force in view of all such as the soldier fill-rate, assault rifle equipped rate of foot soldiers and thermal power.]
Berija	[As is, will the enemy's main force fall not only Leningrad but Moscow?]
Molotov	[So that I must ask you. Can you fly to Stalingrad immediately?]
Berija	[What do you have in your mind?]
Molotov	[Last year when I visited Germany, I gathered that the SS leaders such as Himmler or Heydrich were hooked on occult. At that time Heydrich was boasting the Wenceslaus ruby which existed in German Protectorate of Bohemia and Moravia (the Czech Republic) was under the control of SS. According to what he told me, this ruby is the talisman to stop the invation from Mongolia.]
Berija	[I see. But how does it relate to me?]
Molotov	[I wish you to capture Casper.]

Berija	[He was one of Stalin's doctors till a few days ago, but for what kind of suspect?]
Molotov	[For the suspect of theft of art objects. Keep the seized arts in the sacristy in the basement of the church in Stalingrad. Then, from Stalingrad using the police plain text wireless, a list of the ceazed goods of Timur Barlas ruby in a leather bag and the names of eight Impressionists' oil paintings that used to be the Grand Duke Dormitory. This means…]
Berija	[Though it is too bad for Casper, you wish to ensnare Nazis. But, Your Excellency, this plan is very well considered. If we use the police wire in plain text, Nazis won't be able to notice this is a snare. I have one favor to ask.]
Molotov	[What is it?]
Berija	[To enhance the certainty, I will list 1 x Barlas Ruby of Timur, but will you make it sure to wire back to me instructing me to have the mineral name appraised without fail?]
Molotov	[Okay, then I will have that reply back again to you in plain text. By this plot, Hydrich and Himmler will request their troops to make a useless dispatch of the troops to Stalingrad, and the Impressionists' oil paintings will be an effective bate for Goring.]
Berija	[Can I have the special arrest warrant?]
Molotov	[Here it is. It already is signed by Stalin. This signature of his doesn't have his usual writing pressure so it may show his depression, but it is still

	his authentic signature. As is written on this warrant, once the goods were successfully seized, you can just let him go away under an amnesty.]
Berija	[Understood. Now, I am leaving here for the arrest drama of Casper.]
Molotov	[I'll leave it to you.]

28. Yummy Bait

Around the noon on June 23rd, Berija showed up at the police office in Stalingrad. He requested a truck there and had the police taken him and his party to Casper's retreat.

Berija [Is your name Casper Rubinstein?]
Casper [Do you need to ask that question? What on earth do you need from this old man?]
Berija [We are here to execute the confiscation order for the property that you had gained through illegal gambling.]
Casper [I have absolutely no memory to bet any thing except with Stalin.]
Berija [That Stalin's order with his signature is here. I tell you if you submit those items that you know you possess, we are not supposed to give you any harm.]
Casper [Let me see⋯Barlas Ruby of Timur and the eight impressionists' oil paintings of Grand Duke Dormitory, h'm. Do come in.]
Berija [Don't take it too bad, as I'm just so ordered]

They came to the sofa placed facing the fire place, and Caspar took off the doctor's bag a small leather bag which still smelled of dust and soil and put it on the palm of Berija. Berija unfastened the strings of the bag and picked up a flamingly red transparent stone and using the Pravda newspaper on the table confirmed that the stone was single reflactive.

Casper	[So, Stalin suddenly became sorry to have given it to me?]
Berija	[Stalin has been stunned at Nazis invation.]
Casper	[This signature on the capias is no doubt Stalin's.]
Berija	[Those who want this stone are Himmler and Hydrich of SS, and Goring wants the Impressionists' paintings.]
Casper	[Feel free to take them. You, too, shall not die a good death.]
Berija	[Have it your way! Now, be quick to wrap these oil paintings neatly! Where are the rest of four paintings?]
Casper	[Two are in the dining room and one in the bedroom and the last one is hung at the gateway which you must have seen?]
Berija	[Be quick to pack them!]

In another half of an hour, packing was finished and quickly loaded on the truck.

Berija	[Casper, take care.]
Casper	[You are a Himmler of Soviet!]

The truck of the Police stopped at the front gate of an old charch. The cargoes were taken off the truck and delivered to the underground sacristy which looked having not been used many years since the Russian Revolution time. The place was closed by the stone walls and floor, and the ceiling was covered by the marble stone floor beneath the church altar. On the outside of each package the artist's name and the name of the painting was written in English for an easier recognition by German soldiers than if they were written in Russian.

A small piece of identification paper was sticked to the leather bag which contained Barlas Ruby and the bag was put in a wooden box and was then put in a cabinet in the sacristy.

The cabinet was also duly sealed. In addition, the door of the sacristy was firmly sealed. The key of the underground was kept in the safe in the office of the chief of the police station. After this series of work was finished, the beforementioned addressed to Stalin was sent out and the communication between Stalin and Berija was completed as discussed.

On June 24, a train which is taking NS including Hitler and high class officers of Defence Army arrived at Wolfsschanze in East Prusy Wschodnie. On the first car of the train, Hitler, Keitel and Jodl on the top, some members of the Foreign Ministry relation were aboard the car. On the second car of the same train, Marshall Goring and the Air Force related members, and the alchoholic drinks for use of Goring was being carried. On the third car, with Himmler at the top, SS related members and fortune tellers forming as advisory group and also with Ribbentrop at the top, members in relation with Foreign Ministry were on board. When Himmler and Hydrich went off the train to the dinning room, Goring and Jodl both of whom had already been intoxicated with wine were chattering in a friendly mood.

Hydrich had already read the translated copy of the plain text of

Morse message written in Russian, and finished reporting this news to Himmler. Regarding the significance of obtaining Barlas Ruby of Timur and releasing it to the public and the consequent reaction to it of the fortune tellers from middle asia and Occult related tellers, Hydrich was explaining to Himmler.

Goering [When we have requisitioned the wine cellar called Massandra which is connecting to the Romanovs located nearby Yalta, Crimia, I wish it to be divided between Army Force and Air Force.]

Jodl [Well, Air Force can make just a jump and get it, but Army will have to labor to get it, so, what about 70% to Army?]

Himmler [Your Excellency Goering. I have an information of interest.]

Goering [Very well, tell me.]

Himmler [The police of Soviet seizured eight Impressionists' oil paintings that used to be the property of Grand Duke Dormitory. These paintings are in Starlingrad at the moment.]

Goering [Are those masterpieces?]

Heydrich [As long as those are sealed by Stalin, they should be masterpieces of paintings.]

Goering [Jodl, can you strengthen the support to Army Group South excerting your judgement?]

Yodl [The original plan was to allocate 1.2 million, for the attack from Kiev to Stalingrad another 1.2 million and

	300,000 each for Moscow and Kiev. Hess made this plan change to 1,000,000 each to Leningrad, Moscow and Kiev. He in addition ordered that the reserve forces, too, are to be put in after Leningrad is conquered.]
Goering	[Does Hess has any established reason for this order of his?]
Yodl	[What Hess told us was that we must ruin Zhukov while his destiny was under weak stars and cut the supply route of goods and materials through Arctic Ocean. Accordingly, the order issued by Hitler was to fall Leningrad first, then Moscow. It is too late now to change this plan.]
Goering	[Should the situation allow it, obtain the permission to attack Stalingrad.]
Yodl	[You are a born lover of art products to embarrass me as always.]
Goering	[You can have one from the eight oil paintings. You can choose what you like the best.]
Yodl	[You're a very understanding person. Well, I will think about it but keep it in secret, repeat, secret.]
Himmler	[If we can successfully fall that place, I will be sure to requisition those and bring one of your choice to you.]
Yodl	[The mobilization of the reserve force will need a high prudence.]
Hydrich	[Sounds like you could obtain a good Christmas present for your wife.]

Out of Hitler's knowledge, the plan which had been composed using the advice from Hess' fortune tellers was going to be changed secretly. However, as Hess' exclusive fortune tellers were all arrested on June 9 and since were isolated from the public, even Hitler did not have a chance to listen to those fortune tellers' advice. Himmer, though he had a strong objection to this arresting plan of the fortune tellers, was refraining from meeting those tellers then in the jail. The time when those tellers got a permit and released and afterwards when they again came to display their power was when Mossorini fell and arrested and confined to some unknown place. The passage of this happening was written in the note of Schellenberg evidencing that the prophecy came true and real. Judging from this fact, Hess had long been aware of the destiny of Hitler and for this reason, it can be said he did fly to U.K.

The Third Reich Staff Headquarters again became highly cautious being shown the amazing progress of Nazis German troops.

On June 26, Erich von Manstein who was leading the 56th armed Army Group North was reported by wire that the Daugavpils bridge which was located in the present Republic of Latvia had been seized by Germany, but following the instruction from the General Officers Headquarters he and his troops were forced to stay there till July 2.

This place was also a crossing point of the railways leading to Moscow, Leningrad and Riga and situated about 450 kilometers away from Leningrad. If he had kept advancing for about 200 kilometers in six days, the railway connection between Moscow and Leningrad must have been cut off and consequently Leningrad could have fallen into the indefensible situation. In reality, this standstill of Manstein's troops gave time for Soviet to destroy bridges or to install minefield or to build fortress in order to prevent the advancement of the German troops. Consequently, the final cut-out of the railway line could not be achieved till mid August. Here, the fact that Germany failed to develop its fighting power fearlessly under the luckiest star of the NS highclass officers and the leaders of the German troops caused a problem to Germany and that they failed to terminate Zhukov by the month September was attended with serious consequences.

Putting the above aside, when the supply by transport using railway was not possible, the alternative method was transportation by trucks. Soviet that was incurred by a big loss at the beginning of the battles had to rely on the vehicles that were supplied by America. Such information that could not support the communists' side was completely covered till the time of the colluption of Soviet was due so that the historical researchers in the later era need to riddle search this matter and include the revealed facts in this historical process.

To the American horse cavalry such captured materials as bows and arrows for arms or dried mouses for food were useless. This realty made the concept of logistics (impedimenta) develop quickly in America, which led to the result of their supplying Soviet with a large number of trucks. On the other hand, like Japan or Europe since the middle ages such victorious countries could make use of foods and arms that used to be the possessions of the beated. those countries tend not to value the importance of logistics legitimately.

That Army Group North failed to seize Leningrad or destroy it completely resulted in the cause of the delay of the planned attack to Moscow as Hess' anticipation. This delay which resulted in the fact that allowed Soviet time to construct the large size distribution network via Arctic Sea reduced the possibility of German gaining victory fairly much. In addition, as the main concern of Hitler or Himmler shifted to the furtile black soil region, this deviation of the concern led German miss the timely chance to venture their original plan of targeting Moscow.

While this situation was continuing, U.K. was allowing Hess to read newspapers and books, and to write letters and to keep a diary.

Giving Hess such opportunities, U.K. wished to observe Hess' reactions and behaviors which might show Hess' thinking as to whether he had participated the way The Third Reich would move. A rather surprising fact is that till at this moment of the modern world, information of what Hess' negotiated with U.K. after he had landed there, and what information the U.K.leaders gathered from Hess were not known to the public at all. Presumably, there must have been quite a few written information by Hess while he was in U.K. but in his belongings which were handed over to Hess' bereaved family such written materials did not exist at all.

The reason why all information regarding Hess' was made unavailable was because Charchill so desired. He wanted all data of Hess to be kept for himself alone. On June 26, 1942, Hess was transferred to Maindiff Court Hospital in Abergavenny in Wales diagnosed as a mental patient where he lived till the post-war trials were started. Due to the time passage of more than one year, information that Hess had been holding became totally meaningless, and further more, the new way of desciphering the Nostradamus book with the interpretation of Mary's Book accommodated became no longer pursued.

In middle December, 1942, Walter Schellenberg visited Luc Gauric at National Archives after a while. He looked like coming in the official status as he was dressed in the army uniform of SS Colonel. As Maxime Weygan and his wife were arrested last month in North Africa for being incorporative to NS, Luc pulled himself up suspecting he, too, might be arrested. But Walter came in in the normal manner even without saluting in the Nazis way. Then he started talking to Luc rather politely.

Walter	[Hello, Luc. Long time since we met last.]
Luc	[Mr. Schellenberg, what can I do for you today?]
Walter	[I wish you to lend out those books on this memo.]
Luc	[These are forbidden books so circulation is not possible.]
Walter	[I understand this place is the area controlled by The Third Reich…]
Luc	[Wait for a moment.]

Luc went to the director's office and obtained the director's special approval for lending out, hurriedly opened the book shelf which contained forbidden books and looked for the book Walter demanded and found it. It was quite an old looking book in a leather cover with gold lettering on it.

Luc	[This is the Catherine Book of 『Les Centuries』.]

Walter	[Thanks. The leader of SS Empire will be pleased.]
Luc	[I will write the name of the borrower as Himmler, Okay?]
Walter	[Why don't you make the column blank?]
Luc	[You are lending it out, aren't you.]
Walter	[No name of an individual can be given as it is not used by an individual.]
Luc	[How long do you need it?]
Walter	[Why do you guess I know that?]
Luc	[Keep it to males only that read this book.]
Walter	[Do you have any special reason to say that?]
Luc	[Catherine de Medici, the queen of Henri II, Marie Antoinette, the queen of Louis XVI and Josephine, the queen of Napoleon I, all the kings whose queens read this book ended in unfortunate fate.]
Walter	[The 20th century is a century of science.]
Luc	[I hope this century will not become a scientifical delusion.]
Walter	[Unless you were the fortune teller of the Borgias, you would have been taken to Castle Itter together with General Maxime Weygan.]
Luc	[Time while you can be proactive in your life will be till 1945 only. After this year, hexagram of possible prosecution is showing, therefore, I advise you to be most careful at your peak period.]
Walter	[So, have the Borgias already known it and are well prepared? I reckon that is why they could survive the

past long 400 years.]

When Walter put the book into his bag and were going out of National Archieves, Luc saw a soldier who had been waiting for Walter saluting him raising the right hand. Then he saw the door at the back of the car was opened and Walter put himself into the car. After the soldier rode on the assistant's seat, the car was driven to somewhere.

Schellenberg, taking the book with him, visited the office of the SS Empire leader.

Himmler	[Could you get it?]
Walter	[Here it is.]
Himmler	[During the Christmas time, I will take enough time to read it by the fireplace.]
Walter	[I have a message from Luc.]
Himmler	[Did the fortune teller of the Borgias say anything special?]
Walter	[He said not to allow this book read by women.]
Himmler	[For what reason?]
Walter	[Because the partners of such readers as Catherine de Medici, Marie Antoinette and Josephinne all died in an unfortunate fate.]

Hearing Walter's words, Himmler started talking in a tint of excitement.

Himmler	[Do you know that we unearthed Barlas Ruby of Timur under the ground of a church in Stalingrad at the end of October? This ruby was inspected and

	confirmed by brahmins and lamas of SS Indian travel team. This team was sent there on November 20. That we obtained this ruby means we now have the talisman to rule Central Asia.]
Walter	[May I ask if that talisman has already been taken back to Berlin?]
Himmler	[No, it is still kept in the sacristy under the ground on which the ruins of a church in Stalingrad are standing].
Walter	[Which means this sacristy was surrounded by our 6th troops, am I right?]
Himmler	[As there are not only the ruby but eight paintings of Impressionists are included which His Excellency Goring is eager to obtain, German airforce will sure make a fierce attack and totally crush those communists there.]
Walter	[What do you intend to do when you retrieve the Timur ruby?]
Himmler	[Our intention is to consolidate at least ten armed divisions consisting of Muslims who have antipathy against communists and let them repress the oil fields in Central Asia.]
Walter	[That sounds like a great idea.]
Himmler	[I presume in this book our future must be described, so let me take time to read it carefully. To gather what Hess wanted to read out of the book will be an interesting matter for me to clarify. As regards what you have just said of women reading this book etcetra

	might be used to have such misfortune fall on the communists if by one out of a millions of chance the ambition of The Third Reich should collapse. Furthermore, we may be able to have the wife of the giant of Asia that will come out of the edge of Black Sea.]
Walter	[You're quite right. Then, Merry Christmas.]
Himmler	[Say hello to your wife.]

After the exchange of the above conversation, the Catherine's Book of 『Les Centuries』 fell in hand of NSDAP high official. The writer wishes to tell his readers that there was one book of its first edition that was lost in nowhere under the similar circumstances. What happened to that book in realty was when Berlin fell down it seemed to be taken away as a booty of a Soviet soldier and then passed to the hand of Molotov who could read French, and who stored it back in the Moscow library and made it a book of the deadstock there. In the confusion of the collapsion of Soviet which happened on December 25, 1991, during the time of chaotic cricis of economy, part of the stocked books at the library in Moscow flew out and were sold at random largely because of the deficiencies of an orderly organization of the books at the Moscow library. Later, when allocation of the budget was made possible, those books that had been dead stocked in the shut-out archives were gradually being sorted out. Until then during the era of the communists the control of the stocked books in the library had been totally ignored.

On one occasion, libraries in France received a list of French books which had been written in the past centuries with a request to pigeonhole those books. In that list several books were shown which titles were unknown. In those books the first edition of 『Les Centuries』 which seemed to be Catherine's book was included. To deal with this matter, it was decided that France was to send a librarian to make a research to that French library. What was surprising was the first edition of 『Les Centuries』 alone went missing again. Fact is that the book was put on the black market for someone to get money. At that time people were living at an economical crisis there, too. Even in the situation where people have no clue to get food for that day, there still were some rich people somewhere and for those rich people that they could get a method to learn what would happen in future was something that had never ceasing attractiveness that was irreplaceable.

『Les Centuries 3-94』
  De cinq cens ans plus compte l'on tiendra
  Celuy qu'estoit L'ornement de son temps
  Puis a un coup grande claret donrra
  Que par ce siècle les rendra tre contens
『Les Centuries』 3-94

After more than 500 years people in the world will become aware Of his existence that was symbolizing that era Suddenly a Great Lumiere (film making?) will be published and performed Which will fully satisfy people in the same century

If we take this great ray of hope as a French movie star, it will be something relating to Nostradamus that is to be published or performed. If we base on the statement of more than 500 years, it will come to happen after 2003 counting from his birth year of 1503. This would mean that not only Hess but Himmler must have also become aware of this point. In other words, the age of NSDAP was only after a bit more than 400 years.

When the time came into the 21st century, nationalists namely the group called Neo-Nazi started gathering at Rudolf Hess' grave which was located in Wunsiedel, Bayern on his death anniversary to open a meeting. The Lutheran Church related people there became afraid of the possibility of the Hess' grave be changed to the nationalists' sacred place, so they burnt Hess' body in order to scatter the ash to the North Sea and also destroyed the epitaph showing 『I did challenge』. This series of actions were performed in the morning of July 20, 2011. As a matter of fact, this action of the church was exercised in a sober atmosphere of the right-of-center faction so that the public did not become aware the true purpose of this practice.

The SS Empire Leader Heinric Hitzinger secretly ordered Raja Mitra and also asked Indrajit Devija ,and furthermore sent a request to the Borgias just to be sure, to altogether talk to Luc to persuade him to accept the mission to be present at the unearthing work of Hess' body. While monks were digging the coffin out, Luc and the others performed the prayer in a van which was parked nearby from where the scene could get an obstructed view of this series of work. They desperately prayed hoping to descent the spirit of Hess out from his grave and to get sealed again permanently. Those church related people of the 21th Century who were non-exocists looked not to be aware of the fact that both the coffin and the grave had been sealed to prevent the spirit from its getting reincarnated so that as a result those people were breaking the fixing boundaries for religious practices.

Still now, in the religion that is believed in monsoon region, lots of spirits are filling everything that exists anywhere, and at the same time those spirits are getting reincarnated and travelling between this world and another world for numerous times. Nowadays, the world which is invisible to those people who believe this era is the age of science is widely spread to cover the whole cosmos.

Josef Brunner who was mixed in the monks helping the grave digging work shifted the body of Hess into a coffin made of cardboard for the purpose of cremating it. No attendee there took notice that he kept in his hand some of the hair of the deceased. He left the place and rode on a car parked in the parking space of the church. There, off another van, Louise who was in the mourning dress delivered to him a leather bag sealed by red color wax. Josef checked and confirmed that the seal showed in the old Latin, LVCAS GAVRICVS. He did not open the bag and check the inside, but he was convinced by feeling the thing inside the bag that the object representative of a divine spirit would probably be a large cabochon-cut stone.

On the following day, Josef Brunner went to the castle of Heinrichs Hitzinger. At a place just pass the gate, there a black car was being parked. On one flagstaff of several, he saw the green color manji symbol marked. Josef in the SS military uniform got off the car out of the door of car held open by a soldier, the two soldiers standing at the both sides of the entrance raised their right hand and saluted to him. Josef also raised his right hand and returned the Nazi salute back to them, then the two soldiers politely opened the chestnut made entrance door decorated by a carving of grapes and squirrels and led Josef inside. Josef entered and found Heinrichs nesting himself in a sofa. Next to Heinrichs Kato of green manji was sitting. Josef, approaching to the sofa, clicked his heels and raised his right arm and saluted.

Josef	[Sieg Heil!]
Heinrichs	[Come and sit here. Did you take with you the thing in question?]
Josef	[These are the sealed object representative of sealed spirit and the hair of Hess.]
Kato	[Good, these will be sufficient to try the reincarnation for several times.]
Josef	[With only these things can the reincarnation be truly performed?]
Kato	[We exercise living body reincarnation till it comes back to the age of mid thirties. Then we communicate with the dead and put the spirit into the reincarnated body.]
Josef	[You do this on Hitler, too.]
Heinrichs	[Of course. Then we can plan WW3 and rise it like we did with WW2.]
Josef	[Will you tell me how you do it?]
Heinrichs	[Have you ever read 『Apocalypse』 which is a religion started by the Jewish illegitimate child?]

Josef	[You mean that bizarre writing.]
Heinrichs	[You must know that what turns against God are the Country of Beasts and the old and large Red Dragon Country?]
Josef	[You mean you let these countries commence hostile operations? What kind of plot are you going to use to make such a happening possible?]
Heinrichs	[Here is the Catherine's Book of 『Les Centuries』. Husband of any woman that has read this book comes to meet a very unfortunate fate. Like Catherine du Medici, Mary Antoinette and Josephine.]
Josef	[How do you intend to use these books?]
Heinrichs	[I sold this to a Russian millionaire. Soon the wife of the leader of the Country of Beasts will read them.]
Josef	[So what you mean is that the Country of Beasts is Russia?]
Heinrichs	[Most of the Russian names are the names of beasts. It is Russia that must be the Country of Beasts on 『Les Centuries』.]
Kato	[Those who have obtained money wish to have honor and glory. Even if they do not care to leave the majority of the nation poor and unhappy. No, more correctly, such ambition is primarily a part of the motive power of the progess of civilization of the human race.]
Heinrichs	[In Russia, the groups that should go solid under the flag of The Third Reich are growing their power. When Country of Beasts and Country of Old and Big

	Red Dragon perish, a split internal war will break out and when it comes to the end, we The Third Reich will become The Thousand Year Empire.]
Josef	[So, what we should do first is to hand this book over to the Russian millionaire, right?]
Heinrichs	[Will you fly to Rome tomorrow taking this book? At the airport, Carabinieri is waiting for you, so, go with him by his car.]

Saying nothing more, Josef put the book in his bag and standing up he raised his right arm to Heinrichs.

Josef　　　[Sieg Heil!]

The skull ring was glittering dully on his finger.

End of Apocrypha

Postscript

At the election of Austrian presidential race which was executed on May 22, 2016, the party leader, Norbert Hofer, of Austrian Liberty Party (FPO) lost the election with the percentage of votes of 49.7% and the vote difference of 31,026. However, as injustice was found in that election, it resulted in revoting on October 2. Austrian Liberty Party is declaring 「SS ought to receive glory and respect」. When they elect the party leader, they beatify the new leader with the acclamation of sieg heil in place of clapping. When the candidate Hofer is elected at the second voting, this acclamation may remove the ban on this acclamation.

With the separation of U.K. from EU, the international situation is largely changing. What has to be noted especially is that Scotland is showing the intention to leave U.K. and to join EU. This means that if this materially happens the base of nuclear submarines presently located in Scotland will be forced to be changed to a different place. And naturally the Trident missiles which were loaded on the submarines will be moved to elsewhere. The writer is already aware that there is a statement in Les Centuries which says the Trident soldiers will be gathered in South France. The writer can clearly say that this instance, too, is a sign of WW3.

As you may have noticed, the writer's book illustrator is showing a dragonfly with a Tachi-sword on the front cover of the first and the second volumes of Canon which were already published, as well as on this Apocrypha. This illustration of a dragonfly with a Tachi-sword is used to symborize the writer in its unique way. The

Apocalypse keeps silence about what is what comes out right before the outbreak of pandemic of locusts. However, the writer wonders if Vatican might have been aware of it as shown by the prophecy of Fatima. The writer is planning to publicize a lot more sequels to these three completed books of the two Canons and one Apocrypha. He does wish that the number of readers of his literary works are led to read 『Les Centuries』 will increase and consequently help the key of the new methods of descipherment is unlocked.

 August, 2016

Introduction of the writer's literary works

The age of Apocrypha Volume 1 is concentrating on the age of the past WW2. There, the nidana is shown which comes to exist before the charactors that come on stage of the Canon of near future make a reverse transmigration. This book is written taking particular note of 『Les Centuries (100Psalms)』 which was written by Nostradums in the 1550th years and also is forcusing on Schllenberg, Chief of the SS Secret Military Service who frequently used this book for propaganda against France.

He used to hate Christianism which somehow stroke a chord of Hydrich so he concequently got Hydrich's support. Furthermore, he very much got in good with Himmler, the superior of Heydrich. That the quatrain of Nostradamus was given a twist and this twisted quatrain was spread as one of the tactics of Battle of France was a plot that Schellenberg made up. Getting associated with the fortune tellers that hung out as a large group around Hess or Himmler, he came to gain ability to feel metaphysical existence. In his later years it looks like that he made himself a Catholic due to the change in his mental state.

The point that the writer took a particular notice of was 『The Memoirs of Hitler's Spymaster』. Schellenberg used to minutely record what he had done. Why did he record his deeds so minutely? He was in a position to be able to contact more than several eligible fortune tellers and in that situation he was able to notice when the situation then might change. The writer presumes that Schellenberg was in a position to learn when the glory of SS shall be lost and when the pursuing shall become the pursued. Please note that only who that can see can see.

When NSDAP (Nazi) rose its head, the European occult researchers instantly noticed that that group was the group that had been predicted and not only those researchers but Mussolini and the National Fascist Party related people were also aware of this fact. However, as was usual with any such prophecy, the sign of extinction was intentionally hidden by Nostradamus in order to have it escaped from book burning. For example which the writer showed already, statements in Latin were replaced by the language of relating countries or else by the military terms of that age.

And at the same time the writer understands the timing to re-evaluate the fact that Chanel or the Vichy legislation related people contributed for protection of Paris as the place of transmission of culture has now come. The modern society should be originated in free economical activities, equal participation opportunities and philanthropic spirit for those failurers. Because of the fact that Chanel was grown up as an orphan she had to shift amongst English, Russian and German lovers. The last two having been related to NSDAP, neither Paris nor France admit to have her buried in France. Now is the time that Chanel's personality as a representation of the 20th century French culture be revalued. All what she did was that she loved a man the most who suffered the expulsion that was imposed on him only because he was driven out of his homeland as it became the French territory. Both were buried in Lausanne.

The music that was referred to in this novel was actual songs that were popular before WW1. Such things of expensive value as mistery clocks or Duesenberg cars were based on the fact at that era. Why don't you, dear readers, have some absinth which is now released off regulations and taste the past fashionable age.

あとがき

　2016年5月22日に投票されたオーストリア大統領選ではオーストリア自由党ノルベルト・ホーファー党首が得票率49.7% 31,026票差で落選となりましたが、選挙に不正があったために10月2日に再投票となりました。オーストリア自由党は『SSは栄誉と尊敬を受けるべきだ。』としています。党首選では新党首を拍手で迎えるのではなく、「ジークハイル！」の歓呼で迎えることも行われています。再投票でホーファー候補が選出された場合にはこの言葉はオーストリアで解禁されることになるかも知れません。

　イギリスのEUからの離脱を受けて国際情勢は大きく変化しています。ここで注目すべきはスコットランドがイギリスからの離脱とEU加入への動きをみせていることです。つまり、その場合にはスコットランドにある原子力潜水艦の基地は移転を迫られるということです。そして、その潜水艦に積まれているトライデントミサイルも何処かに移動することになります。レ・サンチュリには南仏にトライデントの戦士たちが集められる記述があることを著者はすでに気が付いています。これもまた第3次大戦への標であることを明言できます。

　既刊の正典2巻分とこの外典1巻にはデザイナーが太刀トンボを加えていますが、これはある意味で著者の象徴です。イナゴが蔓延る直前に出てくるものが何であるのかについて黙示録は何も語りません。しかし、ファティマの預言のようにヴァチカンは気が付いているのかも知れません。本書はまだまだ続編を出版する予定です。本書を読んだのを機に『レ・サンチュリ』を読まれる方が増え新たに言語の鍵が解き明かされることを希望します。

2016年8月

Published List

SS 影の帝国（正典 No.1）日本語版	PASSO ROMANO	
ISBN 978-4-7876-0071-4	April 2011	
SS 影の帝国（正典 No.2）日本語版	ABALON	
ISBN 978-4-7876-0072-1	June 2011	
SS 影の帝国（外典 No.1）日本語版	Queen's Books	
ISBN 978-4-7876-0097-4	September 2016	

SS SHADOW EMPIRE English Edition

  Canon 1   Passo Romano
  ISBN 978-4-7876-0108-7   December 2019
  Canon 2   Abalon
  ISBN 978-4-7876-0109-4   December 2019
  Apocrypha 1   Queen's Books
  ISBN 978-4-7876-0110-0   December 2019

ISBN978-4-7876-0110-0

SS SHADOW EMPIRE Apocrypha Ⅰ
English Edition
SS影の帝国　外典Ⅰ　英語版

令和元年12月7日　第1刷発行
Dec/7/2019　1st edition issued

著　者　author　　Tycoon SAITO
翻　訳　translator　Yoshie HIYAMA
発行者　publisher　Yasushi ITO　伊藤泰士
発行所　株式会社創樹社美術出版

（乱丁・落丁はお取り替えいたします）
©Tycoon SAITO 2019 Printed in Japan